THE TIDE KNOT

by

Helen Dunmore

HarperCollins *Children's Books*

First published in hardback by HarperCollins *Children's Books* 2006

HarperCollins *Children's Books* is a division of HarperCollins*Publishers* Ltd,
77-85 Fulham Palace Road, Hammersmith, London W6 8JB

The HarperCollins *Children's Books* website address is:
www.harpercollinschildrensbooks.co.uk

1

ISBN-13 978-0-00-722897-3
ISBN-10 0-00-722897-X

Printed and bound in England by
Clays Ltd, St Ives plc

FOR ISSY CHEUNG

CHAPTER ONE

Ingo at night. It's not completely dark, though. The moon is riding high, and there's enough light to turn the water a rich, mysterious blue.

I am deep in Ingo, swimming through the moonlit water. Faro's here somewhere, I'm sure he is. I can't see him, but I'm not scared. There's just enough light to see by. There's a glimmer of rock – and a green and silver school of mackerel—

Imagine being lost underwater in total blackness. I'd panic. But it's dangerous to panic in Ingo. You mustn't think of the Air. You must forget that human beings can't live underwater, and then you'll find that you can.

Faro was here a moment ago, I'm sure of it. He's keeping himself hidden, but I don't know why. Even if it was totally dark, I expect he'd still be able to see me through the water. Faro is Mer, and he belongs here. Ingo is his home. And I'm human, and I don't belong.

But it isn't as simple as that. There's something else in me: the Mer blood that came to me and my brother Conor from our ancestors. It's my Mer blood that draws me to Ingo, beneath the surface of the water. I'd probably drown without my Mer blood – but it's best not to think of that—

"Faro?" Nobody answers. All the same I know he is close. But I won't call again. I'm not going to give Faro the satisfaction of thinking that I'm scared, or that I need him. I can survive in Ingo without him. I don't need to hold on to him any more, the way I did last year when I first came to Ingo. The water is rich with oxygen. It knows how to keep me alive.

I swim on. This light is very strange. Just for a moment, that underwater reef didn't look as if it was made from rock. It looked like the ruins of a great building, carved from stone thousands of years ago. I blink. No, it's a reef, that's all.

Why am I here in Ingo tonight? I can't remember clearly. Maybe I woke up in the dead of night and heard a voice calling from the sea. Did I climb down the path, down the rocks to our cove, and then slip into the water secretly?

Don't be so stupid, Sapphire. You don't live in the cottage any more, remember? You've left Senara. You're living in St Pirans, with Mum and Conor and Sadie. And Roger is never far away. How could you have forgotten all that?

So how did I get here? I must have come down to

Polquidden Beach, and dived into Ingo from there. Yes, that was it. I remember now. I was in bed, drifting off to sleep, and then I felt Ingo calling me. That call which is so powerful that every cell of my body has to answer it. Ingo was waiting for me. I would be able to dive down and down and down, beneath the skin of the water, into Ingo. I would swim with the currents through the underwater world that is so strange and mysterious and yet also feels like home.

Yes, I remember putting on my jeans and hooded top, and creeping downstairs in the moonlight from the landing window. Stealthily unlocking the front door, and then running down to Polquidden Beach, where the water shone in the moonlight and the voice of Ingo was so strong that I couldn't hear anything else.

And now I'm in Ingo again. Ever since we moved to St Pirans I've been trying to get back here, but it's never worked before tonight. There's too much noise in St Pirans, too many people, shops, cafés and car parks. But at night, maybe it's different. Maybe the dark is like a key that turns the lock, and opens Ingo.

"Greetings, little sister."

"Faro!"

I turn in a swirl of water and there he is.

"Faro! Where've you been? Why haven't I seen you for so long?"

His hand grasps mine. Even in the moonlight, his teasing smile is the same as ever.

"We're here now, aren't we? Nothing else matters. Sapphire, I've got so much to show you."

He lets go of my hand and backflips into a somersault, and then another and another until the water's churning so fast I can't see him at all. At last he stops in a seethe of bubbles, and grabs my hand again.

"Come on, Sapphire. Time to go. Night is the best time of all."

"Why is it the best time of all, Faro?"

"Because at night you see things you can't see by day."

"What things?"

"You'll see."

We join hands. There's a current racing ahead, the colour of the darkest blue velvet. We plunge forward. The current is so strong that it crushes me. I'm jolting, juddering, struggling in its grip, but I can't break away. It's got me, like a cat with a bird in its claws. It's much too powerful for me, and it knows its own strength.

This is like the moment when you get on to the most terrifying ride of all at a theme park and you're strapped in, helpless to escape. The ride begins to move and you see a mocking smile on the face of the attendants and you realise that they don't care at all. But Ingo is no theme park where people lose their jobs if they kill the customers. Anything can happen here. If I die now, no one will ever know. They'll only say that I drowned, like they said Dad drowned.

Don't panic, Sapphire. Let the current take you where it wants. Wherever you go, you'll be safe. Reassuring thoughts echo in my head and I'm not sure for a moment if they are my thoughts or Faro's. Are we sharing our thoughts again, the way we did last summer? *Relax, let the current take you. Don't resist it, or you'll get hurt.* Jolts of force shake me. I'm afraid, I'm afraid, I can't breathe—

Don't ever think of breathing or not breathing. Air is another country and it means nothing here. Think of now. Think of Ingo. Here. Now.

The words beat in my head like a pulse. *Here. Now. Let go of everything and see what comes to you.* I've done it before, but it's never been as hard as this. Ingo at night is so dark, so vast. Not a safe playground but a wild kingdom. You could so easily lose yourself here. A tingle of pure fear runs through my body. *No, no, Sapphire, that's not the way. Panic is making you deaf and blind.*

I stop fighting. It feels like coming out of a cage. I am free and safe in the heart of the current. There's Faro, a little way ahead of me. His tail gleams blue in the moonlight. I can't see his face, or his hands, or any of him that seems human. Only the strong tail, like a seal's tail, driving Faro through the water. We are travelling faster than I've ever dreamed of swimming, flying through Ingo in darkness.

By the time the current swerves away from us, throwing us off into calmer water, we must be miles and miles from land. I'm exhausted. It seems that even Faro's tired, because he pulls my hand and we swim down and down to the sea bed. Here the sand is deeply ridged, and we sink into one of its sheltered hollows to rest. It is almost totally dark down here.

"Where are we, Faro?" My voice echoes strangely.

"Close to the Lost Islands."

"Why are they lost?"

"They're not *all* lost. Some of them still rise above the surface. There are still humans living there. But the largest islands came to us hundreds of years ago, in a single night."

"Came to you? What do you mean? Was there a battle?"

"Yes, there was a battle, but not with guns or swords. The water rose and the islands fell to Ingo."

"But, Faro, what happened to the people who were living there?"

"Some were lost," says Faro with cool indifference. "Some took to their boats and made for the nearest islands that were still above water."

"Why did the sea rise?"

"It was time for it to rise, I suppose," says Faro. I can't see his face clearly in the gloom, but his voice is maddeningly calm.

"Faro, please don't talk like that. As if everything is – well – *fate*. We should be able to make things better.

Change the future. Those islanders could have built a sea wall, couldn't they, to keep the sea out? That's what people do in Holland. They build dykes and ditches. *They don't drown. They're brilliant engineers.*"

"So I've heard," says Faro thoughtfully. "They're very obstinate, those people in Holland."

"The point is, Faro, that countries don't *have* to drown. Holland proves it. It's the other way round there. They *reclaim* land from the sea. Did you know that?"

"For now, they take land from Ingo," Faro reflects, "but that doesn't make it theirs. What works today may not work tomorrow. Weren't you saying just now that we should be able to make things better, and change the future? I agree. It would make things better for the Mer if Holland were to grow... smaller."

"But why, Faro? Why? Isn't Ingo strong enough already? The oceans are greater than the land. Don't you know that?"

Dad taught me that. He took me way out in his boat, the *Peggy Gordon*, until I could clearly see how small the land looked, and how insignificant, compared to the hugeness of the sea.

"Why do you want more and more and *more*, Faro?"

"You humans are the ones who want more," says Faro fiercely. "You want the whole world to bow to human desires."

Faro's argument is making me uneasy. "Can we... could we go to the Lost Islands?" I ask quickly.

"Everyone's going to the Lost Islands tonight."

"Why?"

"There's a Gathering. Look over there."

"It's too dark."

"*Look*, Sapphire. Open your eyes."

I peer through the deep dark velvet of the water. Yes, there are shapes and shadows, shifting with the pull of the currents. There's a group of them, close together. A shoal of fish swimming to their feeding grounds, maybe. But they're too big for fish, surely; they're as long as – as tall as—

"Mer, Faro! Look! They're Mer!"

I'm seeing the Mer at last. Faro's people. The curtain that has hidden them from me every time I've visited Ingo has lifted at last. They are moving fast, in a group of twenty or so. They're a long way off, and they don't notice us. They seem to shimmer as they swim, as if they're covered in fish scales. But I know from Faro and his sister Elvira that the Mer aren't really covered in scales at all. That's for fairy stories where mermaids bask on rocks, combing their hair and singing to sailors. The real Mer are not like that. They're more powerful, more complicated and much, much more real. I blink, and the Mer have gone.

"What were they wearing, Faro? What's all that shiny stuff?"

"Mother-of-pearl on cloaks of net, I should think. That's what people generally wear to a Gathering when it's moonlight."

"How beautiful. Have you got a cloak like that?"

"What do you mean?"

"Have you got one? A cloak like that? In your wardrobe or whatever?"

"I'm not going to the Gathering tonight, so why would I have a cloak? I'd make one if I was going."

"Do you mean that you make a new cloak every time there's a party? I mean, a Gathering."

"Of course. They take days and days to make. The patterns are complicated."

"Then why don't you keep them? You could have a beautiful collection of cloaks."

"Collection!" says Faro with scorn, then he lowers his voice as if what he's saying is dangerous and not to be overheard. "Listen, Sapphire. A long time ago, some of the Mer started to *keep* things. They grew so proud of what they had *collected* that they became rivals, then enemies. It nearly brought us to war."

"Do the Mer fight wars?" I ask in surprise. Faro has always given me the impression that Mer life is peaceful.

"We almost fought a war then. We were ready to kill each other."

"We have wars all the time. I've seen them on TV. "

"Is TV real?" asks Faro curiously. "I thought it was stories humans make up for one another."

"The news is real."

"It's good to know about the human world," says Faro with decision. "Some Mer say that we should keep right away from it, but I think how you live is interesting."

"You make me feel as if I'm in a zoo, Faro!"

"Zoos! How can you humans keep creatures trapped in cages for pleasure when they are begging to be released?"

"Humans don't hear them. We can't talk to animals, you know."

"I know. I'm sorry, Sapphire."

Faro presses my hand in sympathy. If, like him, you can talk to whales and dolphins and sea urchins and sea eagles, then no wonder he thinks human life is a bit limited...

This seems like the most important talk I've ever had with Faro. It's the first time he's admitted that things have ever been less than perfect in Ingo. In the quiet darkness it's easier to speak openly, and not to start arguing—

"I wish I could see those islands," I tell him.

"We can go now if you like?"

"Really?"

"Yes. I can't take you to the Gathering. It's too early for that, and the Mer wouldn't like to see you there. But we could go to one of the other islands."

We swim out of our hollow. There are currents everywhere – not as powerful as the one we rode on, but little flickering currents that wash over our skin. The light is stronger now, and as we swim along the sea bed I realise that it's because the water is growing shallower.

"I don't want to go back into the Air," I say in alarm. I don't want to burst through the surface of the water, only to find myself marooned on some strange island miles and miles from Cornwall.

"We're not leaving Ingo. But we're coming to the islands, Sapphire. Look ahead."

It's strange – like coming inshore on a boat, except that the land where we're about to beach is underwater, lit by moonlight falling through water. There are the rocks. There's the beach. A long wall juts out. It must have been the harbour wall once. On the drowned shore there are the crumbled remains of buildings which must have been cottages. Their doorways are empty. I suppose the doors have rotted away. The empty window sockets make the cottages look as if they have got hungry, staring eyes. Instead of slate tiles on the roofs, there's seaweed waving gently in the current.

It all makes me shiver. I'm afraid of what might come out of those empty doorways: a scuttling family of crabs, or a conger eel, or a jellyfish with long, searching tentacles. I'm not afraid of any of these creatures usually, but they shouldn't be here, in human houses. There should be fire here, the smell of cooking and the sounds of human voices and laughter. I turn away.

"Don't you like it?" Faro asks.

I shake my head, and my hair floats across my face like seaweed, hiding it. I'm glad that Faro can't see my expression. I don't want to look any more, but the drowned village seems to be casting a spell on me. I stare at the little cobbled road leading up behind the cottages, and the strong, square tower of what must have been the village church, long ago. A weathercock still stands there. I wonder if it still turns from side to side when the tide moves. Does the weathercock still think that the wind's blowing it? It is all so empty, so sad and so silent. Like a graveyard.

"We come on pilgrimage here," says Faro.

"Pilgrimage?"

"Yes. Pilgrims come from far away to see the power of what Ingo has done here. Where there was land, now there is water."

"Great," I say bitterly. "I hope they enjoy it."

"You're angry," says Faro, "but you shouldn't be. In Holland they force the sea back, and you say they are brilliant. Here the sea rises and the land falls, and you think it's terrible. But it's just what happens. Like the tide. At low tide you can walk safely in a place where six hours later you would drown."

"But it's not tides that did this. It's something much more powerful. A whole island has drowned, Faro! How many villages were there?"

"I don't know. Many, I think."

"And how many people drowned?" I say, half to myself. I may have Mer blood in me, but no Mer blood could be strong enough to make me happy here. "It's so desolate," I go on, trying to make Faro understand. "This island wasn't part of Ingo and it didn't want to be. It isn't really a part of Ingo now. It's just dead."

"You're wrong," says Faro passionately. "Every year it's more alive. Look at how much is growing there now. Look how rich the water is." I can't bear to argue with him, and besides, I know we are never going to agree. With a part of myself I see what Faro sees: the beauty of the seaweed waving above the cottages, with thick stems and feathery branches; the schools of silvery, flickering fish; the sea-anemones and limpets that have made their home on the fallen stones. The part of me which is Mer thinks it is beautiful, but the part which is human thinks of all the human life that's been swallowed up by salt water.

"What's the matter, Sapphire? Why are you screwing up your face like that?"

He really doesn't know. Faro knows a lot about the Air, but not that humans weep.

"I'm sad, that's all. It's called crying."

"I've heard of that," says Faro eagerly, "but I've never seen it." He makes it sound as if I was performing a juggling trick. "Show me how you do this crying," he goes on.

"No, Faro, it doesn't work like that. I don't want to cry any more. I've stopped, look. But what do the Mer do when they are sad, if they don't cry? What do you do if someone dies?"

"We keep them in our memories."

"I think we should go," I say abruptly. I want to get away from this place, with its mournful atmosphere.

How could this have happened? How did the sea rise so suddenly that whole islands were swallowed by it, and people didn't even have time to get into their boats and escape?

I take a last look at the drowned village. There are the hulls of fishing boats chained to the harbour floor. They wouldn't float now, even if you could bring them to the surface. Sea water has rotted their timber. What would the people who lived here think if they could see this?

I can't help it. Tears are prickling and stinging behind my eyes again. It hurts more to cry in Ingo than it does in the Air. I don't want Faro to see how upset I am, or to watch me with his bright, curious eyes as I do this strange human thing called "crying", so I put my hands over my face. What was it called, this drowned village? It must have had a name.

Tell me what you were called, I say very softly inside my head. *Tell me your name.*

No one answers. The sea surges around me, lifting me. There's no moonlight any more. I can't see anything. Ingo is dark and full of sea voices that seem to come from everywhere. The sea lifts me again, and carries me away with it.

I wake in my bedroom in St Pirans, struggling out of a sleep that sticks to me like glue. My room is very small, only wide enough for my bed and a narrow strip of wooden floor. There's a shining pool of water on the floor. My porthole window is open. Maybe it's been raining and the rain has blown in. No, I don't think so. I dip my finger in the water and taste salt. Ingo.

The house is silent. Everyone in St Pirans is fast asleep. I look at the digital alarm clock that Roger gave me after I missed the school bus for the third time. Its digits glow green. 03:03. There's a heap of wet clothes on the floor by my bed – my jeans and hooded top – and my hair is wet. I must have changed into these pyjamas after I got back, but I don't really remember. It's all cloudy.

But the memory of the drowned houses is all too clear. The windows looked like empty, staring eye sockets in a skull. I don't want to think about it. I want to push it out of my mind.

CHAPTER TWO

It's daylight again. Safe, ordinary daylight where the things that seem huge and terrifying by night shrink like puddles in sunshine.

I'm down at the beach with Sadie. Mum's already at work, but it's Saturday, so no school. I've cleaned the bathroom and vacuumed the living room and now I'm free.

Sadie is like daylight. When I stroke her warm golden coat, all the shadows disappear. She looks up at me questioningly, wagging her tail. We're standing on the last of the steps that lead down to Polquidden Beach. Am I going to let her run?

I am. Dogs are allowed on to the beach after the first of October, and it's mid November now. Sadie's got a good memory, though, and that's why she's hesitating. She remembers that when we first moved to St Pirans in September, dogs were still banned from the beach. Every year from April to October, when the visitors are here, dogs have to keep away. I think it's unfair, but Mum says you couldn't have dog dirt on the sand where people are sunbathing.

All September I had to keep on explaining to Sadie, "I'm sorry, I know you want to run on the sand, but you can't." The more I get to know Sadie, the more I realise how much she understands. She doesn't have to rely on words. Sadie can tell from the way I walk into a room what kind of a mood I'm in.

Now she's quivering with excitement, but she still waits patiently on the step.

"Go on, Sadie girl! It's all right, you can run where you like today." Sadie stretches her body, gives one leap of pure pleasure, and then settles to the serious business of chasing a seagull in crazy zigzags over the sand. Sadie has never caught a gull, and I'm sure this gull knows that. It's leading her on, teasing her, skimming low over the sand to get Sadie's hopes high, then soaring as she rushes towards it.

I want Sadie to run and run, as far as she likes. I know she'll come back when I call. And besides, I want her to be free.

Since we moved to St Pirans I've been having these dreams. Not every night, not even every week, but often enough to make me scared to go to sleep sometimes. In the dream I'm caught in a cage. At first I'm not too worried because the bars are wide apart and it will be easy to slip out. But as soon as I move towards them, the bars close up. I try to move slowly and casually so that the cage won't know what I'm planning, but every time the bars are quicker than I am. It's as if the cage is alive and knows that I'm trying to escape.

I still can't believe that we are really living here in St Pirans. Can it be true that we've left our cottage for ever? And Senara, and our cove, and all the places we love? Conor and I were *born* in the cottage, for heaven's sake, in Mum and Dad's bedroom. How can you shut the door on the place where you were born?

Mum's promised that she'll never, ever, sell our cottage, but she's renting it out to strangers. The rent money pays for us to rent a house in St Pirans, where we have no memories at all.

It seems crazy to me. Completely crazy in a way that the adults all believe is completely logical.

You'll make so many new friends when you're living in a town!

You'll be able to go to the cinema and the swimming pool.

They've got some really good shops in St Pirans, Sapphy.

Why would anyone who lives by the sea want to go to a swimming pool anyway? Swimming pools are tame and bland and fake blue and they stink of chlorine. The water is dead, because of all the chemicals they put into it. The sea is alive. Every drop in it is full of life. If you put water from a swimming pool under a microscope, there would be nothing. Or maybe some bacteria if they haven't put enough chemicals in.

Even the sea gets crowded in St Pirans. It's quieter

now because the season's over, but everyone keeps telling us, *Wait until the summer months. You're lucky if you can find a patch of sand to put your towel down in August.* There are four beaches and a harbour, and thousands and thousands of tourists who swarm all over the town like bees. Conor and I sometimes used to come to St Pirans for a day while we were still living in Senara. Just for a change. A day was always enough. You can't swim without getting whacked by someone's board. Sometimes there are even fights between different groups of surfers – the ones who are local and the ones who have come here in vans from upcountry. They fight over such big issues as one surfer dropping in on another surfer's wave. Imagine thinking that the sea belongs to you, and fighting over waves. That's another sort of St Pirans craziness. I must tell Faro about it. It would make him laugh.

"Sadie! *Sadie!*" Suddenly I see that Sadie is way over the other side of the beach, bounding towards a tiny little dog. It's a Yorkshire terrier, I think, skittering about by the water's edge. Sadie won't hurt the Yorkie, of course she won't. But all the same I begin to run. At the same moment, a girl of about my age sees what's happening, and jumps up from where she's digging a hole in the sand with a little kid.

"*Sa-die!*"

Is she going to listen? Does Sadie really believe that I'm her owner now? Yes! A few metres away from the terrier, Sadie slows and stops. You can see from her body how much she longs to rush right up to it. She glances back at me, asking why I've spoiled what could have been a wonderful adventure.

"Good girl. You are such a good girl, Sadie."

I'm out of breath. I drop to my knees on the wet sand and clip on Sadie's lead. The terrier girl picks up her dog, which is no bigger than a baby.

"I thought your dog was going to eat Sky," says the girl. She has very short spiky blonde hair and her smile leaps across her face like sunshine.

"*Sky*. Weird name for a dog."

"I know. She's not mine. She belongs to my neighbour, but my neighbour's got MS so I take her for walks. Not that she walks far. Sky, I mean, not my neighbour," adds the girl quickly, as if she's said something embarrassing. "Sorry," she adds, "too much information."

I don't even know what MS is, so I just say, "Oh. I see."

"Is this your dog?" asks the girl longingly.

"Yes." It still feels like a lie when I say that. It's such a cliché when people say that things are too good to be true, but each time I say that Sadie is *my* dog, that is exactly how it feels. Much too good to be true. I worried for weeks that Jack's family would want her back, but they don't. *She's yours,* Jack's mum said. *Dogs know who they belong to, and Sadie's chosen you for sure, Sapphire. Look at her wagging her tail there. I never get such a welcome.*

"She's beautiful." The girl stretches out her hand confidently, as if she's sure that Sadie will like her, and Sadie does. She sniffs the girl's fingers approvingly. I give a very slight tug on Sadie's lead.

"We've got to go," I say.

"I must take Sky and River back, too. That's River, over there at the bottom of the hole. He's always digging holes. He's my little brother."

"River. Weird name for a boy," I nearly say. I stop myself in time, but the girl smiles.

"Everyone thinks our names are a bit strange." She looks at me expectantly. "Don't you want to know what my name is? Or would you rather guess?"

I shake my head a bit stiffly. This girl is so friendly that it makes me feel awkward.

"Rainbow," she says. "Rainbow Petersen. My mum called me Rainbow because she reckoned it had been raining in her life for a long time before I was born, and then the sun came out. My mum's Danish, but she's been living here since she was eighteen."

There is a short silence. I try to imagine Mum saying anything remotely like that to me, and fail. *The sun came out when you were born, Sapphire darling.* No, I don't think so.

The girl – Rainbow – looks as if she's waiting for something. She picks up the terrier, and I say, "Well, bye then."

But then she looks straight at me and says quite

seriously, "You know my name and my little brother's name and Sky's name. Aren't you going to tell me yours?"

I feel myself flush. "Um, it's Sapphire."

"That's great," says Rainbow warmly.

"Why?"

"I'm so glad you haven't got a normal name like Millie or Jessica. *Sapphire.* Yes, I like it. What about your dog?"

"She's called Sadie."

The girl looks at me again in that expectant way, but whatever she's expecting doesn't happen. After a moment she says, "OK, see you around then, Sapphire. Bye, Sadie," and she goes back to where River is digging his hole.

It's only when she's been gone for a while that I realise she wanted to know more about me. But there's nothing I can do about that now, and besides, as old Alice Trewhidden always says, *It's not good to tell your business to strangers.*

You'd have thought I was Rainbow's friend already, the way she smiled at me.

Conor's gone fishing off the rocks at Porthchapel with Mal. Mum was right: Conor has got to know loads of people in St Pirans already. I suppose it's partly because he goes to school here, but it's also just the way Conor is. I don't know all his friends' names, but they're mostly surfers. Conor speaks surfer talk when he's with them. He and Mum and Roger all keep telling me I should surf, but I don't want to any more. If you've surfed the currents of Ingo, why would you want to surf on Polquidden Beach, or even up at Gwithian? It would be like being told that you're only allowed one sip of water when you're dying of thirst.

Conor doesn't feel the same. I tried to talk to him about it once, not long after we came to St Pirans.

"Saph, you're not giving St Pirans a chance," he said. "There's great surfing here. You used to like body-boarding at the cove."

"That was before we went to Ingo," I said. Conor looked at me uneasily.

He doesn't talk much about Ingo now we're in St Pirans. It's as if he thinks we've left Ingo behind, along with the cottage and everything we've known since we were born. Or maybe there's some other reason. I have the feeling that Conor is keeping something from me. Mum says he's growing up, and that I can't expect Conor to tell me everything now, the way he did when we were younger.

"Don't you feel it's pointless, this kind of surfing?" I asked. I wanted to probe what Conor was really thinking. "I mean, compared to surfing the currents, it's nothing. Once you've been in Ingo, you can't be satisfied with messing around on the surface of the water."

Conor's face was clouded. "I can't live like that, Saph, neither properly belonging in one place or another," he said. He sounded angry, but I don't think he was angry with me. "I've got to try to belong where I am. It's no good to keep on wanting things you can't have—"

He broke off. I didn't answer, because I wasn't sure what he meant.

"I know you miss Senara," he went on.

"*Home*, you mean."

"All right, home."

"So, I miss home. That's normal, Con!"

"But other people are living in our cottage now. We can't go back there, so it's no use hankering."

"We could go back if we wanted. Mum could give the tenants notice."

"But, Saph, Mum doesn't want to. Can't you see that? She was glad to get away from the cottage and the cove and everything that reminds her of Dad. Mum's much happier here."

I know that really. I've known it for weeks, but I haven't wanted to put it into words.

"And there's something else, too," Conor goes on. "She wanted to get us away from Ingo."

"Mum doesn't know anything about Ingo! She doesn't even know it exists."

"We haven't *told* her anything. But Mum's not stupid. She picked up that something strange was going on down at the cove. She was frightened for us – especially for you. She even asked me if I knew why you were behaving so strangely."

"You didn't tell her?"

"Saph, why are you so suspicious all the time? Of course I didn't. Mum doesn't *know* about Ingo, but she senses something, and since Dad disappeared she's not taking any chances. Maybe she's right," Conor adds, sounding thoughtful.

"Mum's *right*? Right to take us away from everything? Adults know they can get away with doing what they want, but that doesn't make it right! Conor, how can you say that? It's like – it's like betraying Ingo."

"But if you are always on the side of Ingo, Saph, then *you're* betraying something too. Granny Carne said you had Mer blood, but she didn't tell you to forget that you're human."

I went up to my room. I didn't want to talk about Ingo any more. I was afraid that Conor might say, "Forget about Ingo, Saph. Put it all behind you, and get on with real life."

Yes, I do miss home. I only let myself think about it at night, before I go to sleep. I miss our cottage, the cove, the Downs, Jack's farm. I miss watching the lights of the cottages shine out at night and knowing who lives in every one of them. I miss Dad even more in St Pirans, because not many people here ever knew him. They think Mum's

31

a single parent because she's divorced, until we explain. Everyone in Senara knew Dad, right back to when he was a little boy, and they knew all our family. Even if Dad wasn't there, he was still present in people's memories.

At least I still go to the same school. Conor's transferred to St Pirans school, but I didn't want to. I don't mind going on the school bus to my old school. I had to fight hard, though. Mum said that I should go to school here in St Pirans so that I'd make friends locally and "settle in". Strangely enough it was Roger, Mum's boyfriend, who supported me. He said, "Sapphire's had a lot of changes. She needs some continuity in her life." Mum listens to what Roger says, and to be honest, Roger never talks without thinking first.

That's the trouble with Roger. It would be easier if I could just dislike him. Hate him, even. But he won't let me. He keeps doing things which trick me into liking him, until I remember that I mustn't like him because it is so disloyal to Dad. But it was Roger who made sure I got Sadie. And it's Mum who talks about "settling in" all the time, not Roger. Roger says you have to give everything time, and that we've all got to cut each other some slack, take it easy and let things fall into place. Roger is very laid-back about most things, but he can be tough, too.

Settling in. I hate that phrase so much. Even worse are the adults who tell Mum that children are *very adaptable and soon forget the past.*

"Not Sapphire," says Mum grimly when people tell her how quickly we'll get used to our new life. "Her mind is closed."

Is my mind closed? No. It's wide open. I'm always waiting.

Every day I go down to the beach, to the water's edge, and listen. When we first got here in September, there were still tourists on the beach. Naturally, Faro kept away. I didn't really expect to see him. But if I was going to see him on any of the St Pirans beaches, it would be at Polquidden – the wildest beach. The storms crash in here from the southwest, and at low tide you can see the remains of a steam-ship wreck. I think Polquidden Beach is the closest that St Pirans comes to Ingo. The rocks at the side of the beach are black, heaped up into shapes like the head and shoulders of a man. Sometimes when I'm down there with Sadie, I catch myself scanning those rocks, looking for a shape like a boy with his wetsuit pulled down to his waist. A shape that is half-human, half-seal, but not quite like either of these.

Faro. He came last night. If my mind had been closed I would never have heard the voice of Ingo. That's why I can't settle into St Pirans. I mustn't. I've got too much to lose.

"*Saph! Saa-aaphh!*"

I spin round. Sadie bounds forward. It's Conor, running down the beach.

"There you are, Saph. I've been looking all over for you. Come on."

"What's happened?"

"Something amazing. Come quick—"

My heart leaps. I know what Conor's going to tell me. We're going back to Senara. Mum's tired of St Pirans. Maybe... maybe she's splitting up with Roger. We're going home!

"There's a pod of dolphins in the bay. They're playing off Porthchapel, close in. Mal's dad is taking the boat out, and he says we can both come if we get there quick."

"What about Sadie?"

"We'll drop her at the house on the way."

Our house is in a street close to Polquidden, tucked away behind the row of cottages and studios which faces the beach. We leave Sadie there and race through the narrow streets. Even Conor's out of breath. He ran all the way from Porthchapel so that I could get the chance of going out in the boat too.

"Thanks, Conor!"

"What?"

"For not just going out – in the boat – without me..."

"I wouldn't go without you."

We cross the square, go down the Mazey and we're nearly there. Porthchapel Beach stretches ahead. There's a little crowd of people, and a bright orange inflatable boat in the water.

"Come on, Saph! They're ready to go."

Mal's Dad gives us a lifejacket each, and we fix them on while he starts the engine. Mal splashes thigh-deep in water, pushing the boat out.

"We'll take her out in the bay a bit, then I'll kill the engine so we don't scare them," says Mal's dad. "Mind, they like boats. I reckon there's about twelve of them in the pod, could be more. November – it's late in the year to see them here."

There are a dozen or more people at the water's edge. More are hurrying down the slope from the putting green. I shade my eyes and scan the water. Porthchapel Beach is sheltered and the sea is always calmer here than on Polquidden. Suddenly I see what I'm looking for. The water breaks, and a dark, glistening shape breaches the water. The back of a dolphin, streaming with water as it leaps and then dives back into the sea. Another dolphin breaches, and then another. They swim in a half-circle, in tight formation. Suddenly five of them leap at once, as if the same thought came to them all at the same instant.

One dolphin is much smaller than the others. A young one, probably a calf born in the spring. It's almost a baby, even in dolphin terms.

Dad taught me about dolphins. He loved them. He took loads of photographs of them. He knew the ones that came back year after year, but he said it was wrong to give dolphins human names and human characteristics. *They know what their names are*, he always said. *They have their own language. They're better communicators than we are.*

The dolphin calf is swimming close to its mother. She'll be taking him south soon, to warmer waters.

Wherever the dolphins are, Ingo is there too, I remember that. Even when they show their backs above the water, or leap right through the skin into the Air, they still carry Ingo with them. So Ingo must be very close...

A pod is like a family of dolphins, and here they are, playing in full view of the humans whom they ought to fear. I count them. Six – eight – eleven – yes, Mal's dad is right, there are twelve dolphins here. They don't seem at all afraid of us. But they should be afraid. Why should they trust a boatload of humans?

They're coming closer and closer inshore. People on the beach are waving and clapping. Mal's father switches off the engine and lets the boat rock. A long swell moves under the water's surface. Little waves slap the side of our boat. I sit forward, tense, waiting. Something is about to happen. Every sound seems to die away, even the noises of the sea and the people cheering the dolphins.

One of the dolphins leaps high out of the water.

"She's seen us. She wants to talk to us," I say under my breath to Conor. Mal glances at me.

Conor turns casually and murmurs in my ear. "Be careful, Saph."

Mal's dad stands up, legs braced for balance, camera in hand. "Should be able to get some good shots from here," he says.

I was wrong. It isn't quiet at all. Sound floods across the water in a wave. The dolphins are talking to each other. There are more than a dozen voices, weaving together, clicking and whistling, filling the sea with a net of sound. Cautiously, so that my weight balances that of Mal's dad, I stand up too.

"Careful, Saph," says Conor again.

They want to come to the surface. They want to talk to us. What is it? What's happening?

"Beautiful," says Mal's dad. He has got his shots. "I'm going to blow up these images into posters."

"Hush. Listen."

"What is it?" asks Mal.

"Don't talk. I can't hear what they're saying if you talk."

"They do say dolphins have their own language," agrees Mal's dad.

And now I hear it. It's like tuning into radio stations on an old-fashioned radio. The air waves wheeze and crackle. There's a snatch of music, then something that might be words in a foreign language. One of the dolphins leaps so close to the boat that its wake catches us, our boat rocks and Mal's dad has to struggle to keep his balance.

"This – is – amazing," says Mal in a low, awestruck voice. "I never seen them come in so close. Look at him there."

It's not a male, it's a female. An adult female with broad, shining sides and small, dark, intelligent eyes that look at me with recognition. Of course. Of course. I know her. I know the shape of her – her powerful fluke that drives her through the water, and her dorsal fin. I know what her skin feels like when I'm riding on her back with the sea rushing past me. I know her voice, and the power of the muscles beneath her skin.

"Hello," I say. My voice makes only the feeblest click and whistle, like a baby trying to talk dolphin. She turns, swims away from the boat fast then turns again and rushes the boat. Three metres from us, she stops dead. Water surges and her eyes gleam, catching mine.

"That is just *so am-az-ing*," says Mal again. Even though he's Cornish, Mal likes to sound American, or maybe it's meant to be Australian. He thinks it's cool.

"I reckon she's having a game with us," says his father. "They're playful creatures, dolphins."

She's not playing. You can tell that from her voice. Lots of other voices are breaking in, all of them dolphin voices, some close, some far away. They weave a net of urgent sound, but her voice rises above them all.

kommolek arvor trist arvor
truedhek arvor
arvor
kommolek
lowenek moryow
Ingo lowenek

The dolphin language weaves like music. I hear some of it, and then it slides away. It rushes over my mind, teasing and tickling. I can't grasp it.

"Please help me. I can't understand what you're saying."

She is very close to the boat now. Her eyes look directly into mine, powering their intelligence into me. But I can't decode it; I can't get there. My brain fizzes with irritation, just as it does when I'm on the point of solving a puzzle in maths.

And then the connection breaks.

"Hey, Sapphire, that was fantastic fake dolphin language you were talking!" says Mal, and the dolphin turns and dives back to the pod. I think it's Mal's appreciation which is fake, but I say nothing. Conor is watching me, silently willing me to shut up and not draw any more attention to myself. And I certainly don't want everyone in St Pirans to think that I'm a crazy girl who converses with dolphins.

I haven't conversed with the dolphin. I didn't understand her and I don't think she understood me. My brain and tongue couldn't break the barrier this time, into Mer. The dolphin was so close, struggling to make me hear her, but I couldn't. Maybe moving to St Pirans has taken me farther from Ingo altogether. I'm losing what I used to know. At this rate I will never, ever speak full Mer. A wave of despair washes over me, and I huddle down into the bottom of the boat.

Mal tags along all the way back to our house. Conor asks him in, but I say nothing. *Leave us alone, go away,* I think. As if he picks up my thoughts, Mal says, "All right then, I'll be getting along. See you, Conor. Um… see you, Sapphire."

"Bye."

As soon as we're inside the house, Conor says, "You might be more friendly to Mal. He likes you."

"He doesn't even know me."

"OK, he only *thinks* he likes you. But you don't have to be so hard on him. You don't have to dive away when anyone comes near you."

I hug Sadie so I can hide my face in her neck. Conor isn't going to be deflected.

"That dolphin, Saph."

"Which dolphin?"

"You know which dolphin. The one you were talking to."

"I couldn't talk to her properly. I was trying really hard, but I couldn't. I think it might have been because I was in the Air and she was in Ingo. Even when dolphins leap out of the water, they are still in Ingo, Faro told me that. Or maybe I'm just forgetting everything."

It's the first time Faro's name has passed between us for weeks. Conor frowns.

"Why did the dolphins come? Was it a message from Faro?"

"No. It wasn't anything to do with Faro, I'm sure of that. It wasn't exactly a message *from* Ingo – it was *about* Ingo. The dolphins were trying to tell me something, but I wasn't quick enough. I couldn't pick it up."

"Did you want to?"

"What do you mean?"

"What I just said. Did you want to pick up their message?"

"Of course I did. It was *Ingo*, Conor, trying to communicate with me. With us," I add hastily.

"You don't have to pretend. It was you the dolphin was talking to. But what I want to know is, do you want to listen? Do you really want all that to begin again?"

"Conor, how could I not want it? It's *Ingo*."

Conor's eyes search my face. A strange thought strikes me. Conor is trying to decode me, in the same way as I was trying to decode the language of the dolphins. But Conor and I belong to the same species. We're brother and sister, for heaven's sake. After a while, Conor says very quietly, "You could if you tried. But you don't try, Saph."

I struggle to explain. "It's not like that. I don't have a choice. I feel as if I'm only half here. Only half-alive. Our life here in St Pirans is all wrong for me. I feel as if I'm watching it on TV, not living it. Oh, Conor, I wish I was away in Ingo—"

"Don't say that!"

"It's true."

"I know," says Conor slowly and heavily. "You can't help wanting what you want. I don't blame you, Saph. I do know how you feel. It's so powerful, so magical. It draws you. It draws me, too... But I think that if you try as hard as you can – if you really struggle – you can stop yourself taking the next step."

"What next step?"

Conor shrugs. "I don't know. I was thinking aloud." His voice changes and becomes teasing instead of deadly serious. "But there's something you haven't thought of, Saph. You're so keen to talk to dolphins that you're forgetting Sadie."

"What?"

"They don't have dogs in Ingo, Saph."

As if she's heard him, Sadie pushes up close to me, nuzzling in. She always knows when things are wrong, and tries to make them better. Her brown eyes are fixed on my face. How could I have forgotten Sadie, even for a minute? *They don't have dogs in Ingo.*

Maybe they do. Maybe they could. Sadie's not like an ordinary dog. Could she come with me through the skin of the water, and dive into Ingo? I don't know. I try to picture Sadie's golden body swimming free, deep in Ingo, with her nostrils closed so that the water won't enter them. But it doesn't work: the picture I create in my mind looks like a seal swimming, not like Sadie at all.

Sadie whines. It's a pleading, plaintive sound from deep in her throat. She puts her front paws up in my lap until her whiskers tickle my face.

"You'd never have got Sadie without Roger," Conor goes on." He really pressured Mum."

I know that's true, but I don't feel like agreeing with Conor just now. Besides, why bring up Roger? Roger may have been the one who made sure I got Sadie, but he's also taken Mum and split my family apart.

Sadie gazes at me reproachfully, as if begging me to admit that my version isn't quite true. *Who split your family apart, Sapphire? Was it Roger, or was it your own father, who loved you and Conor so much that he left you both without a backward look or even a note to let you know where he was going?*

Your father, who has never seen you or spoken to you since.

Angry, bitter thoughts rise in my mind. I'm so used to loving Dad, but I'm beginning to realise that it's also possible to hate him. Why did he go? What father who cared about his children would take his boat out in the middle of the night and never return? I can taste the bitterness in my mouth.

No, I'm not going to let that wave of anger drown me. I'm going to ride it. Dad disappeared for a reason. It's just that he hasn't been able to explain it to us yet.

Suddenly an upstairs window bangs. Our house here in St Pirans is tiny, even smaller than the cottage. Downstairs there's one large living room, with the kitchen built into one end. Upstairs is larger because the house has something called a "flying freehold". This sounds more exciting than it is. All it means is that part of this house is built above the house next door. We have three bedrooms and a bathroom. My room is so tiny that a single bed only just fits into it, but I don't mind that at all because the room also has a round porthole window which hinges in the middle and swings open exactly like a real porthole on a ship.

Mine is the only window in the house from which you can see the sea. My bedroom is part of the flying freehold. I like it because it feels so separate from the rest of the house. I can't hear Mum and Roger talking. I'm independent. When I kneel up on my bed and stare out to sea, I can imagine I'm on a ship sailing northeast out of Polquidden, out of the bay altogether, and into deep water—

The window bangs again, harder. The wind's getting up. This is the season for storms. When storms come, salt spray will blow right over the top of the houses. I can't wait to hear the sea roaring in the bay like a lion.

"Better shut your window, Saph."

"Are you sure it's my window that's banging?"

"Yeah. No one else's bangs like that. Your porthole's much heavier than the other windows."

Conor was right. The porthole has blown wide open. I kneel up on my bed and peer out. Beyond the jumble of slate roofs, there's a gap in the row of studios and cottages through which I can glimpse the sea. The wind is whipping white foam off the tops of waves. Gulls soar on the thermals, screaming to each other. We're very close to the water here. I'm used to living up on the cliff at Senara, and it still seems strange to live at sea level.

"I'm going down to the beach," Conor shouts up the stairs.

"I'll come with you."

The wind's really blowing up now. It pushes against us as we come round the corner of the houses and on to the steps.

"Do you think there'll be a storm?"

Conor shakes his head. "No. The barometer's fallen since this morning but it's steady now. It'll be a blow, that's all."

We jump down on to the sand. The cottages and studios are built in a line, right on the edge of the beach. The ground floor windows have big storm shutters that were hinged back when we first arrived, but now they are shut and barred. Some of the shutters are already half buried in sand that was swept up in the storms we had around the equinox, in late September.

Sand could easily bury these houses. Imagine waking up one morning and finding the room dark because sand had blown right up to the top of your windows. Or maybe it wouldn't be sand at all, but water. You could be looking at the inside of the waves breaking on the other side of the glass. And then the glass would break under the pressure, and the sea would rush in.

"I wonder how the sea always knows just how far to come, and no farther," I say to Conor. "It's so huge and powerful, and it rolls in over so many miles. But it stops at the same point every tide."

"Not quite at the same point. Every tide's different."

"I know that. But the sea doesn't ever decide to roll a mile inland. And it could if it wanted, couldn't it? With all the power that's in the sea, why does it stop here when it could swallow up the whole town?"

"Like Noah's Flood."

"What?"

"You remember. God sent a flood to drown the whole world and everything in it, because people were so evil. But Noah built his ark and he survived. And when the flood was over, God promised he'd never do it again."

"Do you believe in God, Conor?"

"I don't know. I tried praying once, but it didn't work."

"What did you pray about?" But I already know. Conor would have prayed for Dad to come back. I know, because I did the same. I prayed night after night for Dad to come back, after he disappeared. But he never did.

"You know, Saph."

"Yeah. Me too."

"Did you pray as well?"

"Yes. Every night for a long time."

"But nothing happened."

"No."

"You know what the story says that the rainbow is? The Noah story, I mean."

"No."

"It's a sign that there'll never be another flood like the one that drowned the world."

"Hey, Con, I forgot to tell you. I met a girl called Rainbow."

But Conor isn't listening. He's shading his eyes and staring into the distance, out to sea. At first I think he's looking for surfers, but then he grabs my arm. "There! Over there by the rock! Did you see her?"

"Who? Rainbow?" I ask, like an idiot.

"Elvira," he says, as if that's the obvious, only answer. As if the one person anyone could be looking for is Elvira.

He never talks about her. Never even says her name. But she must have been in his mind all the time, since the last time he spoke to her. That was just after Roger and his dive buddy Gray were almost killed, when they were diving at the Bawns.

I remember how Conor and Elvira talked to each other, once we'd got Roger and Gray safely into the boat. Conor was in the boat, leaning over the side, and Elvira was in the water. They looked as if there wasn't anyone else in the world. So intent on each other. And then Elvira sank back into the water and vanished, and we took the boat back to land.

"I can't see Elvira," I say. "I can't see anything."

"There. Follow where I'm pointing. Not there – *there*. No, you're too late. She's gone."

"Are you sure, though, Conor? Was it really Elvira?"

"It was her. I know it was her."

"It could have been part of a rock."

"It wasn't a rock. It was her."

"Or maybe a surfer—"

"Saph, believe me, it was Elvira. I couldn't mistake her for anyone else."

I still don't think it was. I have no sense that the Mer are close. Neither Faro, nor his sister, nor any of the Mer. But in Conor's mind, a glimpse of a rock or a seal or a buoy turns into a glimpse of Elvira.

"I keep nearly seeing her," says Conor in frustration, "but then she always vanishes. I'm sure it was her this time."

"You can't be sure, Conor."

"She was out in the bay earlier on, when the dolphins came."

"Are you certain? I didn't see anything."

"She was there; I know she was. I saw her out of the corner of my eye, but when I turned she was gone. I expect it was because Mal and his dad were there. Elvira wouldn't risk them seeing her."

"Do you think they could?"

"What do you mean?"

"Maybe it's only us who can see the Mer. Because of what Granny Carne said, you remember, about our blood being partly Mer. Maybe even if Faro or Elvira swam right up to the boat, Mal and his dad still wouldn't see them."

I remember the words Faro said to me: *Open your eyes.* Maybe that doesn't just mean opening your eyelids and focusing. Maybe it's to do with being willing to see things, even if your mind is telling you that they can't possibly be real—

"Of course they'd see Elvira if she was there," Conor argues. "You're making the Mer sound like something we've imagined. Elvira's as real as... as real as... Saph, why do you think she's hiding? Why won't she talk to me?"

"I don't know."

I don't think I should say any more. Our roles seem to be reversing. Suddenly I'm the sensible, practical one, and Conor is the dreamer, longing for Ingo. *No. Be honest, Sapphire. It's not Ingo he's longing for; it's her.* And maybe that's what is making me so sensible and practical—

"We'd better go home, Conor. It's starting to rain."

"Saph, you said it!" Conor swings round to face me, smiling broadly. "You said it at last. I had a bet with myself how long it would be before you did."

"Said what? What are you talking about?"

"Didn't you hear yourself? You said, 'home'."

CHAPTER THREE

"I'm just taking Sadie out, Mum!" I call up the stairs. It's Sunday night. Mum and Roger are painting the skirting boards in Mum's bedroom. They have stripped off the dingy cabbage-rose wallpaper, and now the bedroom walls are bare to the plaster. Our landlady says we can decorate as much as we like, and I'm not surprised. Her paint and wallpaper are not only hideous, but also old and covered in marks. When we got here, Mum wanted to paint all the rooms white.

"It's a new start for all of us, Sapphy!"

I've painted my room blue and green, so that it looks like the inside of a wave. Our landlady, Mrs Eagle, has been up to see it, and she says it is 'andsome. Mrs Eagle is old. Her name doesn't sound at all Cornish, but that's because she married a man who came to St Pirans from upcountry during the War, she says. He died long ago. She must be about eighty, and she owns six houses in St Pirans, all of them full of cabbagey wallpaper, I expect.

But the rent is low, Mum says, and that's all that matters. Rents in St Pirans are terrible.

Mum appears at the top of the stairs. "It's late, Sapphy. Can't Conor take Sadie out?"

"He's doing his maths homework."

This is strictly true, but I haven't asked him anyway, because I want to go out on my own. St Pirans is different when the streets are empty, and it's dark, and there's no one at all on the wide stretch of Polquidden Beach. I feel as if I can breathe then.

"All right, but don't be long. Let me know when you're back."

Lucky it's Mum, not Roger. Although he hasn't known me very long, Roger is disturbingly quick to grasp when he is being told only a part of the truth, or indeed none of the truth at all.

The wind has died down over the weekend. It's a cold, still night and the air smells of salt and seaweed. The moon is almost full, and it is riding clear of a thick shoal of clouds. I decide to take Sadie away from the streetlights on to the beach, where she can chase moon shadows.

I head down to Polquidden. The bay is full. It's high tide. An exceptionally high tide. It's not due to turn until eleven tonight, but look how far it's come up the beach already. It reminds me of the autumn equinox, when the water came up right over the slipway and the harbour road.

There is still a strip of white sand left, but the water is rising quickly, like a cat putting out one paw and the next. Something else that surprises me is how quickly the sea has calmed. Surely the water should be much rougher than this after all the wind yesterday and today? The stillness is eerie.

Sadie doesn't want to go down the steps. She puts her head down, with her legs braced apart.

"It's all right, Sadie, you're allowed on the beach now, remember?" I give a gentle tug on her lead, but she won't budge.

"Sadie, you're being very annoying..."

I am longing to be down on the sand. I pull a little harder, but she digs in her claws. I don't want to force her.

"All right, then, Sadie. Wait here a minute."

I loop her leash around a metal post. Sadie whines. There's enough moonlight for me to see her face. She is pleading with me to stay, but I'm going to harden my heart this time. I've got to go down to the beach. The urge is so powerful that I ignore Sadie's voice, give her a quick hug and say, "Stay, Sadie!" and then hurry down the steps.

There's a sound of running water on my right. It's the stream that tumbles down the rocks on to the beach.

Children play in it and make dams in summer. The water glints in the moonlight as it pours over the inky-black rock. The sea is still rising. Why does it look so powerful tonight, even though there are no wild waves, no foam, no pounding of surf?

There's not much beach left. I walk to my right, towards a spine of rocks that juts from the glistening sand. A wave flows forward, and I leap up on to the rocks to keep my trainers dry. But I'm still not quite high enough, because now the water is swirling at my heels. I scramble up again on to dry rock, and look back. The bay is full of moonlight and water. The sea is lapping around my rock already.

Sapphire, you idiot, you're cut off! But it's not very deep yet. Even in the dark I'll be able to wade back easily before the tide comes in any farther. I'll just take my trainers off. But I'd better be quick; look how the water's rising—

"You'll have to swim," says a voice behind me. I start so violently that I almost fall off the rock. A strong hand grasps my wrist.

"It's me, Sapphire."

"Faro."

"Yes."

Suddenly I'm angry with him. "Why don't you and Elvira come and see us in daylight, like you used to?" I ask sharply. "Conor keeps looking for Elvira. Where is she?"

"Here and there," he says, with a gleam of laughter in his voice. "Around and about. Just like me."

"Don't laugh at me!" I say angrily. "I hate it when people are here one moment and then they just—"

I swallow the words I was going to say.

"I didn't disappear," says Faro seriously. "I won't ever disappear. I promise you. But in St Pirans it's more difficult for you to see us. Even at night it's not easy. There are so many people. And besides, St Pirans is not our place."

"I know that," I say gloomily. "It's not mine, either."

"But you're human. That's what humans do, isn't it? They crowd together in towns and cities. They love it when everything is covered over with concrete and Tarmac."

Faro brings out the word Tarmac with pride. He loves to impress me with his knowledge of the human world.

"You've been talking to the gulls again. Do you even know what Tarmac is, Faro? Or concrete?"

"Of course I do. It's stuff that humans pour on the earth to stop it breathing."

The moonlight is strong enough for me to see his face clearly. "Faro, have you grown older?"

I know that their time runs differently from ours. Is it possible that Faro has grown a year, when I've only grown a few months? Or maybe he only looks older because of the expression on his face.

"You can enter Ingo in darkness, even from here, Sapphire. You already know that."

A tremor of fear and anticipation runs through me.

"But I can't come to Ingo now, Faro. Mum's expecting me back with Sadie. If I'm away more than half an hour at most, she'll go crazy."

"You don't need to worry about that. Time is hardly moving at all tonight." He says it casually, as if saying that a boat is hardly moving across the water.

"What do you mean?"

"What I say. It's a fortunate night, Sapphire. Come to Ingo now, and you'll be back almost before you've gone. Look up at the moon."

I stare up at the moon. The clouds look as if they are flying away from its bright surface. Moonlight bathes my face with silver.

"You're already in Ingo, Sapphire," says Faro.

He is right. Deep in my heart, I've already left the Air. The powerful, silent swell of the tide is covering my feet, my knees, my waist. The next pulse of water lifts me from the rock, and swallows me into the sea.

Into Ingo. I let out my breath, and it hardly hurts at all. I am breathing without breathing, my body absorbing oxygen from the rich water. My hair flows upward, then swirls down around my face. I push it aside. Ingo. I am in Ingo again, just as I was two nights ago. There's a path of moonlight striking down deep into the water. I plunge forward and follow it.

How strongly I can swim in Ingo. My strokes are far more powerful than anything I can do in the Air. Below me, moonlight catches the glisten of the white sand on the sea bed. The water doesn't feel cold. It feels like – it feels like…

Like home. Like the place where I am meant to be. I open my eyes wide and turn my head, and there is Faro swimming alongside me. The underwater moonlight shines on his tail.

"Look!" He points down. There's a shadowy hulk, half buried in the sea bed. It's not a reef, or a dead whale, or anything that belongs to Ingo. It's something that belongs to Air. Metal. Yes, that's what it is. A metal ship, half rotted away with rust, sailing to nowhere.

"I know what that is," I say. "It's the wreck of the *Ballantine*. You can see her funnels from the beach at low tide."

"The wind drove her onshore and she was broken up," says Faro. "We called and called to warn the sailors, but they couldn't hear us."

"Faro, the wreck happened seventy years ago. Why do you always talk about history as if you were there?"

"Open your mind, Sapphire. Let's talk to each other like we did last summer." He saw my memories, and I saw his. That's what the Mer can do, because Mer minds are not quite separate from one another, as human minds are.

"Do you want to see what happened?" asks Faro. He floats close to me. "Look at the *Ballantine*, Sapphire."

I gaze into the shadowy depths. We could swim down with a few strong strokes, and touch the jagged metal sides of the drowned ship.

I don't want to. The wreck scares me. It must be terrifying to be driven ashore, helpless, caught by storm and tide. To know that your ship is going to smash on the rocks and break up, and that the water is too deep and wild to swim for shore.

The wind is beginning to whistle. I hear voices, crying out in terror. The *Ballantine* surges forward on a huge wave, and crashes on to the hidden reef. The entire ship judders with the shock. Metal shrieks and rips and grinds as the side of the *Ballantine* is torn open and the sea pours into her belly. Then the jumble of sound is pierced by human screams.

"No, Faro! No! I don't want to hear any more!"

Immediately, the window of memory closes. I'm back in the calm moonlit water, with Faro.

"You saw it, little sister," he says with satisfaction. "I wasn't sure if you would have lost your power, living in the town."

I shudder. "How could that wreck be in your memory, Faro? You're not old enough to remember it."

"The memory was passed to me by my ancestors, and so I can pass it on to you."

"I wish you hadn't. I don't want those memories in my mind. Let's get away from the wreck."

"We can go right away if you want. Will you come deeper into Ingo with me, Sapphire? There's someone I want you to meet."

"Who?" My heart leaps. Perhaps – perhaps – could Faro possibly know someone who knows where Dad is?

"My teacher."

"Oh." I try hard to keep the disappointment out of my voice, but Faro picks it up at once.

"He is a great teacher," he says, his voice proud, ready to take offence.

"I'm sure he is. Um… What's his name?"

"Saldowr."

"I can't imagine going to school under the sea. What's it like?"

Faro laughs. "We don't go to school. We learn things when we need to learn them."

"I see…" Faro sounds so sure that his way is the right way "…but wouldn't it be easier just to go to school and learn everything in one place?"

"I've heard about 'schools'. Thirty of you young humans together, with only one old human to teach you. All day long in one room."

"We move to different classrooms for different lessons," I point out.

"Hmm," says Faro.

"We go outside at break and dinner time."

"Human life is very strange," says Faro slowly and meditatively. "All the young ones together, out of sight in these 'schools'. Do you like it, Sapphire?"

"We have to do it. It's the law."

Faro nods thoughtfully. "I would like to see it. I expect the rooms are very beautiful, or none of you would stay. But, Sapphire, come with me to visit my teacher. He wants to meet you."

"How far is it?"

"Not far," says Faro carelessly. "A little beyond the Lost Islands, that's all. We can be there and back by morning."

"Morning!" All of a sudden the image of Sadie floods into my mind. Sadie, tied to an iron pole. She thinks I'm coming back in a few minutes. She'll be worried already, pointing her nose towards the beach and rising tide, whining anxiously. I see her as clearly as I saw the inside of Faro's memory. Usually the human world is cloudy when you're in Ingo, but Sadie's image is bright and sharp. "I've got to get back, Faro."

"Don't worry about the time, Sapphire. Ingo is strong tonight. But I don't need to tell you that, do I? You felt it. You slipped into Ingo almost before you knew it, and it didn't hurt at all. Your Mer blood knows that Ingo is strong. Not only strong but happy. Listen, listen, Sapphire. You can hear that Ingo is *lowenek*."

The word beats in my memory. Who said that to me? Of course, it was the dolphins. But they didn't sound as if they were talking about happiness. It sounded urgent, dangerous. Like a warning.

"I have to go," I say. "I must get back to Sadie. I left her tied to a pole by her leash."

Faro somersaults through the moonlit water. His body spins in a pattern of light and shadow. When he's the right way up again he says, "It seems to me that the one who is tied by a leash is you."

"Me!"

"Yes. You've always got to go home. You stay in the shallows. You want to come to Ingo, but as soon as you're here you want to go back again. Saldowr needs to speak to you. He has something to tell you."

I'm about to snap back, when I realise that Faro is sharp because he is hurt. He offered to take me to his teacher and I refused. The offer must have been important to him. Faro has never spoken to me about his father or his mother. Perhaps he has no parents, and this teacher means a great deal to him.

"I'm sorry, Faro. I'd like to meet your teacher very much," I say, "but I can't tonight, not when I've left Sadie tied up."

"Hm," says Faro, sounding a little mollified by my apology. "We'll see. Saldowr is not like a tame dog, Sapphire. You can't leave *him* tied up and return when you feel like it."

I stumble out of the water, dripping wet, into the chill of the night. The sea is slapping up to the very top step. As I watch, another wave pounces and the steps are completely submerged.

I shiver again, uncontrollably. Quick, quick, I must get home. My fingers shake violently as I untie Sadie. She presses against me, her body warm against mine, and her rough tongue licks my hands. But Sadie is trembling too. She's afraid. Cold makes my voice stammer as I try to reassure her.

"I'm ssssorry I left you sssuch a long time... I didn't mean to ssscare you, Sadie... Please, Sadie darling, stop shaking like that."

I slide my key into the front door lock, creep up the stairs and dive into the bathroom. I strip off my wet clothes, jump into the shower and turn it on full. The hot water prickles like needles on my cold skin. I stand there, eyes shut, soaking up the steamy heat. In Ingo I'm never cold. I'll put my clothes in the washing machine, stuff my trainers with newspaper and leave them by the boiler so that they're dry by morning—

"Sapphy! Sapphire! Is that you in there?"

"Yes, Mum!"

"You were quick. I hope Sadie got a proper walk. Don't use all the hot water, now."

I was quick, was I? So Faro was right. Time is hardly moving at all in Ingo tonight.

"Out in a minute, Mum!" I call.

The next morning I come down to find Sadie lying full-length on the living room rug. Mum's making coffee at the kitchen end of the room. She looks up quickly as I come in.

"Sapphy, I don't want you to worry, but Sadie doesn't look too good."

"What's the matter?"

"I don't know. She's not herself."

I kneel beside Sadie, and she thumps her tail languidly against the floor. Her eyes are dull. Even her coat seems to have lost its shine. But she was fine last night. I'm sure she was...

A cold feeling of dread steals into my heart, mixed with responsibility and guilt. I left Sadie tied up to a post. I went into Ingo without thinking about her. I might have been gone hours. But I wasn't, I wasn't. I was back almost before she had time to miss me.

Time. Is dog time the same as human time? Maybe my absence seemed endless to Sadie. Maybe she was afraid I'd drowned. Could Sadie possibly have guessed where I was? If she sensed that I'd left her behind, along with everything in the Air, to plunge into a strange world where Sadie couldn't survive for more than a minute, how frightened she must have been. She must have thought I'd abandoned her.

"Shall we go for a walk, Sadie?" I say, testing her. But she doesn't rise to the challenge. There's no joyous leap to her feet, no skittering of paws on the wooden floor, no gleam of delight in her eyes. Sadie stares at me sadly, as if to say, "Why do you ask me now, when you know I can't come?"

"She's ill, Mum. She's really ill." I can't help panic breaking into my voice, even though I don't want to alarm Sadie.

Mum leaves the stove, comes over and stares down

at Sadie, frowning. "No, she's not right, is she?" she says at last. "I wish Roger was here. He'd know what to do. But he's up at Newquay today."

"I'll take her to the vet."

"The vet? I don't know. I don't think it's that bad, Sapphy. She's only just become ill. We'll let it wait a day or so, and see how she gets on."

"You're only saying that because the vet is expensive!" I burst out. "I'll pay for it. I've still got most of my birthday money. That'll be enough."

"Sapphy, do you really think I'm the sort of mother who'd make you spend your birthday money on taking the dog to the vet? Do you?"

Mum sounds really upset.

"I don't care. There's nothing else I want to spend it on." But I know I'm being unfair. Mum doesn't see the danger, because she doesn't know what Sadie experienced last night.

"Listen," says Mum soothingly, "stop worrying, Sapphy. If Sadie needs a vet, then she'll go to a vet. But we'll wait and see until tomorrow."

"But she's *ill*, Mum. Look at her. She looks as if all her life's gone out of her."

"It's not as bad as that," says Mum briskly. "You do exaggerate, Sapphire. There's Conor coming down now. Maybe he'll be able to convince you."

But Conor is in no mood for long discussions about Sadie's welfare. He is giving an IT presentation at school today, and mentally he is already there, standing in front of the class. He barely glances at Sadie. "Calm down, Saph. Sadie's tired, that's all."

"Tired!"

"Got to go, Mum. Later, Saph."

"Is that the time?" Mum exclaims. "Oh, no! Why do I keep getting these breakfast shifts?"

Conor grabs his bag, guitar, IT folder, bottle of water and is out of the door.

"The bus, Sapphire! You're going to miss the school bus!"

"It's OK, Mum, you go to work. I've still got to make my packed lunch. The bus doesn't leave for ten minutes."

The door slams, and Mum's gone.

Ten minutes. I open the fridge door and look inside. Milk, eggs, yoghurt... I stare at them. What did I open the fridge for?

Wake up, Sapphire, you're supposed to be making your packed lunch. But just then Sadie whines, very quietly and pitifully. I slam the fridge door and hurry to her side. In a second, the decision is made. I'm not going to school. I am taking Sadie to the vet. I know where his surgery is – on Geevor Hill. My birthday money is in the chest under my bed. Forty pounds. If the vet sees that Sadie's sick, surely he can do something for forty pounds?

"Come on, Sadie. Come on, now, good girl. We're going to see someone who'll make you feel better."

I clip on Sadie's collar and tug gently. She clambers

awkwardly to her feet, and pads slowly across the floor to the front door.

I look up and down the street. No one's about. "Come on, Sadie." We make our way very slowly along the beach road and then up to the corner by the graveyard, where Geevor Hill begins. The vet's surgery is halfway up. Sadie pants like a dog ten times her age. Her head droops to her chest.

"Why ent you at school, my girl?"

Oh, no, it's Mrs Eagle. She'll tell Mum.

"Inset day," I say quickly.

"Never had they in my day," says Mrs Eagle critically. "You belong to be at school on a working day."

I smile brightly, and slip past her. "Just taking Sadie for a walk, Mrs Eagle."

"Don't look to me like she wants to walk up Geevor; looks to me like she wants to go back downlong," grumbles Mrs Eagle. I escape as fast as I can, almost dragging Sadie.

The vet's surgery is the one with the blue door. But on the blue door there is a laminated notice: SURGERY HOURS, ST PIRANS: TUESDAYS AND THURSDAYS ONLY. 10 A.M. – 5 P.M.

It is Monday. No surgery. Sadie looks up at me in mournful exhaustion. All at once I know in every fibre of my body that Mum and Conor are wrong. Sadie's condition is serious. There isn't time to wait for tomorrow's surgery. Sadie needs help now, and there's only one person who might be able to give it. Granny Carne. Everyone round Senara goes to Granny Carne when they have a trouble they can't solve. I think of Granny Carne's amber, piercing eyes, and the power in her. She'll know what's wrong with Sadie. She'll help her, if anyone can.

At the same moment I hear the growl of a bus engine, changing gear at the bottom of the hill. I look back and there is a shabby blue bus with SENARA CHURCHTOWN on the destination board. *Home.* I stick out my hand.

The bus lumbers past without stopping. The driver turns to me and yells something I can't hear, then as he gets towards the top of the hill I see he's indicating left, pulling in at the bus stop to wait for me.

"Can't stop on the hill, see," he explains as I climb up the steps, pushing Sadie ahead of me. "Lucky for you I'm ahead of myself this morning."

"Thanks for waiting."

"I could see that poor old dog couldn't hardly get up Geevor."

I find my fare, and go to the back of the bus. He thought Sadie was old. That must be because she looks so weak.

I flop down on the back seat, with Sadie at my feet. The driver pulls out on to the road again, and picks up speed. On we go past the grey stone houses, past the rugby ground and the caravan site, past the farm at the edge of town and to the crossroads where the school bus turns left. But this bus turns right, on to the open road that leads across the moors to Senara. A streak of pale, wintry sun lights up the hills. The landscape opens wide and beautiful around us. I take a deep breath of freedom. No crowds, no busy streets. Just a narrow grey road rising over the wild country towards home.

CHAPTER FOUR

When the old blue bus drives off into the distance, leaving me at the roadside with Sadie, the reality of what I've done hits me. This is the stop before Senara Churchtown, and the nearest stop to Granny Carne's cottage. There are no houses here, only the road and the hills covered in bracken, furze and heather. There's a wide black scar across the hills, from a gorse fire.

No one is about. The road is grey and empty. But that's what I wanted, isn't it? I didn't want to see anyone I knew. If I walk along the road a little way, there's a footpath that leads up to Granny Carne's cottage.

"Come on, Sadie," I say encouragingly. "It's not far now." But this time Sadie doesn't respond to my voice. She slumps on the rough grass between the road and the ditch, drops her head on to her paws and closes her eyes.

"Sadie!"

Very slowly, with what looks like a great effort, Sadie opens her eyes. They stare at me dully, without recognition. After a few blank moments, her lids close again.

Terror runs through me like an electric shock. I think she's dead. I throw myself down on the grass beside her and press my ear to her side. I can't hear anything. She's gone. It is so terrible that I can't move or speak. And then, very slowly, her ribs move under her skin. There's a rusty, tearing sound in her throat, as if she's trying to breathe through barbed wire. But she's breathing. She's alive.

It's all my fault. I should never have forced her up Geevor Hill. Now she can't even walk. She can hardly breathe. What am I going to do? I look wildly up and down the road. No one's in sight. A sparrow hops out of a furze bush, cocks its head at me, then hops away again. "Sadie!" I try to lift her into my lap. She's heavy, limp and hard to move. But she's warm. She's alive. "Hold on, Sadie. I'll get help for you. I promise. Please, please don't die."

But how can I get help? If only I had a mobile. But even if I had, it would be no good here. Everyone in Senara complains that they can't get a signal. Phone box. There's a phone box down by the church. How long would it take me to run there? Ten minutes maybe, and then I'd have to make the call, and then another ten minutes back. That's too long.

If I leave her now, she'll think I've abandoned her again, and she'll give up.

"Oh, Sadie, I'm sorry, I'm so sorry..." I hug her tight, trying to pour life into her. She can't die like this – for nothing. She wasn't even ill yesterday. She was so full of life.

I put my hand gently on her head, and stroke her as reassuringly as I can. "Hold on. You're going to be all right." But for the first time ever, Sadie twists her head away from my hand. Feebly, she struggles to heave herself off my lap.

"Get up, Sapphire. Stand back from her. Give her air," says a voice behind me.

"Granny Carne!" My words spill over each other in a rush of relief. Granny Carne will know what to do, better even than a vet. "Help me, please help me, I was coming to find you. Sadie's so ill, I think she's dying—"

"Don't say that word in her hearing. You'll frighten the spirit out of her. Stand back and let me see her."

Reluctantly, I unwind my arms and settle Sadie gently back on the cold grass. Granny Carne stands very still, looking down at Sadie. She looks more like a tall tree than ever, with Sadie in her shelter. Her fierce eyes gleam. I can't bear to see Sadie lying like that, so sick and so alone. I start to move—

"No, Sapphire, stand right back. You can't help her."

"I can't stand here and let her die!"

"No one's letting anyone die, my girl. But what Sadie

needs now is Earth power. See the way she lies there, so close to the earth? You ever seen a mother put her baby against her skin when it's sick, my girl?"

"No."

"These days everyone learns so much at school that they end up knowing nothing. But Sadie knows."

"I was going to bring her up to your cottage, but it was too far. She couldn't walk any more."

"Give her time. She'll come round."

For a long while it looks as if Granny Carne isn't doing anything. She stands there, not moving, not taking her eyes off Sadie, watching every breath Sadie takes. Suddenly there's a small, chirruping whistle. One of the sparrows in the furze, maybe. But the whistle comes again, more strongly and sweetly, and I know it's not a sparrow. It's Granny Carne. The sound is coming from her lips, and she's whistling to Sadie. The whistling grows louder, louder. A shiver passes over Sadie's supine body. And another. Big shivers that shake her whole body, as if she's suddenly realised that she is freezing to death. Granny Carne's whistling grows until my ears ring with it. Sadie shivers once more, from her nose to the tip of her tail. Her body looks different. She's not slumped so much. One of her ears comes forward, as if she's listening. Her tail thumps feebly against the grass. Slowly, with great difficulty, she opens her eyes again, and this time her eyes meet Granny Carne's. They shine with recognition for a second before they close.

"Sadie!"

"She'll do now," says Granny Carne. "Give her time."

"Is she better?"

"Not by a long way," says Granny Carne gravely. "Her spirit went a long way from us, on a cold journey."

"Where did she go?"

"Ingo put her in fear. The spirit in her shrank away from it. It was like putting water on a fire. This is no ordinary illness, Sapphire. I believe you know that. Ingo came too close to her. A creature of the Earth like Sadie can't survive there."

"How do you know?"

"I'm not blaming you, my girl. But look at yourself. You've got Ingo written all over you today. Don't tell me you haven't been there. Don't tell me you haven't got Ingo's music in your ears again. And where you go, that dog's bound to follow, since she's yours."

"But I didn't take her with me, Granny Carne. I left her up at the top of the steps."

"That's no protection for a dog like Sadie. She followed you in her heart. She went in your footsteps until she could go no more. She near burst her heart with fear for you."

Sadie is struggling to her feet. I rush to support her.

"No, let her stand. She's best alone for now. Give her a few minutes and we'll be able to walk her up to mine."

I don't ask any more questions. To tell the truth, I'm a little afraid of Granny Carne today. She knows too much.

She makes me have thoughts I don't want to have. I know everyone comes to her with their troubles, but maybe they don't always like the answers they get from her. She won't let me touch Sadie. Surely Granny Carne can't believe I'd ever hurt Sadie?

"Yes, she's been on a long journey," repeats Granny Carne. "You ever seen a man near frozen after he comes out of the sea half drowned, when he's been clinging to a piece of wreckage for hours? You don't sit him by the fire. You let him warm gently, so his body can bear it. Sadie will find her way back to life, but she needs time. She needs the Earth around her, Sapphire. The breath of Ingo is too strong for her, in her present state."

"How's your Conor?" Granny Carne goes on as we set off walking slowly up the footpath. Sadie pads along cautiously, as if she's not sure yet that her paws will hold her up.

"He's fine."

"Happy in St Pirans?"

"I don't know. I think so. He *wants* to be happy there, anyway."

"And you don't?"

"It's not so much that I don't. It's that I can't. Granny Carne, I didn't mean to hurt Sadie."

"I know that. But it's hard to see a way clear in all this. I don't see it myself yet. Only that there's a reason why you and Conor are as you are. It's for a purpose. Could be that a time's coming when there'll be a purpose in the two of you having this double blood. There've been others. The first Mathew Trewhella was one – he that left the human world and went away with the Mer. Your own father was another. But I never knew any with the Mer blood and the human divided so equal as it is in you. Half and half, you are. It must be the way the inheritance has come down to you. It weakens in one generation, and grows strong in the next."

"Do you mean that Conor and I are exactly half Mer and half human?"

"Only you, my girl. Only you. The Mer blood is not near as strong in Conor, and it never will be, for he fights it down every day."

"I know." Now I understand better what Conor meant when he said, *If you really struggle, you can stop yourself taking the next step.*

"Conor doesn't want to be half and half, does he?" I ask. "He wants not to be Mer at all."

"Maybe he does."

Except for Elvira, I think.

"He fights it," says Granny Carne. "Your father didn't fight so hard. Do you understand what I'm telling you?"

"No."

"You're old enough to know now, my girl, that things don't just happen to us. Somewhere in us we agree to them. We let things happen, though even those closest to us might think we're still fighting."

I feel cold and tired. I know what she's saying. She's

telling me that my father wasn't snatched away against his will. And I do know that, really, after all these months. It is seventeen months since he left us now, and his boat was found empty and upturned, wedged in the rocks. Everyone else thinks he drowned. Only Conor and I keep the faith.

For a long time I could convince myself that some mysterious force was preventing Dad from communicating with us, but I can't make myself believe this any more. If Dad wanted to speak to me, he would.

"Nearly there," says Granny Carne. "She did well."

"Brave girl," I say. "Brave girl, Sadie," and I make my voice warm and full of praise, because she deserves it, even if my heart is cold and tired. Granny Carne has been walking between Sadie and me, but now she steps aside. Sadie presses up to me, the way she always does. I stroke her warm golden back. Minute by minute, Sadie's coming back to herself. Already her fur feels sleek and her eyes are brighter. She turns her head and looks at me as if to say, "It's all right, I'm not going to leave you." Why are dogs so forgiving? My eyes are prickly, but I'm not going to cry. Sadie hates it when I cry.

Here's the grey stone cottage that looks like part of the granite hill. Granny Carne pushes open the door and we go inside. There's just one large room downstairs, painted white, with a stove to heat it and a few splashes of brilliant colour from the tablecloth and cushions. The room is very simple, but not bare. Everything looks worn smooth by years and years of use. I remember the last time I came here, with Conor, that hot summer day when Granny Carne first told us about our Mer inheritance. It was the day when Conor talked to the bees. That seems a long time ago.

"I'll bring down an old blanket for Sadie," says Granny Carne. "She'll need to sleep the night here, to get her strength back."

Granny Carne disappears upstairs before I can protest. Sadie can't stay here overnight. We've got to get back before Mum realises I didn't go to school today.

"You'll be staying over too, Sapphire," says Granny Carne, returning with a folded blanket. It doesn't look like an old blanket. It's made of thick, creamy wool and it looks as if it came off Granny Carne's own bed. She lays it down by the stove for Sadie.

"I can't stay, Granny Carne. I've got to get back before it's dark. Mum thinks I'm at school—"

"Sadie needs you here."

"But Mum—"

"I'll get a message to her. Soon as you're settled, I'll walk down to the churchtown and speak to Mary Thomas. She's got a telephone." Granny Carne says this as if telephones are something rare and undesirable. "Your mother will know you're safe enough with me."

Granny Carne has two bedrooms upstairs: a large one, and a smaller room which she calls the slip room. That's where I'm going to sleep. I'm resigned to it now: I can't leave Sadie. There's a china washstand with a jug of water that Granny Carne has brought in from the trough where the spring rises. There's no bathroom. When Granny Carne wants a bath, she heats water on the stove and fills an enamel bathtub, which hangs from a hook on the wall. It's quite small with a shelf inside to sit on. Granny Carne calls it a hip bath. *Try it yourself, my girl*, she says, but I say that a wash will do me fine. There's no toilet in the house either. The outside toilet, which Granny Carne calls the privy, is so cold that I hope I don't have to go at night. She hasn't even got any toilet paper, only cut-up squares of the *Cornishman* stuck on a nail.

It gets dark early. Sadie doesn't want to eat, but she drinks some water. Granny Carne has gone down to the churchtown, so Sadie and I are alone in the cottage. I wonder what Mary Thomas will think when Granny Carne tells her we are staying here? As far as I know, nobody has ever stayed overnight at Granny Carne's cottage. People respect Granny Carne, but they're also afraid of her because of all that she knows. There are a lot of stories about the way she can see into the future, and heal wounds that ordinary medicine can't cure. I don't mean sicknesses like cancer; I mean sicknesses that are inside people's minds. Granny Carne has a power with those.

I still don't know whether or not I really believe that Granny Carne can see into the future. I'm sure that she can see and understand things which ordinary people can't. She has gifts that come from the Earth. Years ago she might have been caught and burned as a witch, because she knows too much. That's what Dad always said.

I follow Granny Carne in my mind as she goes down the path to the churchtown, and then as she takes the road round to the track which leads down to our cottage and Mary's. Our cottage will have lights on in the windows by now. It gets darks early in November. Granny Carne knows her way in the dark. I'm glad that I don't have to walk past there and see other people living in my home. I wonder if the curtains are the same? Those red checked curtains that Mum made when we were little. They always looked so welcoming with the light shining through them when we came home from school on winter afternoons.

I wonder if the people who are living in our cottage ever go down to our cove? I wonder if they will ever catch sight of Faro or Elvira sitting on the rocks by the mouth of the cove, where Conor and I first met them? I hope they don't. I'm not just being selfish in hoping that. If they see the Mer, their lives won't ever be the same again.

But Granny Carne's cottage is at least two miles from the sea. I don't know how far inland the power of Ingo can reach, but Granny Carne's cottage definitely belongs to the Earth. Maybe that's why Sadie is sleeping so peacefully by the stove. I don't feel peaceful, though. I'm going to stay because of Sadie, but I wish I didn't have to. I'm not at home here.

It takes a long time to get ready for the night at Granny Carne's. I help her to carry in more wood from the stack in her woodshed, and fill the scuttle full of coal. The stove's got to be kept going through the night. Before Granny Carne goes to bed, she riddles it out with an iron poker with a hook on its end. By the time Granny Carne finishes, the hook glows red. I help to shovel out the hot ash into the ash pan. Granny Carne says ash is good for the earth, and she'll spread it on her vegetable patch tomorrow, when the ash is cold. She stokes up the stove with logs and a thick layer of fine coal, and closes the damper on the front.

Suddenly I remember something. "We had a stove like this when I was little, before Mum got storage heaters."

"That was the way everywhere, before the electric came." Granny Carne talks as if electricity has only just been invented. "They'll never bring the electric all the way up here, but I don't miss it," Granny Carne continues. She has lit the paraffin lamps. I like the light they give. It's soft and yellow and it gives warm colour to the white walls. She uses paraffin lamps downstairs and candles upstairs. "You don't need a lot of light to sleep by," she says.

The cottage smells of candles and wood smoke, paraffin and stone. There are big shadows in the corners of the room. It's not a frightening place exactly, but it has too much power to be comfortable. I'm glad Sadie's here. If I wake up in the night I'll hear her breathing, and if I say her name she'll wake up at once.

Granny Carne gets slowly to her feet from where she's been kneeling by the stove. She mutters something, too quietly for me to hear.

"Now he'll sleep through the night," she says. "Praise fire and he'll serve you well."

"Does your fire ever go out?"

"He's been alive as long as I have, my girl. Sometimes he's burned low, but he's never died."

"Granny Carne? I ask hesitantly. "How long have you – I mean – how many years—"

She looks at me with her arms folded. Her fierce owl eyes are bright with amusement. She knows exactly what I want to know, because it's what everybody in Senara has asked themselves, one time or another. How old is Granny Carne? How many years has she been living up there in her cottage, with people from the village coming up to see her privately when they have troubles to which they can't find an answer? Years... decades... or even centuries?

"I'm as old as my tongue and a little bit older than my teeth, Sapphire," she says. "Does that answer your question?"

"No," I say boldly.

"You want more?"

"Yes."

"You ask a lot of me, Sapphire." Her voice has grown harsher. Her tone changes. She is no longer an old woman, and I'm no longer a child. I stare into her eyes. People's eyes don't change.

But everything else is changing. As I watch, the wrinkled brown skin around Granny Carne's eyes grows smooth and soft. Colour steals into her grey hair, which breaks loose from its knot and ripples lustrously over her shoulders. Long, dark brown hair, the colour of the darkest earth, and with red lights in it like fire. Her lips are red and full. Her body grows straight and slender as a young birch tree.

"Granny Carne," I whisper. But there's no Granny Carne in the room. The young woman's lips part in a smile, and then she lays a finger on her lips to silence me. This is Earth magic, and it's too potent for me. I shut my eyes. When I open them again, the woman like a birch tree has disappeared, and Granny Carne is standing there.

"Where's she gone?"

"There's been no one in this room but our two selves, Sapphire. All I'm showing you is that time isn't what you think it is."

"But how can you be old and young at the same time?"

Granny Carne smiles. "Ask anyone with grey hair. Ask Mrs Eagle if she feels any different inside from how she felt when she was eighteen. There's little difference."

"Do you know Mrs Eagle?"

"I've known Temperance Eagle from a girl. Temperance Pascoe as she was then. Wild, she was," goes on Granny Carne thoughtfully. "Her father used to scour St Pirans for her on a Saturday night, shouting that he'd take his belt to her when he found her. He was a strong Bible Christian."

But I'm not going to be diverted by tales of Mrs Eagle's youth. Mrs Eagle is most definitely one hundred per cent old now. Granny Carne's old, too, yet she changed before my eyes into a woman like a young birch tree. I know that I didn't imagine it. What Granny Carne did is something completely different from an old person feeling young inside.

"Mrs Eagle can't do what you did," I say as firmly as I dare, "and no one else talks about time the way you do, as if they can go back hundreds of years and see what was happening then."

But suddenly I remember. Someone does. *Faro* talks about time in the same way as Granny Carne, as if history is still happening. As if he'd watched the *Ballantine* smash on to the rocks with his own eyes. And he made me watch it, too, when I saw into his mind.

Granny Carne sighs. She looks very old now. "You ask

a lot of questions, Sapphire. They're hard questions, too, and I can't give you all the answers you want. Let me tell you this much. What you saw just now, not many would see."

"Why did you let me see it?"

"It wasn't me letting you. It was you that had the power to see the old and young standing in the same place. You think all your power lies in Ingo, Sapphire, but that's because you choose to make it so."

"But *you* said I had strong Mer blood, Granny Carne. You told me and Conor that last summer."

"Yes, but there's more to it than that. Your Mer blood may be strong, but your Earth blood is powerful too. Not as strong as your brother's, but strong enough."

"Is having Earth blood the same as living in the Air – being human, I mean?"

"No. Most people live out their human lives without choosing either Earth or Ingo. They don't need to. They're happy as they are. They live in the present time, and in one place. As far as they're concerned, the past is rolled up like a carpet and no one can touch it. And the future, too. Perhaps they are the fortunate ones," adds Granny Carne.

"I don't see what's fortunate about not being able to go to Ingo."

"Ask your brother."

Conor's words echo in my head: *I've got to try to belong where I am.* Conor really wants to be part of St Pirans –

surfing, playing guitar, hanging out with his friends, and yet all the time he's secretly looking for Elvira. Maybe he wishes he'd never met her... maybe it would be easier for him if he hadn't ever gone to Ingo... because he'd be able to belong.

"Time to sleep," says Granny Carne abruptly. She gives me a candlestick, and lights my candle. "Sadie will sleep in my room tonight, Sapphire."

"But—"

"No. She's not strong yet. She needs to be with me. She needs the Earth to make her strong. Don't you feel that? Sadie's an Earth creature. She loves you, and that's what complicates it for her. Tonight Sadie will go into a deep sleep, like the earth's winter sleep. It will heal her. You know how a bulb lies dormant in the earth all winter, Sapphire, growing strong for spring."

"Sadie's not going to sleep all winter, is she?"

"No. She'll go through her winter healing in one night."

"You said Sadie loves me. I love her. I'll look after her. I'd never let her be hurt."

"Never?" The candle flame leaps and a shadow flies over Granny Carne's face. Her eyes are hidden. "Never, Sapphire?"

I left Sadie tied up to a post, and went to Ingo. Sadie almost died... But I didn't mean to, I didn't want anything to happen to her, it was just that Ingo was so strong...

I don't say any of these things, but Granny Carne knows them, I'm sure. She lays her hand on Sadie's head, and Sadie doesn't try to come to me. She looks at me with her soft brown eyes as if to say, "Try to understand. I can't be with you tonight."

The door closes on Granny Carne and Sadie. I wash quickly, and jump into bed. It's cold. I wonder when someone last slept in this bed? Maybe it was hundreds and hundreds of years ago. I shiver.

I wish I had gone down to our cottage. Just to see it. Granny Carne says that Mum won't mind my staying here overnight, but suddenly I feel terribly lonely, longing for Mum and Conor and home. The little slip bedroom faces the side of the hill. It's dark and quiet and earthy. I can't hear the sea. I can't smell salt.

I'm sure I won't be able to sleep. How many hours is it until morning? Hours and hours and hours. Time's moving so slowly. It seems like a hundred years since I left St Pirans with Sadie this morning.

It's cold in here, but it's airless too. Stifling. Like being in a cave, or a burrow under the earth. It makes me feel as if there's a lid of earth on top of me. Like being in a coffin—

Sapphire, stop it. You are not a prisoner. In the morning Sadie will be completely better, and we'll get the bus back to St Pirans. I expect Mum will be angry, even though Granny Carne says she won't be, but I don't care. I just want to go home.

It'll be better if I open the window and get some fresh air into the room. The air in here tastes so old – that's what made me start thinking of coffins. I meant to check under the bed before I got into it, but I didn't. I always have a horrible feeling if I go to sleep without checking that there's nothing under the bed. Or no one. But I'm not going to stay huddled in bed just because I'm afraid of what's under it. That would be ridiculous.

The candle! Why didn't I think of that? I'll light the candle. I'm not too keen on the shadows candles throw on walls, but it's better than the dark. Oh, no, I haven't got any matches. Granny Carne lit the candle for me. Why didn't she give me any matches? What if I have to go down to the privy? I can't feel my way through the cottage in the dark like I can at home. What if I stretch out my arms and touch – something?

I wish Sadie was here. She's only in Granny Carne's room next door, but it feels as if she is miles and miles away. *Sadie's getting better, that's the important thing, Sapphire. Remember how terrible she looked when she lay down at the bus stop.*

I shiver. It's very cold. I wish everything was different, completely different.

I'm in Granny Carne's cottage, up on the Downs above Senara Churchtown. I do wish I'd gone down to our cottage. Even though there are other people living there, it is still home.

Suddenly a brilliant idea strikes me. Is Granny Carne right about time? If I really do have strong Earth blood as well as strong Mer blood, maybe I could try to move around in time in the same way that Granny Carne does. What if I could go down to our cottage now and peep in through the window, into the gap where the kitchen curtains don't close properly, and see time past? We might all be there – Mum and Dad and me and Conor – all round the table, eating our supper. I'd have to be very careful, though, because if the Sapphire of *then* looked up and saw the Sapphire of *now*, she'd be so scared.

We would all be younger. *They* would be younger, that Dad and Mum and Sapphire and Conor. They wouldn't know about everything that has happened.

Perhaps it doesn't *have* to happen. If you move back to another part of time, then the future hasn't happened yet. Perhaps they *should* see me, before time starts moving on towards the time when Dad leaves.

No. If they all see me, it won't work. It'll just be confusion.

But if I could see Dad secretly – the Dad of the past – and he could see me, then I could tell him not to go. I could tell him about all the things that are going to happen. About the memorial service for him in Senara church, and everybody crying, and the way Mum sat staring at nothing, and how we didn't have any money, and how Mum met Roger and now they're together, and how Conor nearly died in Ingo, and how we've moved away from Senara to St Pirans, and all the other things he doesn't know. And then he could stop them all from happening.

I get up very carefully. I crouch on the side of the bed, and then leap to the middle of the floor, landing as quietly as I can. Nothing grabs hold of my ankles from under the bed.

The window must be about here. I fumble for the catch. Yes. It opens easily, and I push the window wide.

Cold, fresh air pours in. It smells of earth. I lean farther out. Although I'm upstairs, the earth bank rises so steeply behind the cottage that I could easily jump out and land safely. It's much lighter out there than it is inside. I can't see the moon from here, but the stars are bright.

A wild idea comes to me. Perhaps I really could do it. I could go down to our cottage now. Granny Carne found her way down in the dark. If time has slipped and we are still there in the cottage – me and Dad and Mum and Conor – then the spare key will still be in its old place under the slate by the front door. I'll wait until they are all in bed, and then open the door and tiptoe into Mum and Dad's bedroom. I'll wake Dad, and tell him everything that's going to happen if he leaves us.

It's a long way to our cottage, down the footpath to the road, through Senara Churchtown and on to the track that leads to our cottage. But there'll be enough light from the stars and the moon. I can do it.

I lean out of the window as far as I dare, calculating which is the safest place to land on the bank. The moonlight is much stronger now. Even though this window is at the back of the cottage, facing into the side of the hill, I can see quite clearly. Light is filtering into the bedroom, too. It makes everything look blue and ghostly, but there is certainly enough light for me to find the path down the hill.

Just then, I hear another sound. I thought Granny Carne's cottage was too far from the sea for the noise of the waves to carry up here. It must be the way the wind is blowing tonight. But no, the air is still. There isn't a breath of wind, but I can hear the sound of the waves quite clearly. They're breaking in our cove, rolling up on the clean pale sand that's exposed at low tide and hidden when the tide is high. They're breaking in the moonlight, in long curls of foam.

Listen. Listen. What was that?

"*Sssssssapphhhhiiiiiiiire... Sssssssapphhhhiiiiiiiire...*"

It's a wave. It's the shushing noise of a wave as it breaks on the sand.

"*Sssssssapphhhhiiiiiiiire... Sssssssapphhhhiiiiiiiire...*"

I stand by the window, frozen. This has happened before. That night when we were still living in our cottage and I heard a voice in the night, and then Sadie started barking across the fields and the owl flew past the window, and the voice disappeared.

"*Sssssssapphhhhiiiiiiiire...*"
"*Sssssssapphhhhiiiiiiiire...*"

Sadie doesn't bark. Nothing stirs but the voice. It makes the skin prickle on the back of my neck. *It is not the same voice as the one I heard last time.*

This voice is Dad's. I know it. I couldn't be mistaken. Dad is calling me. How can this be happening?

One half of my mind wants Sadie to bark, and Granny Carne to wake. Last summer, when I heard a voice at night, I'm sure Granny Carne woke. The owl that flew by my window had Granny Carne's eyes. If Sadie barks now, Dad's voice will fade away and it'll be dark again. I'll go back to sleep. In the morning it will all seem like a dream.

But the other part of my mind tingles with longing. This is not a dream. I'm wide awake, although it feels as if the whole world is sleeping except for me. Sadie has gone far away into the winter sleep that Granny Carne said would heal her. Wherever she is, I don't think she'll hear me or know what's happening to me.

I look up at the sky. Last time, Granny Carne watched over me and guarded me in the form of an owl. But not tonight. Maybe even Granny Carne's power is dormant. Conor and Mum are far away in St Pirans. But I'm not afraid. I don't want any guardians tonight. Nothing and no one is going to stop me from going to Dad.

"Sssssssapphhhhiiiiiiire..."
"SSSSsssapphhhhiiiiiiire..."

How strange that I was thinking of going down to our cottage to find the Dad of the past. I don't have to find Dad at all. He has found me.

CHAPTER FIVE

"I'm coming," I answer softly. "Wait for me."

"Sssssssapphhhhiiiiiiiire..."

"SSSSsssapphhhhiiiiiiiire..."

The voice isn't far away. Not as far as the sea. Dad's near. He's waiting for me, out there in the night. I pull on my clothes, push my feet into my trainers, and go back to the window.

The window is low, and it's easy to clamber on to the sill. The earth bank doesn't look quite so close now. I'll have to spring right out, or I'll fall back against the cottage wall. One... two... three.

I jump out like a cat. The earth rushes up to meet me and I land sprawling, but I grab hold of a tuft of heather and stop myself slithering down the bank. Very carefully, I scramble along the bank, around the side of the cottage.

I come out on to the rough, tussocky grass in front of the cottage. The moonlight is so bright here that I have a sharp moon shadow. I glance up at the windows. No one there.

Dad's voice comes again, stronger now.

"*Sssssssapphhhhiiiiiiiire... Sssssssapphhhhiiiiiiiire...*"

If I follow his voice, I'll find him. I set off on the steep path that climbs down the side of the hill, following the voice. Sometimes it is very quiet, sometimes it's louder. It says nothing but my name. We've left the path now, and the voice is making its own path for me. On and on over the rough ground. My feet seem to know which way is best. I don't trip or stumble. We're above the churchtown, and far in the distance I can see the square tower of the church in the moonlight. It's so bright. Why doesn't everybody wake up? The voice keeps pulling me. I go faster, until I'm almost running through bracken and heather, past furze bushes and looming granite boulders.

At last the voice leads me to the edge of a field. We're not so far from the sea here. It shines in the distance, as bright as if the moon has polished it. The voice leads me to a stile in the granite hedge. There's a bunch of cattle huddled by the stile. What are cattle doing out in the fields on a November night? They snort as I go by, but they're not scared of me. They put their heads up and follow me with their eyes. Their warm safe smell wraps round me for a minute like a blanket, and then I hurry on to the next stile, across the next field and over the field gate. And now I can smell water. It's not the sea with its sharp salt tang. It's fresh water.

I know where I'm going now. I'm crossing to the Lady Stream that runs off the Downs, under the road, through the village, and on between the fields until it plunges into a deep cleft down to the sea. The Lady Stream is quick and strong. There are waterfalls as it rushes down the steep hills, and wide brown pools where trout swim.

The sound of the stream tumbling over rocks is loud now. It's full of autumn rain. My heart beats hard, as if the current of my blood is rushing just as fast as the water. I'm almost in sight of the stream.

Here it is. I've come out by one of the deepest pools, where the water gathers itself before plunging on to the sea. Moonlight flickers on the surface of the stream and shines on the granite boulders beside the pool.

And then I see it. In the centre of the pool there's a round bulk that shouldn't be there, wet and glistening. A boulder on the surface of the water. A floating boulder. No, that's crazy. Granite boulders can't *float*. As I watch, the stone moves. Moonlight stirs, breaks, ripples. The stone *is* moving, rising, coming out into the air—

"*Sapphire*," says the stone.

A stone. A head. My heart turns over as the shape keeps rising. Smooth, wet head. Smooth shoulders. A man's shoulders.

I step back, opening my mouth to scream. But his voice stops me.

"Don't be scared, Sapphy."

And I know who it is. The voice that has drawn me across the fields is the same as this voice. It is Dad.

I can't answer him. Shock has punched the breath out

of me. He's turning to me. Drops of water run down his face and shoulders. His hair is long and tangled, like seaweed. His body looks like stone.

I always thought that if I ever saw Dad again, I would run to him. I would throw myself into his arms.

It's not like that. This is Dad; I know it is. But not the Dad I used to know. I'm afraid to take a step closer. The waters of the pool shine dark and dangerous. They want me to plunge in; I know they do. They want to take me away.

"I can't come any farther," says Dad's voice. He's breathing hard, as if after some great effort. "Come closer, Sapphy. I can't leave the pool."

"Dad!"

"Yes."

"Is it really you?"

"It's me."

"Why can't you come out of the pool?"

"Come closer, my girl. Let me look at you."

I move forward slowly, fearfully, to the edge of the water.

"We've got to talk. I can't stay long," says my father.

"Where have you been all this time, Dad? How did you get here?"

But I know the answer before the question is out of my mouth. I know it with a cold, stony feeling in my heart. Conor and I were right when we were sure that Dad hadn't died. He's alive, facing me. So why aren't I happy? I thought if ever I saw Dad again I would die of happiness.

It's a stranger with Dad's voice and face. Someone who's been changed – transformed…

"Who are you?" I whisper.

"I'm your father," he says in a tired, sad voice that makes me want to run to him.

But I can't. I'm afraid. The stone in my heart grows heavier. I stare at the water. I can see my father's arms, his shoulders and chest, but the rest of his body is hidden.

"Dad," I whisper, "*why* can't you leave the water?"

"You know the reason, Sapphy."

And now I do. The Mer can't live in the human world. They climb up on rocks by the shore sometimes. It hurts them to breathe the Air, but their curiosity is strong and so they do it. But they can't survive inland. And Dad – Dad can't either – because Dad…

Dad has changed, like the first Mathew Trewhella long ago. He's left us, just as the first Mathew Trewhella left his family. And the first Mathew never came back.

No, it's too terrible.

"Come out of the water, Dad. *Please!* I know you can if you want to. Try! *Please* try for me!"

"It's too late." My father's voice kills any hope I've got left. He pushes back his tangle of hair. "I can't stay long, Sapphy. The tide's high. As soon as it turns, I have to leave."

"How… how did you get here, Dad?"

"I came upstream."

I put my hands over my ears. I don't want to listen to this. It's all too strange and too horrible. This is my *father.* Dad's lips move, but I don't hear a word. Suddenly I'm angry. How can Dad say it's too late? Of course it's not too late! We're all waiting for him – me and Conor and Mum. We wouldn't blame him for what's happened; we'd welcome him home again. We'd help him change back again from – from what he is now.

I take my hands away from my ears.

"You *can* come home. No one can stop you. We'll all help you."

Dad sighs deeply. The water of the pool swirls around him. "This is as far as I can reach," he says. "I swam as far as the stream would bring me."

But the Lady Stream isn't deep enough for swimming, not all the way up. Conor and I have followed it many times, jumping from stone to stone. Dad must have dragged himself uphill between the rough bruising rocks, over sharp stones, from pool to pool. He must have struggled to breathe. He must have hauled himself up by his elbows and dragged his weight over the rocks.

"Did it hurt you, Dad?" I ask him.

"No." He twists suddenly, looking towards the sea, then back to me. "Sapphire! Quick, there's no time left. The tide's about to turn. Come close. Listen to me."

"You called me, Dad! You can't go now."

"I had to see you. To warn you—"

"Dad," I interrupt him quickly, "*you* listen. I'll help you. We'll all help you. There must be a way. You made a terrible mistake, that's all. You didn't mean to choose Ingo for ever. You didn't want to leave us, did you? You can come back."

"Sapphy. There isn't time. Come close. *Listen.*"

Slowly, reluctantly, I move forward. I don't want to go to the water. I want Dad to leave the water and come to me. But as I take another step, the shine on the dark water lures me. Another step. Another. It would be so easy to let myself slip into it – deep, deep into the water—

"No!" shouts my father. For a second he sounds like himself. "Get back! Get back, Sapphy!"

I jump back.

"Stay there. Don't come any closer. Listen," says Dad. "Listen. My dear daughter... *myrgh kerenza*. There are things you don't know."

"What things?"

"I've broken the law."

"Dad! What do you mean? Are you in trouble with the police? Is that why you left us?"

"I've broken the law of the Mer to come here to you. But I had to tell you. Warn you. Where are you living now?"

"In St Pirans. We're renting a house by Polquidden."

Why is he talking about where we live? What does it matter, compared to what's happened to him? He doesn't belong to us any more. I can't hug him. He can't come home.

"By the beach? At sea level?"

"What?"

"Your house. Is it on a hill, or down by the water?"

"It's near the beach."

"So what I heard was true," says Dad, half to himself.

"Who told you about us?"

"It was just a rumour," says Dad evasively.

"No, it wasn't! You knew! You knew all about us. You just didn't bother to let us know that you were alive," I say bitterly.

"*Myrgh kerenza—*"

"Don't keep calling me your dear daughter! So *dear* that you haven't spoken to me for seventeen months? So *dear* that you let me believe you were dead? Have you any idea how we've grieved for you?"

The moon gleams on his face and I see it clearly. The expression on it is nothing like Dad's. There are no quick thoughts, and no laughter. Only heaviness and sorrow. Water glistens in the new, deep lines on his forehead and at the side of his mouth. I want to go on raging at him, but I can't.

"You've a right to be angry with me, Sapphy," he says at last. "But there's no time for anger now. There's danger. Ingo is growing strong, do you know that?"

"Yes."

"Ingo is pushing against its bounds. No one knows exactly what that means yet. I'll come to you again. As soon as I know more, I'll come. Look out for danger, Sapphy. Tell Conor I'll come again."

"What danger? What do you mean?"

"I wish you were all safe on high ground again, Sapphy. It's not safe to be so close to the shore."

"We can't keep on moving, Dad. Thanks to you, I've already had to leave my home."

"Tell Conor I'll come again. As soon as I hear of any threat or danger to you, I'll come again. But I must leave now, Sapphy. The tide's turning. God knows I've broken every law to come to you tonight."

"But, Dad, look at your shoulder. You're bleeding."

He glances down. "It's nothing. Maybe I scratched myself on one of those rocks."

It's a deeper cut than that. Blood makes a dark track down Dad's skin.

"Come with me now, Dad," I beg him. "I'll find a bandage. We can make it better. *Please*, Dad. I promise Mum won't be angry. I'll help you. You can lean on my shoulder. It's not far to Granny Carne's cottage. I'll get you there. She'll help us. Please. *Please* come home."

"What would you do with me in the human world, Sapphy? Put me in a tank as a freak for folk to stare at?" asks my father. "You don't understand. I can't change back to what I was."

"Don't show yourself, Dad!" I beg again, as the water heaves. I put my hands over my eyes. I won't see him. I will not see my own father changed into one of the Mer.

"If you don't want to look at me, I shan't force you. But I am what I am, Sapphire. I belong to Ingo now."

His words hit me like hammers. "You have a family, Dad! What about me? What about Conor? Have you forgotten that we're your children?"

"No," says Dad. "I've forgotten nothing. None of it. Not one word either of you ever spoke to me. Not one look, even. Not a single day of your childhood. But I can't come home."

"Don't you want to know about Mum? Aren't you going to ask how she is?"

"Your mother is better off without me," says Dad. "She always feared Ingo, and she was right to fear it."

"Why, Dad, why? Why was Mum always so frightened of the sea?" I remember Conor's story of the fortune-teller's prophecy. Dad has got to tell me everything now. I'm afraid there are more secrets hidden away, waiting to burst out and destroy my family a second time.

"A fortune-teller told your mother that the man she loved would lose her by water."

"What?"

The man you love will lose you by water. Beware of the sea. The sea is your gravest danger," says Dad, and I know he's only repeating something he's heard many, many times.

"And Mum believed it?"

"Yes, she thought that if *she* kept away from the sea, all would be well," says Dad. His voice is sad, but he sounds as if Mum were someone he knew a long time ago, in a different life.

"You don't care about us," I say bitterly. "You've forgotten us. You don't care about us now."

"I haven't forgotten anything," whispers my father. Why's he whispering? Why doesn't he shout at me? *Dad* would shout if I spoke to him like that. *Dad* would yell and slam doors, and then he would come back later and give me a big hug and say, *Sorry, Sapphy. I lost it there for a moment, you were winding me up so much.*

"Dad," I say. Dad is still half-hidden under the water. Sadness rises in me until my anger is swallowed by it. "Dad, where are you? It's me, Sapphire. Your own daughter."

The water seems to be rising too, or perhaps my father is sinking down. Water swells around my father's chest, his shoulders, his neck. The moon shines on his face. He looks strange. Unfamiliar. Mer. He reaches out his arms to me underwater.

I want to go to him so much. I want to hug him tight and never, never let him go again. But I'm more afraid than ever. He is Dad, but he's also a stranger. One of the Mer. The water is like a black, shining curtain which hides my real father from me.

"Tell Conor," says Dad as the water reaches his lips. "Warn him of danger. Good—"

But Ingo takes him before the word is out of his mouth. He sinks down beneath the skin of the moonlit

101

water. His face is still turned towards me, and his eyes watch me until the water covers them. As the pool swallows him its surface stirs and lashes around as if some monstrous creature is fighting for freedom there. I watch the dark underwater shape of my father plunge over the lip of the pool, and vanish downstream.

The surface of the water trembles, and then settles. There's nothing left but granite boulders, leaning over the edge of the pool.

CHAPTER SIX

I can't believe that Granny Carne isn't going to ask what happened last night. Surely she didn't sleep through it all, like an ordinary old woman? But instead of questioning me, she keeps on doing her morning tasks – riddling and feeding the stove, feeding Sadie, making breakfast.

"Did you sleep well, my girl?" is all she says. Her face is inscrutable and it doesn't invite conversation. I nod, and fill my mouth with bread and honey so I won't have to say anything. But there's a glint in Granny Carne's eye that makes me suspect that she's teasing me. I'm glad to be teased. It relieves the dead feeling I have in my heart from meeting Dad.

I had no idea how I was going to get back into the cottage last night. It was easy enough to jump out of the window on to the bank, but it wouldn't be so easy to climb back in. I had all kinds of plans in my head: I'd wait until morning, then pretend I'd been out for an early walk; I'd find a ladder in the shed; I'd manage to open one of the downstairs windows. But when I tiptoed up to the cottage door and tried the door handle, it turned as smooth as silk. The door swung open without a sound. Maybe Granny Carne never locked her door, or maybe she knew that I had gone out and had left it open for me. I crept up the stairs, opened the door of the slip bedroom and slid into bed.

It felt as if a hundred years had passed since I'd said goodnight to Sadie and Granny Carne. My heart was still beating hard. I was back in bed, safe, I told myself. *Calm down, Sapphire.* The booming of my blood in my ears was so loud, I was sure Granny Carne could hear it.

I wasn't safe. Nothing was safe. Dad was in Ingo, and he wasn't like my dad any more. He wouldn't come out of the water. No, it was worse than that: he couldn't, even if he wanted to, because he'd made his choice. He belonged to Ingo now, and not to us. The only way I could live with him was if I chose Ingo too. That was too huge and frightening to think about.

I'd been waiting so long for him to come home. Month after month after month, when everyone else had given up hope, we'd kept the faith. Conor said, "As long as we keep the faith, we'll find Dad one day." We swore and promised that we wouldn't rest until we found Dad. Now what am I going to tell Conor?

I'd found Dad – or he'd found me – and it solved nothing. We didn't hug and kiss and cry. I didn't even touch him. Did he even ask about Conor? Not really. Not the questions a father should ask about his son when he hasn't seen him for a year and a half. But I remember what it's like being in Ingo. The human world fades quickly.

I turned over in bed restlessly. Maybe my heart was booming so loud because it was empty. *Away in Ingo.* My dad could never come out of Ingo now. Unless... unless there was some magic that could change him back again into a human being. Earth magic. Granny Carne's magic. Surely there was some hope.

Away in Ingo... away in Ingo...

But now you know where he is, you can go to him. You can slip through the skin of the water and into Ingo. You can go where he is.

I tossed in the bed as if there were lumps of rock in the mattress. I would never be able to sleep. How was I going to be able to tell Conor about Dad? I should have asked more questions. I should have made Dad tell me everything that had happened to him from the moment he left us. Maybe Conor would blame me for being so stupid, but with the moonlight and everything being so mysterious and terrifying, I didn't have time to think of questions.

No excuses. *You had the chance, Saph, and you let it slip away.* As for telling Mum, that would be out of the question. Even if she believed me, she wouldn't be able to help Dad. She'd hate him for abandoning us. She might even say we were better off without him.

Poor Mum, I thought. She didn't choose to fall in love with Roger and go to St Pirans to live. It was all chosen for her because Dad left. And I'd blamed her so much, almost hated her sometimes when she smiled at Roger and sang so cheerfully around the house in the mornings.

I would never be able to sleep. I would have to lie awake until morning. Or was it morning already? The sky seemed to be growing lighter – but perhaps that was the moon—

I woke with a shock to hear Sadie barking joyously downstairs. I didn't know where I was, and then everything jumped into place. White walls. Granny Carne's cottage. Was Sadie better? She sounded better. She was barking as if she had never been ill in her life.

And now here I am in Granny Carne's kitchen, eating bread and honey while Sadie sits on the flagstone floor beside me, quivering with life, her eyes fixed on me. Sadie looks as if she's been dipped in a pool of sunlight. Her coat gleams, her eyes are bright and moist, her tail is a golden plume. She can't wait for the day to begin, with all its adventures, and she can't believe that I'm being so slow and dull, munching breakfast when I could be outside, leaping downhill, chasing rabbits.

"She's got plenty of life in her this morning," says Granny Carne, looking up from her green notebook. While I've been eating, she has been writing steadily with an old-fashioned pen that she dips into a bottle of ink. I've never seen a pen like it. I did try to read the writing from upside down, but I couldn't. It is black and spiky and there are long letters which look like *f*s without the line across. It's probably her spell book, I think. *Eye of newt and toe of frog,* like in Macbeth, which is the play we are studying at school. Something must show on my face, because Granny Carne looks at me quizzically.

"Um… are you writing a recipe?" I say quickly. Anything to distract Granny Carne from what I'm really thinking.

"No," says Granny Carne, "I'm writing Sadie into this life book."

"Is that like a biography?"

"A life book's more than that. A biography's all about the past."

"Oh."

"Sadie's got her past, but she's young yet. Her future's dominant."

"Do humans have a life book, as well as animals?"

"Of course. Every one of us is written in the book of life."

As soon as Granny Carne says this, I long to see inside the book, to know the future, as Granny Carne does. If only I could see Dad coming back to us – not Mer, but human—

"Does anyone ever read inside the life book, Granny Carne?"

"No," says Granny Carne. She puts down her pen. "Never try that, my girl. These words can blind you." Her eyes blaze at me.

I take a deep breath. My voice squeaks with nerves, but I'm determined. "I need to, Granny Carne. I wouldn't ask otherwise. I really need to."

"No, my girl."

"Please! You don't know how important it is."

Granny Carne stares at me hard. "*You* don't know what you're asking." She weighs the book in her hand, then suddenly she seems to change her mind. She holds up the green notebook, open and facing outwards.

It's just a book with writing in it. Not a spell book or anything ridiculous like that. Granny Carne's magic isn't of that kind.

"The life book has no power of its own," says Granny Carne slowly. "It's what you put into it. What *you* put into it, my girl."

The writing faces out towards me. I can't read it, though. The writing is too small – or maybe it's too difficult for me...

Granny Carne begins to turn the pages, slowly at first and then faster. There are far more pages than a small notebook could possibly hold. The pages flicker as if a strong wind is blowing them. I stand up and lean forward, desperate to pick some words out of the blur, to catch just one drop of the future. But instead of making sense, the words swarm like bees all over the creamy paper.

Can words move like this, once they've been written? They're writing themselves, coiling and clustering and buzzing all over the page. They're angry. Angry bees that have been disturbed by a stranger at their hive. Any moment now they will fly off the page and straight at me, stinging and stinging until I'm blinded. I put my hands up in front of my face to ward them off. The hum of the words rises dangerous and threatening, filling my ears. I step back. A chair clatters. I stumble, reach out to get my balance, and nearly fall. The word bees are swarming close, ready to attack.

"Granny Carne! I didn't mean it! Don't let them—"

Suddenly, the noise is gone, as if a door has been shut on it.

"It's all right now, my girl. The book is closed."

Slowly, I let my hands fall. Granny Carne's green notebook is shut. It looks so innocent.

"You have to handle things right," says Granny Carne. "Go to the bees in anger and they'll give you anger back. This book is not for your eyes, Sapphire, no matter if you put your life into it. It's not for you to read. Remember that, no matter what the temptation."

I nod. I feel too shaky to answer.

"You want to make things go back to what they were before last summer, but the pages have turned," goes on Granny Carne. Her voice is stern now. "You cannot turn them back, except by blinding yourself. Go forward, my girl. There's good and bad coming that won't be cured by looking back. I can't see the scope and nature of it yet, but I can read its power. Keep your eyes open. Ingo is growing strong, and the Mer blood in you is racing to meet it.

"But remember something. Remember that you are Earth too, even when you are angry with her, as a girl is angry with her mother when she's growing away from her. That's what you carry, my girl: the gifts of both sides. Two ways they can be used – to split you in half, or to heal what needs healing. There are hard times coming. Troubled times."

We stand frozen for a few moments. Granny Carne's amber eyes are as wide as the eyes of an owl hunting in the dark. Sadie is like a statue, and I can't move or speak. And then the spell breaks and we're just an old woman drinking tea, a girl eating bread and honey, and a dog who wants a walk.

"Go on home now," says Granny Carne. "Best you don't stay here any longer. Hurry now, the bus'll be at the corner at ten past nine, and if you miss it there's another two hours to wait."

But I go straight past the bus stop on the road to the churchtown. I keep my head down, hoping that no one will recognise me, but of course they do. First the post van stops for a chat, then Alice Trewhidden is on her way up to catch the bus, then the vicar appears at the church gate just as I'm going by.

"How you doing, Sapphire girl? How's life down in St Pirans?"

"Your mum all right, then? She like it down there?"

"Ah, Sapphire, good to see you! How are you all? How is your mother?"

"She's all right."

The vicar's face is smiling but his eyes are sharp. He drops his voice and suddenly it's a person talking to me, not a vicar. "It's hard," he says. "Don't think I don't know that."

I don't know what to say to this. "S'OK," I mumble. The trouble is that whenever I see the vicar my mind flashes back to Dad's memorial service. I don't want to think of it.

"Give your mother my love," he adds, and I don't know what to say to that either. Mum always liked talking to the vicar. Dad never went to church, but Mum did sometimes, just on her own.

By the time I get away, I wish I'd caught that bus. But I can't go back to St Pirans without seeing our cottage. It doesn't matter if the people who are living there now see me. They won't know who I am. When they came to look round, before they decided to rent it, I went out for a long walk. I didn't want to meet them.

I reach the top of the track that leads down to our cottage. Everything is so familiar, yet slightly different. Even the baling twine tied round the gate is a different colour: green now, instead of orange. There is a Jeep parked outside the cottage. It's old and dusty but it looks in good condition. Dad always wanted a Jeep.

Our front door is open. Radio music spills out into the garden. To my surprise the vegetable patch has been completely dug over. The gooseberry bushes have been pruned, and the roses. The window frames are freshly painted.

The curtains Mum made are no longer blowing at the kitchen window. Instead someone has put up smart new curtains, the colour of cornflowers. I try not to like them, but I do.

Sadie sniffs eagerly around outside the gate. I walk very slowly, trying not to dawdle too obviously, trying to make it look as if I'm just having a relaxed walk with my dog. "Come on, Sadie girl," I say loudly in case anyone inside is listening. But Sadie is more intelligent than to believe I really want her to move on.

I drink in every detail of the cottage. It's so nearly the same, and yet completely different, because we don't live there any more. This must be what it's like to die and come back to haunt a place you used to love.

"Can I help you?" asks a voice. I jump violently, and feel a blush start to spread over my face.

"No, no, I'm fine, my dog's just—"

A woman swings out of the doorway. She's on crutches, but she handles them easily, as if she's been using crutches for a long time. She's younger than Mum, wearing a long red skirt and a sweater. "Were you looking for something?" she asks. Her eyes are penetrating. Has she guessed who I am?

"No, no, I'm going for a walk with my dog – down to the cove maybe—"

You idiot, Sapphire. Why did you mention the cove? Maybe they haven't discovered it yet.

"The cove," repeats the woman. "Do you know it?"

"Yeah."

"I'd really like to see it. I can get to most places, but I can't do that climb down just now. The only way I'll get there is if they swing me over the cliff in a basket. I'm on these crutches for the time being."

She smiles, a quick warm smile that I can't help responding to, even though I had no intention of liking the person who's living in our cottage.

"Do you live here on your own?" I ask her.

"No. My husband works up in Exeter with the Met Office. He stays there during the week."

"It must be lonely," I say, testing, probing. But she shakes her head.

"Lonely's in your head. I don't find it so," she says. "The neighbours are good. I wasn't sure, coming down here."

"What's the Met Office?"

"Meteorology. Weather forecasting. Rob doesn't do the day-to-day stuff, though. Long term climate change is his thing, and the role of extreme weather occurrences."

"So he looks into the future," I say, without knowing I'm going to say it.

"Yeah, in a way he does. You interested in climate change?"

I think of the sea horses and sunfish that come into Cornish waters now, where they never used to come. The changes Faro has talked about, and the dangers they bring.

"Yes."

"You must meet Rob. D'you live around here?"

"Yes— I mean no, um… not very near." The words stumble over one another just when I want them to be smooth. Suddenly she's looking at me closely. Her face changes. Something comes into it that shouldn't be there: recognition

"I know who you are. You're the girl with the seaweed hair."

"What do you mean?"

"That's what I call you. Rob calls you the little mermaid."

"*What?*"

"I'm sorry. I didn't mean to offend you. I've really messed this up, haven't I? You didn't want me to know who you were. It's that picture of you, the one that's set into the dresser."

"Oh. *Oh.*"

"You know the one."

I know the one. Dad took it about three years ago. It's a colour photo, and I'm wearing a sea-green dress that I wore to a New Year's party. My hair is loose and very long. I'm not smiling. Dad always loved that photo. He said I looked as if I came from another world. He had the photo made into a tile and set it into the kitchen dresser. We couldn't take the dresser with us to St Pirans because it was built into the wall.

I look down. I feel so stupid. She'll think I came here spying on her. But her voice doesn't sound angry. "It's a beautiful picture, you should be proud of it," she says. "Rob says you look like you came from another world."

"Oh! That's exactly what Dad used to say."

"He took the picture?"

"Yes."

"I'm sorry. The letting agent told me about the… accident."

She has found the kindest word she can, but I still have to clench my hands and dig my nails into my palms.

"We should introduce ourselves. I'm Gloria Fortune."

"I'm Sapphire Trewhella."

"Of course. I should have remembered. Mary Thomas told me your name."

I'm not sure I like this. Mary is *our* neighbour.

"It must have been tough, leaving this place. Every day I wake up and look out of the window, I have to pinch myself, it's so beautiful."

"It's my home." I'm not angry any more. I don't even want Gloria Fortune to leave our cottage. It's just that coming back here has made me know for sure that no matter how long I live in St Pirans, it will never be home.

"Then you'll come back," says Gloria, looking into my face.

"Do you see into the future?"

"No." She smiles. "But I know a single-minded person, because I'm one myself."

"I must go."

"You going down to the cove now?"

I glance down at Sadie, and gently stroke her head. No, Sadie doesn't deserve that. As soon as my feet touch that hard white sand, I'll look at the rocks at the mouth of the cove, and I'm sure I'll see a figure there, and then I won't be able to stop myself. The cove will be too powerful for Sadie. That's where Conor and I first entered Ingo. The cove is a gateway, I am sure it is, and it's another reason we've got to come home. Dad left the human world through the cove, so perhaps the cove is his way home.

I'm not going to accept that Dad has changed for ever. He still has human blood in him, just as I have. If a human being can change to become one of the Mer, then he must be able to change back again somehow. There will be a way. Somebody, somewhere, must know.

Faro's teacher! He's supposed to be so wise. Perhaps he can help me. I won't tell him why I want to know. He's Mer, so he'll want Dad to stay in Ingo. But surely all the changes can't be one way?

"Are you all right?"

"Oh – yeah, yeah, I'm fine, I was just—"

"You were miles away," says Gloria Fortune. "Penny for your thoughts?"

"You wouldn't want them," I answer. "They're just a mess."

"OK, OK, I didn't mean to pry. You go on down to the cove."

"Maybe not today."

"Come back another time, then," says Gloria. "You can help me with that basket and pulley."

"Um… you know, I think that could be quite dangerous."

"I wasn't being entirely serious. I smashed the top of my thigh bone and things didn't mend so well, so I've got to have a hip replacement. But I'm putting it off, because I don't like hospitals."

"I've never been in one."

"Not even to be born?"

"No. I was born here, in Mum and Dad's bedroom. It's the one that faces away from the sea."

There's a pause. Luckily Sadie creates a diversion by diving towards a hole in the garden wall, pretending she's smelled a rabbit. It's a hole where I've seen adders sunning themselves in August, so I pull her off sharply, even though any adders should be hibernating now.

"Come again," Gloria repeats. "But maybe you wouldn't like to come inside the cottage, with us living here."

"I don't know."

Gloria nods thoughtfully. There's something about her face – I don't know what it is. A look that is strange yet familiar. It's elusive, but it's there, like a ripple of water moving over her features. *Water!* Yes, that's what it is. Salt water. Ingo. Ingo has touched her face and left its look there.

It sounds like a wild, crazy guess, but it's not. I *know*, deep inside me, because it's the look I see on my own face sometimes in the mirror. And on Conor and Faro and Elvira... and on my own father.

I open my mouth to speak, but then say nothing. It's too much of a risk. If she doesn't know, is it safe to tell her? I have the feeling that if she were to go down to the cove, Gloria too would see a figure sitting on the rocks. A figure that looks like a surfer in a wetsuit from a distance, but when you come close it looks like a boy, and then like a seal, and then like a boy again. But Gloria's leg is injured, so she can't climb down the cliff path. Maybe that is just as well.

"Were you born by the sea?" I ask abruptly.

She stares at me. "Why do you ask that?"

"I just had a feeling."

"That is weird. You're right. I grew up in London, but I was born on Skye, up in Scotland. Our cottage was down by the shore."

"You don't sound Scottish."

"No, I'm a Londoner, really, like my dad. He came over from Jamaica when he was two months old. But my mother was Scottish. She came from Skye, and we lived there until I was six. We had to move down to London then because my father got a job there. Maybe that's why I love this place so much. It reminds me of when I was little. Skye is so beautiful. I remember the seals. I used to think I could talk to them, and they'd talk back to me. The place we lived was so remote that I conversed with the seals more than I did with other children."

Her face is soft with remembering. That strange yet familiar look is growing stronger. I was right. She really has a look of Ingo on her. Maybe she doesn't yet know what it means.

I'm burning with excitement. I can't wait to tell Conor. There are others, not just ourselves. We are not freaks. We are part of something much larger than we knew. Maybe there are other gateways, other people going through the skin of the sea and into Ingo, all over the world…

I bend down over Sadie, pretending to adjust her collar, and whistle, very low, a few bars of *O Peggy Gordon.*

I wish I was away in Ingo
Far across the briny sea,
Sailing over deepest waters…

I glance up cautiously. Gloria's expression is faraway, and she's listening intently. "What tune is that you're whistling?"

"It's a song called *O Peggy Gordon.*"

"Is it a Scottish song?"

"I don't know. It could be. My father knew a lot of Scottish songs."

"I'm sure I know it. My mother used to sing me a lot of songs. Do you know the words?"

I shake my head. It's too risky. It was the song that began it all, that Midsummer Night before Dad disappeared. He was singing *O Peggy Gordon* then, and he was listening, listening... but then I didn't know what he was listening for.

I mustn't tell Gloria the words, or speak the name of Ingo to her. Not here. Not now. What if Ingo starts to call her when she's alone? It might tempt her as far as the cliffs. She can't climb down them on crutches, but I know how powerful the pull of Ingo can be. Gloria might try. She might fall. It's safer for her if she doesn't know too much. Not yet.

"I've got to go now," I say aloud, "but I'd like to... I'd really like to come again, and bring my brother Conor to meet you."

She nods. "That'd be good." Does she recognise a look on my face, too? Does she have that feeling we're not really strangers, but more like distant cousins from a family that's been scattered for generations?

Get a grip, Sapphire. If you say anything like that, this woman will think you are completely crazy. She'll keep the door locked next time you come.

I want to come again. Not now, maybe not for a while.

But deep inside me, I'm sure that I'll see Gloria Fortune again. Somewhere in the future, where only Granny Carne can see it, our lives are linked.

"Goodbye, then," says Gloria, smiling. "I'll tell Rob I've met the little mermaid. He'll be sorry he missed you. You look exactly like your picture."

CHAPTER SEVEN

I hoped Mum would be at work when I got back early this afternoon, but no. She had swapped her day shift for an evening shift at the restaurant, and was waiting for me. I was sorry when I saw how tired and tense she looked, but then she began to shout and I began to shout back.

Not only was Mum waiting behind the front door, but Roger was on patrol in the living room. With a pincer movement, they got me into a chair so they could lecture me while they stood over me like judges. Most of what they said (or in Mum's case shouted) was what I'd expected.

You've missed two whole days of school. Do you expect me to write a pack of lies to your teachers about you being ill?

Don't you realise how dangerous it is to go off without telling anyone where you're going? Anything could have happened and we wouldn't have known.

If Mary hadn't phoned to tell us you were at Granny Carne's, we'd have had the police out looking for you. What do you think it's like to have a neighbour telling you where your own daughter's got to?

I knew you'd be safe with Granny Carne, but that's not the point. You've got to be more responsible, Sapphy.

Your mother has been seriously upset, Sapphire, and when she's upset, I'm pretty unhappy too.

There was a lot more, but I was ready for it. I'd known there would be major trouble when I got back, even though the most important thing was that Sadie had been cured.

"But look at Sadie," I said. Sadie cocked her head towards us from where she was sitting, as far away from the row as she could get. Her eyes glowed, and her coat shone with health. "She's completely better. Granny Carne healed her. I *had* to go. She was so ill she might have died."

"Rubbish!" Mum shouted. "She was ill, but she wasn't *that* ill. You're just using Sadie as an excuse to do exactly what you want."

I thought about the accusation. It wasn't true this time. Sadie wasn't an excuse, she was the heart of the matter. But Roger hadn't seen how ill Sadie was, and so he backed Mum. "If Sadie could cope with the journey to Senara, she can't have been as bad as you say."

"She was. She was nearly dying. She collapsed on the ground by the bus stop and she couldn't get up."

"Don't exaggerate, Sapphire!"

I took a breath, ready to yell back at Mum, but Roger

put up his hands. "Wait. Let's cool it here. Sapphire, you have to understand that your mother has very proper concerns about your welfare, and she has a right to be angry with you."

"Why are you being so pompous?" I flashed back. "You can't tell me what to do. *You're* not my father."

As the words came out of my mouth, I saw Roger flinch, just a little. And then a picture of Dad rose into my mind, exactly as he'd appeared the night before. Drops of water glistened on his shoulders. His hair was like seaweed and his face was torn with anguish. He *was* my father, and yet he was like a stranger. I couldn't even put my arms around him. It must be like that when you have to visit your dad in prison, and talk to him through one of those glass screens they have, and not be able to hug or kiss him.

"You're not my father, Roger," I repeated quietly. "It's not that I don't like you, but—"

I expected Roger to react angrily, but he didn't. "I know that. All the same, I care what happens to you."

"Only because you don't want Mum to be upset."

"Yes, that's part of the reason, but it's not the whole of it. Why do you find it so hard to believe that people like you for yourself, Sapphire?" I had nothing to say, which was just as well since Roger still had plenty.

"I don't want to tell you what to do, Sapphire. I think you're probably right, and Sadie did need help, but you've got to go about it the right way. I want *you* to take responsibility for your own life. Make your own life good. Running back to Senara isn't going to solve anything. That's not where we live now. St Pirans has a lot to offer, but you're walking around with your eyes shut so you won't get involved."

I tried to take a deep breath to calm myself, but it hurt. My chest was tight. I wanted to get out of the house, out of the town, out of this tangle of Mer and human, to a place where I could be one thing and one thing only. But perhaps that place did not exist.

"Promise me you'll never do anything like that again," broke in Mum.

All the things that had happened since yesterday morning flashed over my mind. Sadie lying on the verge of the road, so desperately ill. Granny Carne pouring life back into her. The dark night and Dad's voice calling me. The eerie silence by the moonlit pool after Dad had disappeared again. Granny Carne's life book with words that swarmed like bees. The look of Ingo that I'd seen on Gloria Fortune's face...

So much had happened. No, I would never do those exact same things again, though I might do other, different things. It was safe to promise. "I promise I'll never do those things again," I said, perhaps a little too readily, because Mum looked at me with suspicion.

"You really promise, Sapphy?"

"I really promise. Mum, where's Conor?"

"He stayed over at Mal's. They were going surfing at

first light. They've got a late start at school this morning for some reason."

I bet, I thought.

"Did he come back after school yesterday?" I asked with apparent casualness.

"No, he went straight to Mal's," said Mum innocently.

But Roger had seen what I was getting at. "Sapphire," he said warningly.

But I went on as if I hadn't heard, "So Conor's been away for exactly as long as me, but he won't even be back until tonight. Much later than me. Aren't you worried about *him*?"

"No," said Mum sharply, "because I know where he is."

"Mary Thomas told you where I was."

"It's not the same thing. Conor's older. Besides, I can trust him—" She broke off again.

"And you don't trust me. I told you that Sadie was dying. It was true, Mum, but you didn't believe me because you don't trust me. I do the things I do for a *reason*. Not just because I want to. Because I *have* to do them."

Both of them were looking at me now. I didn't feel like yelling at them. I didn't want to burst into tears. A year ago, I'd probably have done both those things.

Roger leaned forward. "What things?" he asked very quietly. "What things do you do, Sapphire, because you have to do them?"

Perhaps I should have told him then. I don't know. Ever since the day when Roger dived into Ingo without knowing what he was doing, and was almost killed by the guardian seals, I've had the sense that he knows something. Deep in him, there are memories that he can't quite touch. But sometimes, perhaps they come close to the surface.

I didn't tell him. I looked back at him as seriously as he was looking at me, and answered, "I can't tell you that."

Mum did something surprising then. She knelt down by the chair where I was sitting, and put her arms around me. She hugged me so tightly that it hurt, as if she never wanted to let go of me. "Don't grow up too fast, Sapphy," she whispered in my ear. I couldn't believe what I was hearing. Mum always wants us to be independent, and we are. "I don't want to lose you just yet."

Lose me? I had the feeling that Mum understood, suddenly, how far away from her I sometimes was. She didn't know about Ingo, but she realised that something was changing me and drawing me away from her. I'd thought she was happy about it, because it left her free to get on with her life with Roger, but perhaps I was wrong.

I hugged her back, hard. It felt so nice, and I could tell that for once she wasn't thinking of Roger or work or Dad, or even Conor, but only of me.

So now I am grounded, and Conor's not back yet. Grounded, grounded, grounded. No TV, no using Roger's computer, no using the phone either.

"Do some extra homework," said Mum before she went off to the restaurant, "and make up for the school you missed."

I take out my maths book, but the figures won't do what I want. I try to read, but I can't keep hold of the thread of the story. By eight o'clock I'm lying on my bed because there is nothing else to do. I might as well rest my eyes. Of course, I won't go to sleep yet; it's much too early. I'll just lie here for a while, and listen out for Conor.

I wake with a shock out of a deep, dreamless sleep. I'm completely disorientated, and have no idea how long I've slept. It must be morning. But my alarm clock reads 21:32, and someone is banging on the door downstairs. And shouting. It's Conor. His voice is loud and urgent. There's something wrong.

I jump up, fling open my door and rush downstairs. Roger is already at the front door, and there's Conor on the doorstep, with Mal, both of them streaming wet with rain.

"Conor! What's happened?"

"Dolphin stranded on Polquidden," gasps Conor. He must have run all the way up. "Mal's dad was night fishing – found it lying on the sand just now. Must've got stranded after dark. He's down there now."

"Is it alive?"

"Just about. In a bad way though. We've called the emergency number and there should be a rescue team here soon. Is Mum still at work?"

"Yes," says Roger. He's already pulling on his boots and waterproofs. "I'll come down with you, Conor. I've done basic training on live strandings."

Of course, you would have, I think. Is there any field in which Roger is not competent? I slide my bare feet into my own boots, and find my waterproof. I don't care if I'm grounded, I'm going, and no one's going to stop me. Roger glances at me, but says nothing except, "Don't bring Sadie. She'll stress the dolphin even more."

We slam the door, remembering too late that none of us has a key. Conor left his at Mal's. But there's no time to think, because we're already running down the street, turning the corner, and down the slippery rain-wet steps to the beach. The tide is out. It must have turned by now, but it's still far away. The dolphin would have got stranded on the falling tide. What happened to make it come so close inshore? Maybe it was sick or injured, or it had been hurt in an encounter with a trawler, or something else had disorientated it...

We splash over the wide, empty beach, through the shallow pools that the sea has left, over hard ridged sand, towards a faint, bobbing light over by the rocks way down on the left hand side of the beach. The light is shrouded by rain.

"Where's Mal gone?"

"To fetch more help."

We run as fast as we can towards the light. It seems near, then far, and sometimes there seems to be nothing but rain and darkness and our own labouring breath. But we're getting close. Now we can see shapes in the darkness ahead. Roger raises his torch. There's a man – Mal's dad – and a curved bulk on the sand. It glistens with rain, like a wet black rock rising in a hump from the sand. But it's not a rock, it's the dolphin.

I have never understood what "stranded" means, until the moment I see the dolphin lying there. The most graceful creature of Ingo lies helpless as a sack of sand. It cannot move. It cannot escape.

Roger's up ahead of me and Conor, shouting to Mal's dad. "All right, Will? How are things?"

"Female, weighs about half a ton. It's not looking so good," Will calls back. "She's struggling."

Struggling to survive, he means. She's not moving. Out of her element, stranded on the hard sand. She lies on her side.

"Don't reckon the tide'll come in fast enough for her."

"Low water was about eight, that right?"

"That's right. Where are we now, half past nine? Water should be back to her by half ten, eleven time."

"Is she injured?"

"Bleeding from cuts on her flank. They're not too serious though. It's the pressure that's getting to her."

"What pressure?" Conor asks.

"Once she's out of the water," says Roger quickly, "her own weight starts to crush her internal organs."

Mal's dad swears softly. "How many strandings is that round Cornwall this year? 'Bout eight hundred?"

"Twice what it used to be."

"Terrible, it is. I blame those trawlers pair-fishing."

All the time they're talking, they're moving around the dolphin cautiously, assessing her condition.

"Problem is," says Will, "could be a while before the emergency team gets here tonight. There's a live bottleneck stranded over at Gwithian. They're still busy up there. Can't leave it. Bottlenecks are rare enough, let alone a live stranding."

So this dolphin has only got us to help her. But the tide's rising, so maybe things are not so bad. "Won't the sea float her off safely as soon as the tide comes in?" I ask.

"It's not as easy as that. Soon as she's out of the water, see, her own weight starts to damage her, like Roger here said. We don't know what that damage may be. We need pontoons to support her, and a vet."

More lights are coming down the beach. "I hope Mal's not roused too many," says Will. "A crowd's the last thing she needs. Die of stress, a dolphin will."

But it's only Mal and a couple of older boys I

recognise from the surf shop. And another figure – not as tall, face hidden by a cagoule hood.

"Sapphire?"

"Rainbow!"

She pushes back her hood. Her short, bright hair shines in the light of the lantern she's carrying. Her smile is warm.

"Why are you here?" I ask. "Sorry, I didn't mean you shouldn't be here…"

"Patrick told me about the dolphin. That's Patrick over there. He's my stepbrother."

They've brought more torches as well as the lantern, buckets and a bundle of what looks like cloth. Tarpaulin, Patrick says.

"Flat sea tonight, thank God," says Will, "Heavy surf come in on her now, she'd stand no chance."

No chance. No chance. But the dolphin mustn't give up. I kneel on the wet sand by her head. Rainbow crouches beside me.

"Don't touch her," says Roger sharply.

"We're not touching her."

I want to shield her from the light of the torches and lantern. It's too much for her. She'll be even more afraid. She has never known a world without the strong salt sea all around her, buoying her up and taking her weight.

"Hold on," I whisper to her. "We're trying to help you. Please hold on."

She says nothing, but her eye looks into mine. She is very tired, very far away. She has retreated deep inside herself, trying to survive. She doesn't want to give up her life here on this cold, hard earth.

"What can we do?" Rainbow whispers. "She looks as if she's dying."

"Don't say that. She'll hear you."

"I'll get some water to pour over her skin. You're supposed to keep a dolphin's skin wet, aren't you?"

It's still raining hard, but maybe sea water would be better for the dolphin than rainwater. It might comfort her. "That's a good idea."

Rainbow stands up, takes one of the buckets and heads off to the sea. She's right: it's good to do something practical to help. But I can't leave the dolphin. She feels so alone. She doesn't understand the Air and the smell of land and the way we tramp round her in our big boots. Everything hurts.

Behind me there are low, angry voices. Mal's dad is arguing with the boys. "You can't lift a live dolphin in a tarpaulin. That's for a dead stranding. You'll do more harm than good."

"She'll die if we do nothing," insists Mal. "Isn't it worth trying?"

"Manhandling a dolphin like that? You'll kill her. She's suffering from shock as it is."

"I'm only trying to help."

"Well, you're not helping, boy."

"Call the rescue service again," suggests Conor. "Ask them what's best to do if they can't get here themselves."

The dolphin is so big and so helpless. Another squall of rain hits us, and the roar of the tide is suddenly loud. But the white edge of breaking waves is still too far away to save her. No new lights bob down the beach. No rescue is in sight. Rainbow comes back with her bucket of sea water, and pours it carefully over the dolphin's back, avoiding her blowhole. She runs down to the sea again with the empty bucket. Does the dolphin like the salt water? Yes, I think it comforts her. But it torments her too. It has the smell and touch of home. Her home is within sight, but it might as well be a hundred miles away. The dolphin is helpless to move. I feel so frustrated I want to scream. The tide's rising, but not fast enough to save her.

Before long the water here will be so deep that I won't be able to stand. In less than an hour, maybe. Then the dolphin will float free. But by that time she might be dead.

The dolphin is so afraid. She is so alone. She is calling inside herself for the other dolphins of her pod. But they are somewhere out in the dark water, and they can't hear her. They'll be desperate too, trying to call her and find out where she is, but the air blocks their voices. She's so afraid of dying alone, out of the water, among strangers.

"You're not alone," I whisper to her. "I won't leave you, whatever happens."

I lean closer. She wants me to touch her. She can't bear the touch of the sand, and yet her weight is making her sink deeper into its gritty harshness. Roger said her own weight could crush her internal organs. That means her heart, her liver, her lungs, all those vital parts of her. The thought of the dolphin's heart being slowly crushed makes me shudder.

"I'm sorry. I'm so, so sorry."

Rainbow is back again. She sluices sea water over the dolphin's back, then kneels down beside me. The dolphin's tension and fear rise in her like a tide. She doesn't know Rainbow. Rainbow is part of Earth, and threatening.

"Rainbow," I begin awkwardly, not sure if she'll understand or be deeply offended. "The dolphin, she's getting stressed with both of us here. She doesn't understand that you're trying to help."

"I don't want to be with her," Rainbow answers, getting up. Her voice is full of pain. "It's horrible to see her suffering like this, and we can't do anything to help. I wish – I wish it was all over."

"Don't say that! Fetch more sea water."

Roger and Will are also down at the sea's edge, filling buckets. Rainbow wipes her hands on her jeans and picks up her own bucket again. Then, like an echo of my own thoughts, she says, "Tell her I'm sorry."

Mal and the other boys are digging a channel in the sand, so that the rising tide will reach the dolphin as soon as possible. Should I help them? I weigh it up quickly, and then make my decision. The dolphin needs the trench to be dug, but her shock and fear are the greatest threat to her life. I am sure – almost sure – that I can support her.

"What are you doing, Saph?" asks Conor quietly in my ear.

"She's so afraid, Con. She'll die of fear before the tide reaches her."

"Roger said you shouldn't touch her."

But my Mer blood is rising, growing stronger in answer to the call of the dolphin's desperate need. Ingo is powerful in me tonight. I know it. The touch from my hands is a Mer touch now, salt and reassuring. I am sure I feel the dolphin's anguish ease a little under my hands. But that won't be enough to save her. If only the sea would come quickly. If only Ingo would come to her daughter's rescue now. I stare down through the darkness at the pale line of foam where the tide is coming in. With all my heart I wish for Ingo to come. *With all my heart I wish for Ingo to come.*

I put my arms around the dolphin. I can feel her heart beating inside her with slow, deep strokes. Her gaze in the lantern light is full of suffering. She must not die. I can't stop myself, I'm crying now, swallowing tears and tasting the salt.

"Hold on. Hold on, *hwoer kerenza.* They are all waiting for you out there. As soon as the water's deep enough, they'll come in to help you. Don't give up hope now."

"Saph!"

I look up at Conor.

"Saph!" he whispers urgently. "Don't let anyone hear you. You're speaking Mer—"

"What?"

"Conor, give us a hand here!" yells Mal from the trench. Lights are coming up from the water. Roger and Will's torches. They are lugging two heavy buckets, and behind them—

"Conor! Look! The tide's coming in!"

Mal and the others sit back on their heels as the first tongue of white foam touches them. Rainbow races up the beach, her bucket swinging from her hand. A wave splashes over Conor's boots. Roger and Will are knee-deep and wading. The wave retreats, but there's another coming, and another—

"We won't need the trench!" shouts Conor, grabbing the lantern and lifting it high. "Here's the tide already."

"I never seen it come in as fast as that," pants Will. "Near had to run, didn't we, Roger?"

"We've got to keep her blowhole clear of the water now," says Roger. "The state she's in, she could drown before she gets free. Sapphire, Rainbow, you two better go back now. The tide's coming in fast."

I say nothing. Roger thinks because the boys are taller and stronger, it's all right for them to stay. But I am not going anywhere. She needs me here. A swell of fresh sea water breaks around the dolphin's sunken body. The sea water surges and bubbles, then drains away. Roger's right, we've got to help her, support her until the tide's strong enough to take her. Just a few more vital minutes. If we can get her through these minutes, she might survive.

But Rainbow is staring at the onrushing water. Suddenly I see that she's afraid. The speed of the tide frightens her as much as the hard, harsh sand frightens the dolphin. Rainbow must be like Mum – all Earth without a trace of Mer in her. The shore is dangerous for her now.

"Go on up the beach now, Rainbow!" yells Patrick. "NOW! This tide'll knock you off your feet!" And she does. She turns her back after one more fearful glance at the waves, and begins to wade clumsily through the water up the beach.

"No time to do things by the book," orders Roger. "We'll have to hold her. Get round here, boys. Mind her tail now. All on this side now and hold her, before the sea rolls her."

There are six of them on the dolphin's landward side now, supporting her as the water begins to surge in around her body. This is the most dangerous time, as the sea grows deep enough to drown her but still not deep enough to release her from the trap of land. I stay by her head, as close as I can. I can help better here than by trying to hold her. The sea is over the top of my boots and the incoming waves buffet me, pushing me off-balance, even though the sea is calm tonight. Mal's dad is right. What would this be like in a storm?

"It's all right now," I tell her, "the sea is coming for you. Only a few minutes more and you'll be free. Don't be afraid. Please don't be afraid. I know it's hard, but try to keep still and not thrash your tail or you'll hurt yourself more. We're trying to free you."

I think she knows it. In spite of her exhaustion and despair she controls herself, and allows the six of them to hold her so that the incoming tide can't roll her over and submerge her blowhole while she is still trapped. But the battle is a terrible one. She is huge and heavy and now her skin is alive with sea water and slippery. The water is thigh-deep – waist-deep. Is she going to do it? Is she going to find the strength? The lantern has gone out. Mal's dad has the torch between his teeth. Shadows jump crazily over the water.

"Look out! She's starting to roll!"

"Get back! Get back, boys!"

The sea lifts me off my feet. The dolphin and I are face to face now. Her stupor of pain and fear is lifting. Ingo is growing strong around her. One more wave, and now another. Her body rolls, quivering like a beached boat finding the sea under its keel.

"Don't struggle. Please don't hurt yourself any more. Wait for the sea. Let the sea take you."

"Sapphire! Where's that girl?"

"*Sapphire!*"

I am treading water, my hair all over my face and blinding me. My mouth is full of salt. A surge of water lifts her. She rises. Is she free? No, she falls back. Another wave lifts us both, and this time I feel the change as her whole body enters its element.

"Go now," I say. "Go now."

She eases herself away so gently. She turns herself into the tide, into the open water. She pauses, as if she's listening to something. I listen too. The sea is still rising, over my head now. For a few seconds I dip into Ingo, and hear the voices as she hears them. Skeins and skeins of dolphin voices urgently guiding their sister out into the bay, towards them. It's not like human language at all, but like music, layer over layer of it, making meanings that sing to the injured dolphin of rescue, healing, safety and freedom.

Very slowly, hesitantly, her injured body gathers itself, and begins to move. She brushes past me, and for a second I think wildly of climbing on her back, as I climbed on a dolphin's back and rode through Ingo last summer. But already she's sliding away into the darkness. Slowly at first, and then faster, faster, as she begins to believe in her own freedom. Her tail curves, the water swirls, and she disappears.

I can't believe that she's gone. I stretch out my arms to touch her one last time but my hands close on water. There's no one. She's gone, and I rise to the surface.

"*SAPH!*" It's my brother's voice. But where is he? I thought we were all together by the dolphin, but the dark sea is empty around me. Where am I? I tread water, holding my hair out of my eyes. Everything's dark. I can't see any lights. I can't see any landmarks. Where has everyone gone? A flash of pure terror goes through me.

"SAAA-AAAPPHH!"

The voice comes from behind me. I turn, and there, about a hundred metres away, a torch is flashing. Behind it there are the lights of St Pirans, up above the beach. I wasn't lost, I was facing the wrong way, out to sea. I turn and begin to swim inland, but I don't call out an answer in case Conor plunges into the water to rescue me.

I'm in no danger. The November water must be cold, but I can't feel its chill any more than I feel cold when I'm swimming through Ingo with Faro. Is it possible that I'm still in Ingo now, within Ingo's protection, even though I'm breathing air? The feeling of Ingo wraps around me, safe and free. I could swim all night. I don't really want to swim for shore; I want to stay out in the deep water. But Conor will think I got caught by a current. I've got to tell him I'm all right. I swim faster, towards the light of the torch.

The cold hits me as soon as I wade out of the water. I start to shiver so violently that I can barely call out to the others. They see me anyway, and run towards me.

"Saph! Are you all right?"

"She – she got away. She's free. She's b-back in Ing—"

"Quick, Saph, the tide's still coming in fast. Pat, get hold of her other arm. She's soaked through."

Everyone is soaked through after the battle to launch the dolphin. We stumble up the beach, shivering like dogs. The tarpaulin's gone, and the lantern. The last remaining torch is weak and yellow. But here are the steps at last.

This is when Roger remembers that we haven't got the house key. "Can't go into the restaurant looking like this," he mutters. "It'll scare Jennie rigid."

I am too cold to think what to do. I just stand on the steps, shaking.

"Come *on*, Saph, you can't stay here," says Conor, grabbing my arm and pulling me along. "We're going to Patrick's – it's the nearest."

"Can't – can't m-m-move m-m-my legs."

"Yes you can. Two minutes and we'll be there."

Patrick's home is right by the beach – part of a row of old fishermen's cottages which overlook the water. The lights are on. The door is flung open almost before Patrick has banged on it, and there is Rainbow, her face pale and anxious.

"Are you all OK?"

"Everybody's fine. No worries," says Roger, "but we're homeless. Can we all come in?"

"Of course," says Rainbow, and opens the door wide.

CHAPTER EIGHT

We crowd into the narrow porch, stripping off wet cagoules and pulling off boots. Mal and his dad and Roger go on into the living room with Patrick and his friend. Charlie, I think his name is. There's a fire lit there, Patrick says. My hands fumble with my cagoule zip, trembling. Rainbow sees I can't manage it and starts to help me, but to my embarrassment I start to shake so hard that my teeth chatter the way they do in books.

"You're ill," says Rainbow. "What happened?"

"She went in deep," says Conor. "Are you OK, Saph?"

"C-c-c-cold..."

"Come up to the bathroom," says Rainbow decisively. "You need to get all that wet stuff off, and have a hot shower. I've got some jeans and a top you can borrow." Conor and Rainbow help me up the stairs. I can't believe I'm being so pathetic. This has never happened to me before, no matter how long I've stayed in the sea.

"Do you want a shower or a bath?"

"B-b-bath." I'm cold to the core. It's a funny little bath – short but deep. Rainbow runs it full of steaming water.

"Will you be OK on your own? You're not going to faint or anything?"

The steamy heat of the bathroom is making me feel better already. Rainbow goes out, leaving the door ajar in case I feel ill.

"I'll sit on the stairs so no one else can come up," she promises, and I pull off my wet clothes and slide gratefully into the water. It's so hot that it hurts at first, but deliciously. I dip my head down under the water, which is quite hard to do in a bath as small as this. The smell of the sea has gone. Rainbow has left a chunk of rose-scented soap, and I wash myself with it slowly, luxuriously, thinking of absolutely nothing at all.

There's a tap on the door. "I've brought you some tea. It's just outside the door when you want it. Are you feeling better?"

"Loads better."

I clamber out, wrap a towel around myself and fetch the tea. Rainbow is still sitting on the stairs, guarding them. She jumps up. "I'll get you some of my clothes. They're all clean, I promise! Everyone's sitting round the fire, warming up. But they didn't look as bad as you. What happened?"

"Nothing. I had to swim, that's all. I must have got pulled out by a current."

"Did she get away safely? The dolphin?"

"I think so."

I don't really want to talk about it any more, but Rainbow goes on awkwardly, "I'm sorry I didn't stay. It was the water coming in like that. I've never seen it rise so fast."

"I know."

There's a pause, then Rainbow goes on in a rush, "It's like that with me. I get scared of the tides sometimes. I think the sea's not going to stop where it should, it's going to go on coming in and coming in right over our house. I know it's stupid."

"It's not stupid," I say slowly. "My mum is afraid of the sea, too. She's much worse than you are. She won't even go on the beach if she can help it."

"But you're not, are you, Sapphire? You love the sea. You love it more than you love the land."

"How do you know?"

Rainbow shrugs, suddenly looking much younger and less certain. "I don't know why I said that. But when we were with the dolphin, I had a feeling— No, you're going to tell me I'm completely mad."

"What sort of feeling?"

"You were talking to her. But it wasn't English, was it? What language was it?"

"It can't have been another language. I don't know any."

Rainbow looks disappointed, and unconvinced.

"Where are your parents?" I ask quickly, to prevent her asking any more questions.

"In Copenhagen. My mum likes to go back to see her friends. My stepdad's gone with her. He's Patrick's father."

"Oh."

"We're fine on our own. They took River with them, so I don't have to look after him. Anyway, Patrick's sixteen," she says quickly, as if she's had to explain all this a few times.

"How long are they away for?"

"Not long," says Rainbow carefully.

"So you just go to school and everything, even though they're not here?"

"I don't go to school. I learn at home."

"What – never?"

"No."

I bet she doesn't learn much while her parents are in Copenhagen, I think. Great chance for a holiday from schoolwork. Unfortunately my sceptical thoughts show on my face.

"I speak English and Danish and German," says Rainbow quietly. "But music is what I do most of the time. And cooking. I want to be a chef when I'm older."

This sounds so much more impressive than anything I've achieved at school so far. "You must be really clever."

"I'm not. You could try it. Home-schooling, I mean. See if it works for you."

"Maybe. But I suspect my mum sends me to school for other reasons, like getting me out of the house," I say drily, and suddenly we're both laughing.

Rainbow fetches the clothes. Her jeans are a bit big for

me, but her cream top is so beautiful that I wish I could wear it for ever. I take a secret peep in the steamy mirror.

"It's so good with your dark hair and eyes," says Rainbow. "It looks loads better on you than it does on me. Keep it."

I look at her in amazement. A beautiful top like that! It must have cost loads. "It's only a top, Sapphire," says Rainbow, as if she's amused. "You're welcome to keep it."

Maybe they're rich. That must be it. But, no, rich people don't live in tiny cottages like this. I ought to say no, but I'm longing to say yes.

"It's yours," says Rainbow firmly.

"Thank you," I mutter. I always find it hard to sound grateful, even when I really am.

When we go downstairs, they are all sitting around the fire. There aren't enough chairs, so Patrick has put big cushions on the floor. He has also brought out some beers, and everyone is telling their part in the story of the dolphin's rescue.

I stay silent, drinking my tea. The dolphin is safe in Ingo, and here I am in a warm, lighted room, with the fire leaping up in the grate, and everyone's faces flushed with relief and beer. The door is firmly shut against the night and the rain. These cottages are very old. Some of them have been standing for more than four hundred years, resisting the storms that sweep in from the southwest. Rainbow's living room has a feeling of permanence and safety. Even though it is so close to the sea, it feels anchored to the rock of the Earth.

The small room is crowded with people and voices and laughter, and it feels good to be here and part of it all.

Rainbow comes over to take my empty mug. "Do you want more tea? Are you still cold?"

Conor puts his arm around my shoulders. "You've stopped shivering at last. I was worried about you, Saph. Your lips were blue."

"It didn't feel at all cold when I was in the water."

"You were numb," says Roger. "Lucky you're not suffering from hypothermia."

If I was, I'm sure you'd know what to do, I think to myself.

"Sapphire speaks the most amazing dolphin language," says Mal innocently. "Did you hear her? What were you saying to the dolphin, Saph?"

Everyone looks at me, smiling as if it's a joke.

"Only Conor calls me Saph," I answer coldly. Mal flushes and turns aside, and I feel a moment of regret because I've broken the atmosphere. But Rainbow grabs a towel and begins to rub Mal's long surfer's hair dry, teasing him about how he must miss his hairdryer, and suddenly everything's all right again. I pass the chocolate biscuits to Mal in a way which I hope looks friendly, but unfortunately the plate wobbles and four biscuits slide into his lap.

"You're shaking again," he says in surprise, picking up the biscuits.

"The cold must have got right into her," says Roger. He takes one of my hands and chafes it. "Cold as ice. Did you say you had a hot bath?"

"I don't feel cold."

They are looking at me in concern. Rainbow fetches a duvet from upstairs and puts it around my shoulders.

"You need more flesh on your bones," says Mal's dad. "Have another chocolate biscuit."

The talk turns to the sea. Why is it that so many dolphins are being stranded – more than ever before? Is it the trawlers' nets trapping the dolphins, or sickness, or some kind of secret underwater military sonic systems disrupting the dolphins' sonar...

Mal's dad blames the trawlers; Patrick believes there's something more to it, something we don't know.

"It tears you up to see a beautiful creature like that thrown up on the sand to die," says Mal's dad.

I wish Faro could hear this. He divides the world so sharply. He believes that humans have no concern for Ingo, because all they want is power and money and more and more living space. To Faro, humans are a source of pollution, danger and damage.

But these people are all humans. They don't even know about Ingo, but they all fought to save the dolphin. They risked their lives. Next time I see Faro, I'm going to tell him that.

"We ought to be getting back," says Roger at last, getting up. "Your mum will be finishing her shift."

It's hard to leave the warmth and company. It must be great to be Rainbow and Patrick, with the house to themselves, knowing they can wake in the morning and do exactly what they want. I wonder how long their parents really will be away?

"When's your mum and dad back?" asks Mal's dad as if he's picked up my thought.

"Couple of weeks," says Patrick easily.

"You two seem to manage pretty well." Mal's dad is approving. He thinks kids these days get brought up too soft – all of them going to college and doing media studies and living off their parents when they should be earning. Patrick has a full-time job in a surf shop. But Conor has already told me that Mal wants to be a doctor, which takes years and years of training. Why is it that whatever kind of child parents get, they always think the opposite kind would be preferable? My mum would think she had died and gone to heaven if I said I wanted to become a doctor. She has always told both of us that she won't let money stand in our way if we choose a career that needs a long training.

"We haven't got a lot of money, you know that, but I'll beg, borrow and steal to get you through, once you make your mind up what you want to do. I can easily take a second job." When she says this, Mum looks so determined and fiery that I wish I had an ambition that was big enough for her.

We leave Rainbow and Patrick's cottage, and go up the rain-wet street.

"We'll stop by the house and see if Jennie's back. If not, I'll go down to the restaurant for the key," says Roger.

The lights are on behind the drawn curtains. Mum is probably making herself a cup of tea. She likes to relax for half an hour before she goes to bed, with the TV on low so as not to wake us. She'll think Conor and I are asleep in our beds, but in a few seconds we'll appear on the doorstep. She's not going to be pleased. Roger hesitates. "Obviously we've got to tell your mum what happened to some extent, but there's no need to worry her," he says.

"We'll just give her the general picture, shall we," suggests Conor.

"That's right," Roger agrees seriously. "No need to mention Sapphire going into the water, for instance."

"Of course not."

"We never do," I add, and Roger gives me a sharp glance. But it's too dark for him to read my expression.

We'll go inside, and in a little while Conor and I will go up to bed. And then I'll have to tell Conor about Dad. There's no putting it off any longer. He would be furious if he thought I'd kept something so vital from him for a second longer than necessary.

I think back to the day of Dad's memorial service, when Conor and I first swore and promised that we two would never give up hope until we found him. Everyone except us was mourning Dad, but we knew he wasn't dead.

Maybe it would have been easier if he had died. Easier than having to tell Conor now that Dad is alive, but he says that he can't come back to us.

CHAPTER NINE

Conor doesn't react as I thought he would when I tell him the whole story of what happened last night at Granny Carne's. He listens intently, without saying a word. Even when I tell him about Dad with water running down his shoulders and his hair like seaweed, Conor remains calm. He doesn't seem as shocked as I thought he would be. At last I reach the end.

"And then Dad sank back into the pool and I couldn't see him any more."

There's a silence. After a while I say, "Conor, you do believe me, don't you?"

"Yes."

"Then—"

"Give me a minute, Saph. I need to think."

We are sitting on my bed, huddled in my duvet. I should be tired, but I feel wide awake. It's a relief that Conor shares my knowledge now. I won't have to keep going over and over the events of last night in my mind, trying to work out if I did everything I could. Conor clasps his knees, frowning in deep thought. At last he looks up with a faint smile and says, "Don't look so scared, Saph."

"I thought you might blame me for letting Dad go again."

"No. None of it was your fault."

"I wish you'd been there, Conor."

"I wouldn't have been able to stop him. He couldn't stop himself, don't you see? He wasn't free. But listen, Saph. It's not what happened last night that's important now. It's what we do in the future."

Conor is so composed, as if he's understood and accepted in about five minutes everything that has taken me hours to absorb.

"Conor, aren't you even surprised?"

Conor shakes his head. "No. As soon as you told me, everything slipped into place. I must have known inside myself for a long time, but I didn't realise it. There were so many clues. I'm sure Granny Carne was trying to tell us. Why else did she talk so much about how the first Mathew Trewhella disappeared? Didn't *you* know, somewhere inside yourself?"

"I'm not sure, Conor, I... Yes. Maybe."

"But that's not what matters now. What matters is that Dad needs us. He's not free. He can't do what he wants.

He's trapped, like you said, and he can't come home. He's like a prisoner."

I am more and more amazed. I thought Conor would rage against Dad for going into Ingo, for leaving us, for letting his human self weaken and his Mer self grow strong. I was sure that Conor would blame Dad.

"A prisoner," Conor repeats. "He's a prisoner in Ingo and he's a prisoner inside a body which isn't his any more."

"But maybe he wants to be there."

"Saph, don't you understand? If Dad doesn't have a free choice, then how can anybody know what he wants?"

Suddenly I think of something. "Conor, listen. *We've* only been able to go into Ingo since Dad was there, haven't we? Maybe there's a connection."

"Or a reason."

"What do you mean?"

"Dad can't leave Ingo, but we can enter it. Think about it, Saph. We've got the power to go to Ingo, where Dad is. We mustn't waste it."

"Do you mean we could sort of – visit him there?"

Conor laughs. "You mean like access visits when parents get divorced? *It's my dad's turn to see us this weekend, only unfortunately he lives under the sea.* No, Saph, I don't mean visiting Dad. I mean giving him the choice to leave Ingo."

"Rescuing him?"

"Finding out how he can gain his freedom. We know

that human beings can go to Ingo and become Mer. It happened to the first Mathew Trewhella, and now it's happened to Dad. It might have happened to other people. But I don't believe that all the transformations go in one direction. Hasn't any of the Mer ever tried to live in the human world? Even if only out of curiosity?"

"There's a story about that. I think there was a mermaid who came up on land and her tail got cut to pieces on the stones."

"That's just a fairy story. Why shouldn't someone be able to leave Ingo, even if it means that his body has to transform? We know that Faro and Elvira can stay in the Air for a while. One of the Mer might have done it for longer, even permanently. If there is a way, we've got to find it. We've *got* to find it, Saph. Dad isn't completely Mer yet; he can't be. He's still partly human. Once we've found the way, Dad *has* got a choice."

Excitement is starting to burn in me at Conor's words. If Conor is right, and Dad hasn't chosen to leave us permanently, then it's still possible that everything can be reversed. But I'm not quite as hopeful as Conor. Maybe it's because I feel the pull of Ingo so strongly myself. If I had to choose between spending the rest of my life in St Pirans, among streets and houses and traffic and crowds, and living in Ingo, it would not be so easy to decide. But if Dad comes home, then we'll return to the cottage. The cottage, the cove, all our old free life will open up again as if it's never been interrupted.

But even as these happy thoughts float through my mind, there's also a trace of doubt. Gloria Fortune will have to leave. Mum will have to change back into the person she was – the one who loved Dad and had never met Roger. Roger will have to disappear – and somehow I can't see Roger agreeing to do so without a fight.

But I won't think of all that now. All we need to think about is rescuing Dad.

We make plans until three o'clock in the morning. Conor's convinced that we need to go to Ingo together, as soon as we possibly can. He insists that we go together, although I have to point out that he's going to find it hard with only me to rely on. Conor cannot take in enough oxygen underwater to swim independently. There is too much of Earth and Air in him, I think, although I don't say that.

"It's a long time since the summer. We'll both have grown stronger," Conor insists. "I might be fine in Ingo now."

But I am sure Conor has grown farther away from Ingo over the months since we left Senara. My Mer blood is certainly stronger, but I daren't rely on it to keep us both alive. What if we're deep in Ingo, a hundred metres below the surface, and my strength fails until it's only enough for me, but not for Conor?

I've seen before that this can happen. I've watched the life and colour drain from Conor's face. And we were in relatively shallow water then. We were doubly lucky, because Faro was at hand to rescue us, but next time he may not be, unless—

"Faro should come with us, Conor."

"I don't want him. This is family business. It's private."

"But, Conor, how can we do this on our own? We don't even know how to begin to look for Dad. Ingo is so vast. We could search for years and not find him. We haven't got a map. The Mer don't even *have* maps. Or – or if you don't want Faro, then maybe Elvira would help us?"

I glance slyly at Conor's face to see how he reacts to Elvira's name. I think his colour deepens. It's hard to tell with Conor because his skin is so brown.

"She wouldn't come," he says quickly.

"Then I'll call for Faro. I daren't go into Ingo with you unless Faro is there. I'm not strong enough."

Conor seems to be on the point of agreeing when another brilliant idea strikes me. Saldowr. Faro's teacher. If he's so wise, if he knows so much, then he is the person to ask. Maybe that is why Saldowr wanted to meet me. Faro said he did. Perhaps Saldowr knows that I'm searching for Dad. Perhaps he wants to tell us something.

My thoughts race on, pulsing with excitement. We'll find Saldowr, and he'll be ancient and white-haired and wise, like a wizard in a children's book. He'll be very tall, with a flowing beard. He'll stare down at us in an all-knowing and ancient way and say very solemnly, "I am glad you came to me, my children. Your quest is over." And he'll raise his arms and his robes will spread wide, and then he'll unveil the mystery—

"Saph! Wake up!"

"Wasn sleep…"

"You were. Your eyes were completely shut. Did you hear what I just said?"

"Something bout a wiz— No."

"Listen, Saph. This is important. How much do you trust Faro?"

Faro calls me his little sister. Faro and I can see into each other's minds and discover the memories and images there. How much do I trust Faro? I think of his eyes sparkling with glee as he outwits me, and his dark, passionate anger against what humans do to Ingo. "Quite a lot," I say cautiously.

"Enough to tell him about Dad?"

Perhaps Faro already knows where Dad is. He surfs the currents all over Ingo, and I'm sure there are many things he knows which he has never told me, because of my human blood. I wonder whether or not Faro would be capable of concealing from me what had happened to my own father.

"I think so," I say to Conor now.

Conor continues to plan aloud. He's fired up now, and I know he won't rest until he's organised exactly what we're going to do.

Tomorrow's a school day, and there is no way that Mum will let me miss school again. By the time I reach home, there'll be only an hour or so left before dusk. Conor won't consider going to Ingo in the dark, even though I try to persuade him that it's not too hard to find your way, especially if there's a moon.

"It's too dangerous, Saph. We won't know where we are."

After this I tell Conor about Saldowr, and my idea that Faro's teacher might help us. Conor is not as interested in Saldowr as I expected.

"He won't tell us anything the Mer don't want us to know. We've got to be more subtle than that. Faro's our best chance."

It's all decided. On Saturday Conor will tell Mum we're going out together for the day, and maybe meeting up with some of the others. But without Sadie. What's a good reason for us not taking Sadie? Simple. We don't want her to get exhausted when she's only just recovered from her illness.

I would prefer to add some convincing detail to this story but, as usual, Conor is scrupulous about keeping as close to the truth as he can. We are going out for the day: that's true. We may meet some of "the others" if things go according to plan: that is not a lie, either. And so Conor is satisfied. No need to specify what kind of "others" we hope to meet.

We're going to walk along the coast, past the Morvah rocks. There are some sheltered little pebble inlets beyond the rocks. Most of the walkers go the other way, following the coast path up where it swerves inland. The inlets can't be seen from the coast path or from the town. Sometimes people come to watch seals there, but if we're lucky, the place should be deserted on a November morning. Conor thinks we can get into Ingo there. It's far enough from St Pirans, and it's outside the shelter of the bay. The Mer should feel safe to come there: as safe as they ever are within sight of land.

"So we'll just call for Faro?" It all sounds so vague and unlikely to succeed. Up at Senara, at our cove, I could easily slip through the skin of the water and into Ingo. Ingo was all around us there – its magnetism drawing me even when I didn't want to be drawn. But imagine standing by the water on an ordinary Saturday morning, calling and calling in broad daylight as if I were calling for my dog, but hearing no answer except the mocking surge of the waves and the screams of gulls. Or stepping into the water, but feeling nothing except the cold around my ankles. I'd be like a kid paddling out of season.

"Conor, I still think we'd have more chance of entering Ingo in darkness, from Polquidden."

"It's too risky. If we *have* to go in darkness, then we will, but we'll try this first. I'd even rather do what you did and go up to Senara than try to search for Dad at night here. But you've got to believe Faro will come, Saph. You remember how you called him when we were in danger last summer, and he came? There was something in your voice then. I was feeling so terrible by then that I couldn't even see, but I could still hear you. You had power in your voice. And Faro came, didn't he? If you call like that, he'll come, Saph. Believe me, you can do it. Dad's depending on us."

After Conor's gone off to bed, I lie awake for a long time. I keep reminding myself how tired I'm going to be the next day, but still I can't sleep. I wish I could be as sure and certain as Conor about what has happened to Dad. It sounds so logical. Dad is in Ingo and cannot leave, and therefore Dad is in Ingo against his will. By Conor's logic, that means Dad is like a prisoner, waiting for rescue.

If I believed this as confidently as Conor, the problems would melt away. All we would need to do is find a way to release Dad. It might be difficult, or dangerous, but it would be like a journey where you know your destination.

But I'm not as sure as Conor. I don't really know where my journey will end. I've seen Dad with my own eyes, but that has only made his disappearance more mysterious.

I turn over and beat the pillow into shape again. I have got to get some sleep, and I never will if I keep on like this. I'm going to need all my strength for what lies ahead. *Stop thinking, Sapphire. Conor is certain enough for both of us.*

CHAPTER TEN

"You ready, Saph?"

"Yes." I bite my lip. It's a lie. I'm not ready at all. Carrying the heavy weight of responsibility for my brother's life – no, I'll never be truly ready for that.

There are rocks behind us. Two curving arms of rock protect us from view, on the left and the right. Ahead of us is the open sea. The water is calm today. Too calm, Conor says. In November that silky blue surface can't be trusted. The barometer's falling, and bad weather is on its way.

"Will there be a storm, Conor?"

"Maybe. There'll be a blow, at least."

"Could the bad weather get here while we're in Ingo?"

"If time were exactly the same in Ingo as it is here, I'd say we should be back safely before the weather turns. But you know it doesn't work like that."

"I really hope there won't be a storm."

When the gales blow, waves sweep right over these

rocks where we're standing. The sea boils and rages. We'd never be able to climb out of the water again without being smashed against the rocks. I glance nervously at the horizon. Cloudy strands of mare's tail streak the blue. Those clouds mean the weather's about to break. Conor's right.

"Let's get going, Saph. We might not have much time."

We're both speaking quietly, even though there's no one else around and we're hidden from view. But Ingo has ears everywhere. A gull swooping through the air, or a seal lolloping up on to a rock could hear us, and send on the message that we're coming to Ingo to search for our father. Would it matter? I don't know. But if Conor is right, and Dad is somehow trapped in Ingo, then we need to keep our journey secret. *If* Conor's right...

The water shelves down sharply here. Once we've waded in a few steps, it will be over our heads. Ingo is almost within touching distance.

"Saph, get on with it!"

Conor thinks I should call Faro now. He is sure Faro will come for me. I stare at the water, watching, listening. I can't tell what's going to happen. Is Ingo going to open for us, or will we have to go home disappointed and shivering, our clothes soaked through for nothing?

Suddenly a shiver of excitement runs through me. Faro's close. I'm sure of it. The part of my self that is at home in Ingo is starting to wake. Senses that I don't possess in my daily life are stirring. Somewhere beneath the surface of the water, somewhere beneath the surface of my mind, Faro makes his presence felt. It's like a very soft knock on the door of my understanding. A greeting.

Here I am, little sister. Come and find me!

I scan the rocks, the water. Nothing. No smooth dark head breaks the surface. I swing round, half-expecting to see Faro perched on a rock, watching us with that familiar half-mocking smile. He isn't there – and yet he is, he is. I grab Conor's arm. "Faro's here somewhere, Conor. He's close."

But Conor is peering round the side of the rocks. "Saph, quick, there's a man up on the path with fishing tackle. He's coming this way."

We didn't think of that. This is a good place for mackerel, and once that man settles down to fish he might stay all morning.

"Quick, before he sees us."

"What about our stuff?"

Conor has planned everything. We have spare clothes in a plastic bag for when we come out of the water dripping wet. Conor has wedged the bag into a crevice above the tide line, along with our trainers.

"Hurry, Conor, Faro's waiting for us."

We take one step, then another. The land shelves steeply here. As soon as we enter the water I know all will be well. It doesn't feel cold. This is not the chilly sea of ordinary November beaches. It laps up my legs, soaking my jeans. I wade forward carefully so the fisherman won't hear any splashes. We're still hidden here, but soon we'll be beyond the cover of the rocks. We'll have to dive down quickly.

Conor and I glance at each other. He has to trust me now. His mouth is set hard. He's ready for the dive, even though he can't be sure that I'm strong enough to hold him safe in Ingo. I'll never really know how much courage it takes, because Conor won't tell me.

"Come on, Saph, he'll see us," Conor mutters, as if the only thing that worries him is the fisherman.

"Hold my wrist tight." He nods. "Don't breathe, whatever happens. Pull my arm hard if you aren't getting enough oxygen. I'll bring us up to the surface."

I take a step deeper, and so does he. The water rises waist-deep, chest-deep. It begins to lift us so that we can't keep our balance. We glance at each other one last time, then lean forward and give ourselves to the water.

We go through the skin. I open my eyes. Bubbles stream past me: the last of my breath rising to the surface. My lungs are empty of Air now. I draw in the rich oxygenated water of Ingo, and my body floods with energy and life. Conor is beside me, his hand tight on my wrist, his eyes shut.

The next moment, as I knew, as I hoped, as I believed, Faro is there, swimming alongside Conor, holding his other wrist. He smiles that secretive Faro smile, as if he knows something we don't. "About time," he says. "I was wondering how long I'd have to wait for you. Quick, we must swim farther out. The water's too clear here. They could see us from the cliffs."

We're swimming into deeper water. The sea bed glides smoothly beneath us, falling away as the sea grows deeper. White sand, dark weed and rocks. The camouflage patterns of Ingo, where anything could be hiding.

"I knew you were close," I say to Faro.

"Not too difficult, considering how loud I was calling you."

"I wasn't sure."

Conor says nothing. I turn to check that he is all right. His colour is good, but his face is a mask of pain. "What's the matter, Con? Aren't you getting enough oxygen?"

Faro is holding his wrist. Conor should be fine.

"It's not to do with that," says Faro. "It's the pain of entering Ingo. Going from Air to Ingo is hurtful for humans. Don't you remember?"

How could I forget? That burning pain in the lungs, the feeling of being crushed and unable to breathe—

"I'm so sorry, Conor. I forgot it would hurt you."

I forgot because the transition didn't hurt me at all. I slipped into Ingo like a fish into water. What does that say about me? I glance down at myself quickly. My feet and my legs in jeans look puny next to Faro's powerful seal-dark tail. They are definitely human feet and human legs. Whatever's going on in my mind, my body is still completely human.

After a few minutes, Conor feels well enough to speak. "That was the worst yet," he says grimly. I squeeze his hand.

"But it should be getting easier each time. Isn't that right, Faro?"

"Not for everyone. Sometimes each journey across the elements is more difficult than the last. You have too much Air in you, Conor. Too much Air and too much Earth."

"How would you like it if I said you had too much Mer in you?" retorts Conor.

"I am what I am."

"That goes for me, too."

There is always this sense of challenge between Conor and Faro.

"Where's Elvira?" I ask, because Conor will want to know, but will never ask.

"She's with our mother. They went away together. Elvira is learning the healing of coral wounds."

"What?"

"Elvira is a healer – or she will be one day."

"When did they leave?" asks Conor abruptly.

"This morning."

Conor says nothing, but I guess what he's thinking. *If Faro knew we were coming, then Elvira must have known too. She could have come with Faro, but she chose not to.*

We are moving steadily away from shore on the back of a gentle current, about twenty metres below the surface. The light is clean and clear. Forests of weed reach up towards us like arms that want to hold us tight. Small mackerel flicker through the weed. Their green and silver and black stripes shimmer in the underwater light, and they look as if they're playing a game of hide-and-seek. They look so free. They don't know about the white marble slab at the fishmonger's down by the harbour, where their brothers and sisters lie in rows, waiting to be sold. I swim faster. I don't want to catch the mackerel's innocent eyes.

"We want to meet your teacher," says Conor to Faro.

"He means Saldowr," I add.

"It's possible," Faro agrees. "Although you have chosen your time for meeting, not his."

"Could we go to him now?"

"Why not?"

I'd forgotten Faro's way of answering a question with another question, and just how annoying it is. As soon as this thought crosses my mind, he gives me a quick, cheeky grin.

"Get out of my thoughts, Faro! They're private."

"You'll have to learn to stop me, then."

"All right. You wait!"

I think of a portcullis I once saw in a film about a medieval castle. It was a huge black grate of metal with sharp spikes pointing up where someone might try to climb over. Once it slid down into place, no invader could get past it. I'm going to slide a portcullis down over my mind to guard my thoughts. Faro won't be able to climb over the spikes. But I'm not sure that it will work. Faro is as slippery as water. I might not be able to keep him out.

"Did he read your thoughts, Saph?" demands Conor.

"Only because I let him. And I don't feel like letting him any more."

"I would hate anyone to read my thoughts. It must be like being burgled inside your head."

"Conor, you've become even more human since I saw you last," Faro observes wryly.

"I'll take that as a compliment," answers Conor.

Faro always wants to draw a clear line between the Mer and humans. I check myself hastily, because I don't want Faro to see this thought. But it seems that I'm safe this time. The portcullis is in place.

"So, tell me. Why do you want to see Saldowr?" asks Faro. "What need have you of his wisdom?"

"He's wise, then, is he?" asks Conor. I'm a bit shocked. Of course Saldowr must be wise, if he's Faro's teacher.

"He has more wisdom in one of his fingers," says Faro haughtily, "than the greatest philosophers of Air have in the whole of their cloven bodies."

Conor winks at me. "Fine. Sounds like he's our man," he says aloud.

Does Faro suspect why we want to talk to Saldowr? Probably. Suddenly I have an idea. I want to see how Faro reacts if I let an image of Dad rise in my mind. It's hard.

I don't want to do it. I want to swim along like this, in the peace of Ingo, between my brother and my friend. I don't want to remember Dad as he was in the pool in the moonlight, close enough for me to reach out and touch him, but caught between two worlds.

Dad's face is there in my mind. Every feature is heavy with pain. It's there in brilliant detail, like a portrait. I let the portcullis rise. I open my mind, and as I do so Faro swerves violently, as if he's seen a shark.

"When did you see this?" he demands.

"A few nights ago."

"He broke the law of the Mer in coming to find you. What did he tell you?"

"She doesn't have to tell *you* that," says Conor, not aggressively but as if stating an obvious fact. "And why should our father be ruled by the law of the Mer when he is human?"

"Conor, please, *don't!*" We're in Ingo now, and Conor depends on Faro. The stakes are too high for a quarrel.

"Your father chose Ingo. That means that he also chose to live under the law of the Mer. He can't go back on his choice now, unless he wants to become a renegade. A traitor to the welcome he found in Ingo's arms."

"But we aren't sure that it was a free choice, and besides, Faro," Conor goes on calmly, "this argument is one we must have another time, and not with you. Do you know our father?"

Faro and Conor are swimming close to each other, because Conor must hold Faro's wrist. They turn, face to face, then look away. I'm struck by the similarity between them, which is as strong as the sparks of hostility that leap between them. Both have dark hair, dark eyes, brown skin. The resemblance goes deeper than that, to the fire of their sudden anger, and their determination not to back down. But they are different, too. Faro is watchful, teasing, secretive. Conor's spirit is open and generous. They are both strong. I don't know which of them, if either, is the stronger.

"I know him," answers Faro at last. "He is—" but he breaks off.

"He's what?"

"You must ask Saldowr. I was about to say something that Saldowr should tell you, not I."

I'm afraid of what's unfolding so quickly now. I have longed and longed for answers about my father, but now it seems as if we may get them, I'm afraid. I don't know what to feel about Faro, either. Has he deceived us by keeping his knowledge of our father from us, or wasn't it his secret to keep? I don't want to believe that Faro has deceived me, or played games with me. Not about something as important as this.

"How far is it to Saldowr?" I ask at last.

"It's not far to the current which will take us there. And then half a day's journey."

We make our journey on a current that is broad-backed and immensely strong. It is much too strong for us to enter it directly. The force would knock us aside, or even injure us, Faro says. Instead we join it by means of a smaller current which flows into the larger like a tributary into a river. The three of us swim close, pressed together inside the surging rope of water that hauls us through Ingo a hundred times faster than we could ever swim. Ingo swirls around us. The sea bed is so distant it's invisible. Inside the current, at its heart, there's a strange peace. We rush onwards, face down, staring into the Deep below us.

"Have you ever been to the bottom of the ocean?" asks Conor.

Faro says the Mer can't swim down that far, or the pressure of the Deep would crush them. Only strange creatures which have adapted themselves to the dark and the weight of water can live at such a depth. Sometimes they float to the surface like monsters.

"I thought you'd be able to go anywhere in Ingo," I say, surprised.

"Can you go anywhere on Earth?"

I remember Everest and the Antarctic and the Sahara. "I suppose we can, but it's not easy. You have to have special clothing and equipment."

"Typically human," Faro remarks. "Show you a place where you aren't meant to live, and immediately you want to go there."

"We aren't meant to live in Ingo, and here we are."

"Of course you're meant to be here," says Faro as if he's stating the most obvious thing in the world. "Do you think that every human creature who ventures into our world gets such a welcome? No. From the moment my sister first saw your brother—"

But at that moment the current humps its back like snake, and begins to whip round on itself in circles that whirl faster and faster, dragging us with it. Faro's face changes. With a shock I realise that for the first time since I've known him, he's afraid.

"Rogue current!" he shouts. "We've got to get out! Sapphire, kick out! Swim for it!"

Faro lets go of me to grab Conor with both hands. One moment we're together, and then I'm torn away by the current. I catch a last glimpse of them whirling away from me, and then they vanish. The current snatches us apart like the wind blowing rubbish along a gutter. I tumble over and over, blinded by my own hair, rushing down an endless tunnel in the current's roaring heart.

I'll never know how far I travelled. I think I must have lost consciousness. I don't remember anything except what felt like a hand wiping across my mind, wiping me into sleep.

I wake in the dark. Hollow, booming, echoing dark.

But it's not complete darkness. There are grains of light in it. Thick shadows loom and then vanish. I try to move my hand, but it's so slow, so heavy. The water weighs me down, as if a mountain has fallen on top of me.

Painfully, I turn my neck, searching for Conor, Faro. Nothing but dense, dark water everywhere. I peer upwards, searching for the brightness of the surface. Perhaps I'm looking in the wrong direction. I've got to find the surface. That must be the sea bed down there. But no, perhaps I've been tossed over and over so many times that I'm floating upside down without knowing it. If I swim towards what I think is the surface, then I might be swimming down into the depths of the ocean.

Conor would never be able to breathe down here. He must be with Faro; he's got to be. When the current struck, Faro knew he had to help Conor. That's why he grabbed hold of Conor with both hands and let go of me, because he knew I could survive alone. Yes, Faro and Conor must be together, safe, searching for me. No other possibility is going to enter my mind.

I'll swim in any direction for a while, and see what happens. If it grows darker, I'll know I'm heading the wrong way, down to the sea floor. If it grows lighter, then that must be the way to the surface.

And what good will it do if you come up to the surface hundreds of miles from home?

I'm not going to think of that. I am strong in Ingo. I am

Dad's *myrgh kerenza*, his dear daughter. I'm here to speak to him, that's all. It's not a crime.

Perhaps the current heard us planning Dad's freedom in our minds. Perhaps it knew we intended to frustrate the law of the Mer. Perhaps that's why it went wild, breaking its own law to hurl me into the Deep.

I'm alone. Completely alone. Not just alone until Mum comes home, or alone because I don't want to be with the others. *Alone.* If I died here, nobody would know. The pressure of the sea bearing down on me is so strong that I don't think my body would even float to the surface. No one would ever guess what had happened to me. I could call for Faro, but he wouldn't hear me. Faro said that the Mer don't come to the deep ocean. There's no one to help me here.

Only yourself, says a small voice inside my head. *Only yourself.* The words sound hollow and lonely. I can't even see my fingers. It's too dark.

But I'm still here. I'm not dead. I'm not even hurt. My body is able to bear the weight of the Deep. Perhaps it is not so deep after all.

Faro told me that monsters live here. Giant squid with tentacles as long as a basking shark…

He must have been teasing. Of course he was. Don't think of tentacles now. I have still got myself, even if that's all I've got. I must keep my head clear and not let panic crowd its way in and stop me from thinking. I've got to be brave, like Conor when he entered Ingo without knowing whether I could keep him alive here. Be brave, Sapphire.

I'll start swimming, and I'll keep on until I find something or somewhere that lets me know where I am. I won't think about the weight of water above my head.

Only yourself, repeats the cold little voice in my ear.

Yes, myself! I'm angry now. I'd rather be angry than terrified.

I swim along cautiously, feeling my way through the thick dark water, trying not to use up too much energy. I can't swim fast anyway. My arms and legs seem to have weights on them, dragging me down. It's the pressure.

Conor's safe. He escaped the current with Faro. I've got to believe that. The alternative is too terrible. For a second I see Conor's body turning over and over as it sinks slowly into the mouth of the Deep, and then I shut my mind. The Deep can't hurt Conor. He's safe with Faro. The Deep doesn't want to hurt me either. Probably it doesn't even know that I'm here. I'm like a gnat on the shoulder of an elephant. I'll keeping swimming along, not too fast, not too slow, at a pace that I can keep up for hours if necessary. If you believe things, sometimes they start to happen. I'm going to believe that I'm swimming to safety.

The whale sees me before I see it. I am quite close before I realise that the whale is anything but a deeper part of the darkness. And then the whale's body slowly swings. Water swirls against my body. The whale is denser than a shadow, and alive. I'm looking at one of those puzzle-book pictures where a shape is hidden. As soon as you find the shape, you can't believe that you ever missed it. The whale shape comes out of the dark. Blunt, squared off, looming head, body still in shadow.

The whale is so huge that I'm like a dinghy in the path of a tanker. It's lucky that the whale is swimming slowly. Maybe it has to conserve energy, too. I wouldn't like to be caught in the onrush of a whale travelling at full speed.

I don't know what kind of whale it is. I rack my memory, trying to recall what Dad used to tell me about whales. It's too dark to be sure, but this must be one of the biggest. Blue whales are so rare now. What's the other big one called that Dad said could dive a thousand metres deep? They don't come often to our waters, but they do sometimes. I can't remember their name.

The strange thing is that I'm not afraid of the whale's vastness. It is like meeting a friend in an alien world. A distant cousin, maybe. This whale is a creature of warm blood, a breathing creature like me. A fellow mammal.

I lift my hand in greeting. It sounds crazy, but I find myself so glad to see the whale that I start talking to it, telling it my name. I don't know whether I am speaking Mer or not, but I believe that my words reach the whale.

I feel something like a wave of intelligence flowing over me, questioning what I am and what I'm doing here. I repeat my name. "I'm Sapphire. I'm looking for my brother, and for Faro. The current drove me here."

The intelligence probes me again. It wants more.

"I don't want to be here. This is too deep for me. I need to be back where the Mer are, in Ingo."

A ripple passes through the water between me and the whale. The whale is laughing. Not mocking laughter, but the way Mum used to laugh when I pronounced words wrong when I was little. I used to say "windowsilver" instead of "windowsill" and I didn't know it was wrong until I went to school. Mum said she liked it so much that she didn't want to tell me it was wrong. Suddenly I am absolutely sure that this whale is female.

The whale's laughter changes. It turns into sound, shapes, syllables. She fills the dark water with pulses of meaning. She is talking to me.

"You say you need to be back in Ingo, little one. But this is Ingo. How could it not be Ingo, where I am?"

"But I thought… The Mer don't come here, do they?"

"Ingo is more than where the Mer are. But what's a little barelegs like you doing down so deep?"

"The current brought me."

"You said that. But the Deep doesn't let little barelegs live, so how are you here?"

"I don't know."

"And where are you going?"

179

"I want to leave the Deep, but I don't know which way to go."

"Poor little barelegs. Don't they teach you which way is up?"

The deep trembles with the whale's enormous joke.

"Nothing they teach us works here."

"Come here, little one."

I am extremely hesitant about this. A whale is a whale. And it's quite possible that whales hold their memories in common, even though they are not fish. They might remember terrible things about humans harpooning them, dragging them for miles with blood pouring from a dozen wounds, and then cutting up their carcasses for oil and blubber. Something nags at my mind. Those whales – the ones that could dive deep – they were hunted for a particular reason. I wish I could remember their name.

"I don't think you are big enough to cause me harm, little barelegs," rumbles the whale.

Clearly she thinks I am about six years old, and she also doesn't seem to realise that my legs aren't bare at all, since I'm wearing jeans. But she offers my only hope of help, and there is something about her which I can't help trusting. I swim cautiously towards her flank.

"Come closer."

Her body is like a cliff. I brush against it and it feels rough, like a huge shrivelled orange. I swim upwards over the landscape of her skin, towards her head. It is much too dark for me to see her eye, but she seems to see me.

"Why do you swim so weakly?" she asks.

"I can't go any faster. My arms and legs are so heavy."

"Your mother should have taught you better."

Now that I'm in the shelter of the whale, I feel safer. She is an air breather, though she can stay underwater for a long time. I wish I could remember how long. But she will have to go home to the Air, and maybe she'll take me with her.

"So slow, so slow," grumbles the whale. "Come up to my forehead, little one."

I climb higher, feeling my way along the pitted surface of her skin.

"Would you like me to swallow you, little barelegs, and spit you out again once we leave the Deep?"

My body shrinks with horror. My mind babbles with panic.

"I am not serious," says the whale reprovingly. "My children would have known that I was not serious."

For a second I imagine the whale's children rolling their eyes at yet another of their mum's not very good jokes.

"I must leave the Deep," I say. "I have to find my brother and Faro, and go to see Saldowr."

"Saldowr?"

"He's a teacher, a wise one."

"I know who Saldowr is," says the whale.

"Do you know where he is?"

"I know a current that will take you to where he is. But are you sure, little barelegs, that this is what you want? We whales never visit Saldowr. He has too much knowledge."

"But I want to know something."

"Of course," muses the whale. "I was forgetting, little barelegs. I was thinking of you as one of my own. Your world is full of knowledge. As soon as you meet any creature, you have to know what is inside it." Her voice has changed. It is full of a sadness as profound as the Deep.

My memory clicks open. Whales like her were hunted and killed in thousands, because the hunters had learned that inside their bodies was oil and a precious wax called ambergris. I remember asking Dad what the wax was used for.

Perfume, he said.

But, Dad, how could people ever have discovered they could make perfume out of whales?

By killing enough of them.

"So you must go to Saldowr and find your answer," the whale goes on, "whatever pain it causes. And I must rise."

"Do you need to breathe?"

"Yes, I need the Air. I have filled my hunger for food, and now my hunger for air begins to grow. Rise with me, little barelegs, unless you prefer the Deep."

"But how can I?"

"Have you seen dolphins ride the bow-wave of your ships?"

"Yes. No. I mean, I know that they do it."

"Dolphins are full of play. You have to be the cleverest of creatures to play as much as they do. We whales can't complain, but our lives are heavy. The dolphins ride free. That's their gift, little barelegs. They turn their whole lives to play."

"Don't whales play?"

"Certainly," rumbles the whale, "certainly we try to play. We have many jokes, but everyone is afraid to laugh."

"Oh. I see."

"That is the burden we whales have always borne."

There is certainly nothing playful about the way the whale brings me up from the Deep. Heavy surges of water throw me from side to side. It's like being batted through the water by a giant in boxing gloves. The whale's huge wake curls from her sides and I'm tucked inside it, rolling over and over, blind and sick and dizzy but rising, rising, drawing away from darkness, slowly at first then faster, faster, as the whale's strength bursts the grip of the Deep.

CHAPTER ELEVEN

I don't want to say goodbye to the whale. In her company I feel as safe as if she were my mother. I wish that she would tell another of her ponderous whale jokes, and this time I would make sure to laugh. She'd be pleased about that.

There's no time left. She slows, and halts about fifty metres from the bright surface. I can see her clearly now. Her skin is wrinkled, almost shrivelled-looking. I wonder if she is very old. She is like a mountain of protection at my side.

"Leave me now," she says. "you are safe here. Climb on this current and it will take you where you want to go. I must rise quickly." She needs to breathe. She's probably risen more slowly from the Deep than she should have done, for my sake.

"Goodbye, dear whale. Thank you thousands of times."

"Goodbye, little barelegs."

She backs away from me. Slowly, like an air balloon

sailing up into the sky, her huge bulk rises with majestic grace to the surface.

"Goodbye, dear whale!" I call after her. I wonder if we'll ever meet again. I hope we will.

There's the current she told me to take. A warm, bright, bubbling current. I swim slowly towards it. Every muscle in my body aches with exhaustion. I feel weighed down, as if I still haven't escaped the pressure of the Deep. I turn into the current and a warm fountain of bubbles explodes against my skin. I stretch out, and the flow of water buoys me up like a pillow. *Relax*, the current whispers, *I know where I'm going and I'll take you there safely. Just relax and trust me. Close your eyes.*

And I do. I must be crazy. The last current I trusted turned on me like a tiger and dragged me into the Deep. But what choice have I got? I don't know where I am. The whale has already disappeared. I wish I'd asked her name. I hope we meet again...

It's so peaceful. The current rocks me gently as it moves along. There are no monsters here. I can relax. In fact the light is so strong after the dark of the Deep that it stings my eyes. I'll just close them for a little while...

I slept. You know those warm delicious sleeps full of dreams that are so wonderful that you never want to wake? That was the sleep the current gave me. Sleep full of sea colours and sea music. Sleep full of singing voices, so far away that I could only catch a few lines of the song...

Sea nymphs hourly ring his knell
Hark, now I hear them
Ding dong bell, ding dong bell
Ding dong...

It was a sleep that felt as gentle as a rock pool after you've been swimming in rough, cold water. I must have travelled on for hours, or perhaps it was only minutes that stretched out to hours, as they do in dreams. Sometimes I felt myself rising to the surface of sleep, but then I drifted back to the lulling sound of the current in my ears. The current wrapped itself round me like a blanket. I almost forgot that I'd ever had another life except this one, drifting wherever the current wanted to take me. There was nothing to fear, nothing to grieve for, no more mystery to solve.

I forgot Conor and Faro. My life in the Air was as remote as a toy I'd had when I was a baby. I dreamed of a woman with a seal-dark tail, singing her baby to sleep. I looked into the baby's cradle and saw it had dark feathery hair, and little hands like starfish, and a tail like its mother. I dreamed of a home deep under the waves, and a bed made of sea moss and sea emeralds, curtained by swaying seaweed.

Sometimes, between dreams, I remembered the

whale. I never thought about Dad, or the reason we'd come to Ingo. Each time I woke up and then drifted back into sleep, the dreams grew more enchanting. Each time, the waking world grew more shadowy. Why wake at all? Why go back there when the current offered everything I had ever wanted...

Ding dong bell, ding dong bell
Ding dong...

The voices chimed more sweetly than any human voice I'd ever heard. Going away would be easy if it meant going to join those voices. I would leave everything to follow them... leave everything—

"Sapphire! Sapphire! Sapphire!"

A voice was saying the same word, over and over. I listened dreamily. After a long time I remembered what the word meant. It was my name. I was Sapphire.

"Sapphire! Sapphire! Sapphire!"

Why did the voice sound so sharp and urgent? Why was it trying to wake me up? All that mattered was the dream. Nothing must break the dream. I would rather stop being Sapphire than break the dream.

"Sapphire!"

The voice would not leave me alone. It was an echo

booming in a cave. It was a bee buzzing in my ear. I twisted in the current, trying to close my ears—

And then something caught hold of me. Something grabbed me by the arms and hauled me out of the current. Something tore me away from the dream, and it shattered into a million brilliant drops, like drops of water, as I was pulled back into the world.

"She's awake."

Someone is bending over me. A face I know I ought to know.

"Saph! Don't you recognise me?"

I stare at the face. Brown skin, dark eyes, dark hair. The face is peering at me anxiously. "You're... yes, I know you. Your name is Conor."

"Saph! Why are you talking like that? It's *me*. Conor. Your *brother*, Saph. Wake up!"

"Leave her," says another voice, much deeper. I know this voice at once. It's the one that called my name and made me lose my dream.

"Why did you do it!" I exclaim angrily. "I was so happy, and you destroyed it."

"It would have destroyed you," goes on the deep, rich voice. Another figure is leaning over me now. His hair is threaded with white, his eyes are green and silver. He looks as old as the world, but his face is unwrinkled. Is he young or is he old? His tail is like a seal's tail dipped in frost.

"She looks so ill," says the one I recognise as my brother. "What do you think happened to her, Saldowr?"

At the sound of his name, a shudder runs through me. *Saldowr.* It is all flooding back, and I want to build a dam to keep out the knowledge. It was so peaceful in the current, so beautiful. Why did they pull me out of it? Saldowr. *You must go to Saldowr and find your answer, whatever pain it causes.*

"She has been in the Deep," says Saldowr. "She has survived the Deep, which no human child or Mer child should survive. It has not crushed her body, but it has crushed her heart. It left her weak and empty, and the current knew it. It filled her with its false dreams. I hope that we have caught her in time, before the dreams took her so far away that she could never return."

"Were you really in the Deep, Saph?" My brother's face bends over me. He looks worn and anxious. There are black hollows under his eyes.

"Yes," I say calmly. "But you don't need to worry. I was perfectly safe."

Conor's face twists. How strange he looks! "What's the matter with you?" I ask.

"He's weeping," says Saldowr. "It's something humans do. He has been watching and waiting, hoping against hope that you had survived the Deep. He has not eaten. He has not rested for a moment."

I stare at my brother. Something niggles at my mind. Something is different – unexpected—

"Why, Conor! You're not holding on to Faro."

"He is with me within the Groves of Aleph, within my protection," answers Saldowr. "He does not need any other help."

"So where is Faro?"

"Saph, stop it! Stop asking all these questions as if they're maths puzzles! Don't you *care* what's happened to him?"

"Care what happened to him... That's why I asked."

Conor's looking at me as if I scare him. "But that's not the same thing, Saph. Don't you see?"

"Give her time," says Saldowr. "In your world, when a person has been lost in the snow and her feet and hands are half frozen, you don't bring her in to sit close by the fire. Your sister has been in the Deep, where life and feeling are pressed as thin as a sheet of paper. Let her come back to us slowly."

He turns to me. "Faro is well. He is resting. He brought your brother to me."

"He did much more than that, Saph! Faro took a terrible risk. After he'd got me safe to Saldowr, he tried to dive into the Deep to find you. He's lucky to be alive. He blacked out from the pressure, and Saldowr's been treating him ever since. Don't you understand, we've been desperate, thinking you were dead?"

"I wasn't dead. I was still in Ingo."

Saldowr is watching me closely. "Part Mer, part human," he murmurs. "The mixture is potent, but unstable... You were still in Ingo, you say?"

"That's what the whale told me. She said, *How can it not be Ingo, where I am?*"

"Say those words again," demands Saldowr.

"How can it not be Ingo, where I am."

There is a long silence. Why are they staring at me like that? Saldowr so intent and sombre, Conor so strange, his face struggling... *He's weeping. It's something humans do.*

But *I'm* human. Why did Saldowr talk as if I wasn't?

"Saph, what have they done to you?" asks Conor despairingly. "You've changed. You're not yourself any more."

"I don't understand what you mean."

"Leave her, Conor. She must rest. She must come back to herself slowly."

For the first time, I look around and take in my surroundings. I am lying on a bed of soft sea moss, like the bed in the dream. We are in a grove of underwater trees, as thick as oaks. Their trunks are knotted, shiny and reddish brown in colour, with roots rising like knuckles above the pale sand. Above our heads, thick branches sway in the water. We are no more than thirty metres below the surface, but the trees hide us.

"Watch your sister, Conor," says Saldowr, and he swims away into the thickest part of the grove, where a dozen trunks are twisted together.

"That's where he lives," murmurs Conor to me. "His cave is among those trees. Faro is there, for healing, but we can't enter because our Mer blood isn't strong enough."

Conor's words lap at my ears. I know I should concentrate on what he's saying. From his expression I can see that it's important, but I can't focus on Conor or Saldowr or anything else. If I do, I might never hear those singing voices again. I'm sure they are still singing somewhere, just out of earshot. If only I could find that current again, and lay my head on its pillow, and let it carry me away—

"Saph!"

Conor bends over me, his face drawn with the pain which Saldowr said was a human thing. Weeping seems strange to me. Human things seem very far away now. "Saph," Conor pleads, "come back, before it's too late!"

Something gathers at the corner of his eyes. Water. All the water in Ingo is salt, but this is not ordinary salt water. It does not blend into the waters of Ingo, and lose itself there. A drop glistens as it rolls down Conor's cheek. He leans close to me, and the drop falls. It remains as separate as a drop of mercury as it falls through the water and on to my forehead.

The tear tingles as it touches my skin. The tingling spreads outwards. It hurts, like pins and needles in a foot that's gone to sleep. I screw up my face in pain. What I see hurts me. What I hear hurts me. The enchanting curtain that the current drew between me and the world has been ripped down. But there's my brother. Suddenly I remember how terrified I was down in the Deep when I thought I might never see him again. Conor has survived. We are back together, both of us alive against all the odds.

"Conor!"

"Saph!"

"Conor, what happened to you? How did you get that cut on your forehead?"

"Saph!" He grabs my hands and squeezes them in his. "You're back! It's you!"

"Conor, I feel so weird. I feel as if I'm waking up from a dream. Is it really you?"

"Of course it's me, you idiot! Who else would it be?"

We can't stop smiling stupidly at each other. We can't let go of each other's hands. Everything is so sharp and bright that it makes me blink. I can hardly take in what's happening.

"You *were* weird," Conor says. "It was like someone had put a spell over you. Horrible." He shivers. "As if you were here in your body, but absent in your mind."

"I don't know what happened to me. I knew things but I couldn't feel them. It was like looking at you through thick glass. But are you hurt? What's been happening?"

"It's a long story, Saph."

We sit side by side on the bed of sea moss, Conor's

arm round my shoulders, while he tells me everything. How they watched the current sweep me away, and struggled to reach me, but in a few seconds I disappeared. They were tossed over and over, battered by the water, battered against each other, but the current didn't swallow them.

"It was like being chewed up in a monster's mouth," says Conor. All he could do was cling on to Faro, and Faro never let go of him. They were both covered in cuts and bruises, but at last they got out of the current. They must have been closer to its edge than I was, and Faro had the power of his seal tail to drive them through the water.

"But I still don't think we'd have escaped on our own. I think the current didn't want us. It spat us out."

Once they were out of the current, there was no choice. Faro wanted to dive to find me – Conor realised that later – but he couldn't until he'd got Conor to safety. The only sure place was where Saldowr was, in the Groves of Aleph. By the time they reached the Groves, they were both exhausted, but Faro wouldn't give up. He handed Conor over to Saldowr, then before they realised what he intended to do, he swam back and tried to enter the Deep.

"It was an incredibly brave thing to do. The Mer can't survive in the Deep, and he knew it. The Deep was too powerful for him, and it threw him back. He was unconscious, and Saldowr brought him back. I don't really know about that part, because I was out of it too.

Faro's recovering now, Saldowr says. I haven't seen him yet."

"Does he know I'm alive?"

"Yes. Saldowr told him."

So this is where we are: the Groves of Aleph. It's like an underwater forest. The trees are thick and close together, as if they've crowded up to protect whatever lies in the heart of them. I wish I could see Faro now. He risked his life going into the Deep for me. He must have thought he'd failed, and I was dead.

The Deep should have killed me, but it didn't. The whale didn't expect to see one of my kind there. Mer can't survive there, and nor can humans. I know that I am part Mer and part human, so I don't understand why I'm still alive. It's making my head hurt to think about it all.

"Conor."

"Yes."

"You are really here, aren't you?"

Conor squeezes my hand, hard. "Does that feel real enough?"

"Yes, get off, you're hurting— But, Conor, it was so scary being alone down there. I'd have died without the whale."

"What whale?"

"She looked after me. It's strange, isn't it, Con – human beings have been killing whales for hundreds of years, and yet she helped me to get out of the Deep. I'd never have done it without her. She was like a – a bit like a mother—"

We stare at each other in consternation. Mum! I had completely forgotten about her.

"How long do you think we've been in Ingo?"

"I don't know. Not too long, I hope."

"Mum'll be so worried—"

"We couldn't have done anything else. I couldn't have left Ingo without you."

"Maybe we should leave now, Con."

But Conor is resolute. "No. Not before we've asked Saldowr about Dad. Not after we've come all this way."

By the time Saldowr returns, we are sitting silently, pondering everything that has happened. Saldowr is carrying something – fruit that look a little like grapes, except that they are flatter in shape. They are a rich, dark turquoise. "I brought these for your sister, to help her to return to us," he says to Conor, "but it seems that it's not necessary. The deep has released her already. All the same, you must both be hungry. Eat."

I've never thought of being hungry in Ingo before. I've never even wondered about what the Mer eat or drink. Conor looks cautiously at the sea grapes. "I'm all right, thank you," he says politely.

Saldowr smiles as if he knows exactly what Conor's thinking. "They are quite safe to eat," he says.

I reach out, take a grape, and put it in my mouth. The

skin bursts, spilling juice. It tastes so good that I take another and then another, greedily, until half the bunch is gone. "Conor, I'm eating them all. You have your share."

"I'm really not hungry, Saph."

"You like our fruit, child," says Saldowr to me. "How do the grapes taste to you – salt or sweet?"

"I don't know. They don't taste salt or sweet to me. They're just right."

"Then eat them, *myrgh kerenza*."

My hand is reaching out to pick another grape from the bunch, but at Saldowr's words it freezes. "Why did you say that?"

"Because you know what it means."

Myrgh kerenza. Dear daughter.

"But you're not my father."

"My child, you must understand that you are not only your father's daughter. You are a daughter of Ingo. You have a purpose here, with us."

"Saph, what's going on? What's he saying?" asks Conor.

Saldowr touches him lightly on the shoulder. "Your sister is speaking full Mer to me now. I am telling her that she has a purpose in Ingo. But we will go back to speaking the common language. Understand this, Conor: it is neither a strength nor a weakness in your sister that she is as she is. She did not choose it: it chose her. She is part Mer and part human: you are both that. But in her, Mer and human are strangely and powerfully fused. She has gone to the Deep and returned alive."

"You're just like Granny Carne!" exclaims Conor, staring at him.

"Who is Granny Carne?" asks Saldowr.

"A wise woman."

"Saldowr isn't at all like Granny Carne, Conor, he's the complete opposite. She's Earth—"

"Yes, I know, but Saldowr is to the Mer what Granny Carne is to humans," says Conor impatiently. "She belongs to Earth and he belongs to Ingo, but they're like two sides of the same thing"

Saldowr is watching Conor closely, as if he wants him to say more.

"Do people – Mer, I mean – do they come to you when they have troubles – when they want to know what to do?" goes on Conor eagerly. Saldowr nods.

"I told you, Saph! They are doing the same thing, but in different – what's the word? *Elements.*"

"You seem to know a great deal about me," observes Saldowr dryly. "Those who come to me usually come with questions, not answers."

Conor flushes. "We have come with a question," he says.

"Then ask it."

But Conor turns away. His fists are clenched. "In a moment," he says in a stifled voice. I'm sure that Saldowr already knows our question. Conor is right: they would recognise each other, even though he is not the same as Granny Carne. I raise my head and meet Saldowr's eyes.

"Our father is in Ingo," says Conor slowly, "and we think… we believe that he is unhappy here. We believe that he made a choice without knowing what he was doing. It wasn't a free choice if he didn't understand it, was it? We want to know if that choice can ever be… changed."

"You want him to return to you," says Saldowr sternly. His green and silver eyes flash as he draws himself up to his full height. "You think that he can return to the Air, just as your sister returned from the Deep." He frowns, and looks from one of us to the other. "It will take more than human tears to restore your father to you. Are you truly ready to know what has happened to him? Are you ready to know what choice he made?"

I can't speak. Conor answers quietly but steadily, "We are ready."

"A true answer can cut like coral," warns Saldowr. "But if you want to know more, come with me now."

Without a backward glance to see if we are following or not, Saldowr swims away, towards the heart of the grove.

CHAPTER TWELVE

We halt in the thickest part of the trees, not far from the cave. Its entrance is hidden by a curtain of silvery weed that sways gently to and fro. I wish I could go into the cave and thank Faro for what he did. Diving into the Deep like that, risking his own life to help me. I feel a rush of gratitude, and a shiver of fear for what could have happened to Faro, and to me too. I've got to thank him.

As if Saldowr catches my thought, he shakes his head. "Wait here," he orders, and then he dives through the curtain of weed.

We wait. The light glows a soft, deep red as it filters through the dense branches above us. The rocks around the cave entrance glisten with mother-of-pearl. The sand is silver. It's beautiful here in the heart of the Groves of Aleph, but it's not a peaceful sort of beauty. It makes me tingle with anticipation. Something's going to happen – or maybe it's already happening, only we can't see it.

Suddenly, Conor nudges my arm. "Look up," he whispers. "Look up between the branches."

"I can't see – what are they?"

"Look carefully. I think they're sharks, swimming above the trees."

"Sharks! What - what kind of sharks?"

"I can't tell."

"I wish Saldowr would come back."

"They're not coming any closer. They're just swimming up and down. Like they're patrolling—"

"Patrolling! Conor – you mean like the guardian seals?"

The guardian seals patrol the borders of Limina, where the Mer go to die. The seals are prepared to kill anyone who threatens the peace of Limina. They almost killed Roger and his friend Gray. I shudder, remembering how the grey seals tossed him and Gray through the water like rag dolls. "Conor, do you think those sharks are patrolling the Groves of Aleph?"

"Maybe." Conor stares up intently. His eyesight has always been sharper than mine. "They do look as if they're on guard, like those seals in Limina. But it's all right, Saph. Don't be scared. We're here under Saldowr's protection, aren't we? They're not going to hurt us."

I move closer to Conor, and look up where he's pointing. A familiar shape slides into focus. Long, sleek, submarine body, underslung jaw. The shark glides across my vision, and with a powerful flick of the tail doubles back on itself. And over there, a little higher, there's another one—

"Why didn't they attack us when we came here?"

Conor shrugs. "Just be grateful they didn't."

Saldowr is on his way back. He has put on a cloak which is the inky-blue colour of a mussel shell. It swirls around him, wrapping itself over his right arm. There's something in his hand, hidden by the cloak. Saldowr's face is sombre. His eyebrows are drawn together, frowning, but I don't think he's angry with us. His cloak swirls again, inky blue and black and pearl.

He stops, facing us. He spreads both his arms wide, and the cloak falls back. In his right hand, there's a mirror. It's only a small mirror, about the size of my hand, made of a dull metal like pewter. There's no decoration on it. In fact, it's rather disappointing. I thought it would be something more important. I stretch out my hand to touch.

"No!" cracks out Saldowr's voice. I snatch my hand back as if I've touched fire.

"You may look, but not touch. One at a time. Who will go first?"

"You first, Conor. You're the eldest," I say quickly.

"But you're the most curious," murmurs Conor, then he catches Saldowr's stern gaze. Conor straightens his shoulder, and steps forward. Saldowr holds out the mirror.

"Look, but don't touch," he repeats.

Slowly, Conor bends over the mirror, his hands at his sides. I can't see anything. The mirror is hidden by Conor's back.

Suddenly, his hands clench into fists. His whole body tenses. I think he's going to cry out, but he says nothing.

Nobody speaks. Conor just keeps on staring into the mirror as if it has enchanted him. Saldowr holds the mirror steady. The shadows of the swaying water-weed above us flicker over the surface of his cloak. I watch the patterns they make, and after a few seconds I start falling into a dream, as if someone is hypnotising me.

With a huge effort I drag myself back. I've got to make sure that Conor's all right. How long has he been staring into that mirror? It's probably only seconds, but it feels like minutes or even hours.

Saldowr's our friend. He wouldn't be trying to hypnotise me and Conor; I'm sure he wouldn't.

At long last Conor steps back and stands next to me again. I reach out and squeeze his hand, but he doesn't squeeze mine back. He tries to smile at me, but his eyes aren't smiling. They're blazing with anger.

"Are you all right, Con?"

"I'll tell you later." He sounds out of breath, as if he's been running a race. Saldowr's hand falls to his side, and his cloak wraps around the mirror, hiding it again. Isn't he going to let me look into it?

"The mirror must be cloaked," says Saldowr quietly.

"But – but you let Conor look into it."

"Do you want to see what the mirror will show you, my child?"

"No," breaks in Conor, "that's enough. Saph doesn't need to look at it."

"Don't you think your sister has the right to know the truth?"

"Saph doesn't need to see it! I'll – I'll tell her what's in the mirror, Saldowr."

Saldowr shakes his head. "It doesn't work like that. She must see with her own eyes, and hear with her own ears."

I stare at the folds of Saldowr's cloak, where the mirror's hidden. I do want to look into it, but I'm afraid of what the mirror's going to tell me. But if I don't see with my own eyes, I'll always be left wondering about what I might have seen if I'd been just a little bit braver. Very slowly, I step forward. I'm glad that I don't have to hold the mirror myself, because my hands are trembling. Saldowr's face is expressionless as he raises his arms again, throws the cloak back and reveals the mirror. Slowly, he brings the mirror forward. There is no choice now.

At first I see nothing but the dull sheen of its metal surface. Perhaps I'm not going to see anything. I don't know if I'm relieved or disappointed. Dull, silvery metal. It's not even a very good mirror. You couldn't see to comb your hair in it.

As if the mirror has heard my thoughts, a change comes over it, as sudden as a squall over the sea. Shadows gather and then race over the mirror's surface. Shadows of branches, and a breaking pattern of red and purple and blue. Dark blue, inky blue. The reflection of Saldowr's cloak, that's all it is. But suddenly the racing shadows part, like a curtain at the opening of a play. Yes, it's just like a play. The actors are already on the stage, waiting for the audience.

A woman is sitting with her back to me. She must be a Mer woman because there's her beautiful strong, solid tail, like a seal's tail, curled to one side. She's leaning forward, absorbed in whatever it is she's looking at, as if it means everything to her.

Her rippling dark hair streams over her back. She's wearing a fine woven green bodice. Elvira wore a bodice like that once. As I watch, the woman lifts her head. Slowly she turns, and looks into the mirror with a faint, happy smile on her face. Her face is a little like Elvira's too. She has green eyes, like Elvira's, and the same short, straight nose. But her smile is quite different.

The woman's smile widens as if she recognises someone. Is she looking at me? Can she see me? No, her eyes don't meet mine. She's looking at someone else, coming towards her inside the world of the mirror. As I gaze at her, I realise that she's much older than Elvira. She's a woman, not a girl. She could be Elvira's aunt, or an older cousin. She's not old enough to be Elvira's mother.

The woman moves a little to one side, still smiling. Now I can see what she was looking at. In a cradle of smooth stone, lined with silky weed, there is a Mer baby. The baby is asleep, eyes shut, feathers of hair drifting in the soft movement of the water. There are no coverings on the baby. I suppose you wouldn't need to wrap up a baby here in Ingo. The baby's arms are curled around its head. Its tail is the colour of a pearl. Perhaps Mer babies are like seals, and their tails grow darker as they grow older.

As I watch, the woman lifts her hand in greeting, and smiles. Her face is full of warmth and love. I wish she *was* smiling at me. I'd like to swim inside the mirror and get to know her.

There's a shadow at the edge of the mirror. A figure. A man. One of the Mer, swimming towards the Mer woman. He lifts his hand too, and waves at her. As he turns in a swirl of bubbles, I see his face.

The Mer man swims to the cradle, and kisses the sleeping Mer baby on the forehead. Very gently, very lovingly. Dad always kissed us on the forehead like that before we went to sleep. My heart stops beating and then thumps violently, as if an electric shock has jolted through it. The mirror goes dark.

We say nothing for a long while, me and Conor, but we draw close to each other, shoulder to shoulder, touching.

"A true answer can cut to the heart," says Saldowr at last. "I am sorry for it."

"A true answer," says Conor through his teeth. "Is that what you call it?"

"Yes," says Saldowr.

"I suppose everyone here knew except us," goes on Conor in the same cold, angry voice. "Does Faro know? Does Elvira?"

"Yes, they know. How could they not know? The Mer are not like you. We find it hard to have secrets from one another."

I don't want to even think about Dad. I want to wipe the image of him out of my mind.

"She looked like Elvira," says Conor, "that – that *woman*. Is she related to Elvira?"

"She is their mother's sister. But it is easier for Faro and Elvira, because her husband, their uncle, is dead. They can be happy that Mellina has found happiness after long grief."

"Can they," says Conor grimly. "Did they know this all the time? Right from when they first met us last summer? I suppose they must have done."

"You'll have to ask Elvira and Faro yourselves."

"We may not want to," says Conor.

Saldowr says no more. He just watches us thoughtfully. I can't think of anything to say. If I open my mouth I'm afraid I'll cry or yell like a baby. Faro knew all this time, and he said nothing. I thought he was my friend. We were so close we could see into each other's minds. Didn't he know how much it hurt that Dad had gone? Didn't he know how we would feel about this Mer woman? How could Faro be happy about something that made me and Conor so unhappy? *Little sister,* Faro called me. I never understood why. Maybe he was trying to tell me we were more than friends: we were almost related.

"You have to understand that it is different for the Mer," says Saldowr. "We do not own each other as you do."

"*Own* each other? It's got nothing to do with owning. My father was *married.* Married to my mother. End of story," states Conor.

"But it wasn't the end of the story for him. His love began to flow elsewhere."

"She made him love her. He didn't want to," I say hotly. "That woman, Mellina. She sang to him. He'd never have known she existed if she hadn't sung to him."

"The point is that your father listened."

"He should never have listened," says Conor. "He had no right. He was married to Mum."

"I cannot talk to you in this way about the forces that drive men and women," says Saldowr sternly. "*Should, would, could, might, ought.* Those are human words, and even in our common language they mean nothing. We must live with what *is,* not what *might* have been or what *should* be. You saw the child. He has been born. He cannot be unborn again to suit your desires."

"So you're saying that our father can never return to us," says Conor slowly.

"I am not saying that. I am only showing you what *is*."

Conor draws himself up, and says with sudden dignity, "Thank you for showing us what you showed us. We have no more questions."

I look at him with admiration. I'd been on the point of babbling out hundreds of desperate questions about Dad, about the Mer woman, and about that little baby with the pearly tail who is—

Our half-brother. That's the right word for him. But I've only got one brother, and that's Conor. And I don't want another.

Our half-brother, and Faro's and Elvira's cousin. The Mer baby's mother is their aunt. His father is our father. It's all so bewildering and strange that it makes me feel dizzy. Conor's right. We need to go away and talk in private. It's no good looking to Saldowr to solve the problem for us.

Saldowr is also looking at Conor, measuring what he's said. Finally he bows his head in agreement. "As you wish," he says. "But there is another reason for your being here, I think."

"No. There's no other reason."

"Go with your sister now. Comfort each other, but then return to me. There is another subject on which I must speak to you."

"Don't you think we've had enough?" asks Conor savagely. "What else can there be?"

"It is a matter of the gravest urgency. Compared to it, what you saw in the mirror will lose its power to wound you. Each of us will die one day, and our loves and sorrows will die with us." Saldowr shrugs. "Our troubles are not as important as we think. *We* are not as important as we think."

"So I see," says Conor. There is a bite in his voice I've never heard before. "Now I've looked into your mirror, I see that I'm much less important to my father than I thought I was."

"I will speak to you again later. Now is not the time; you cannot hear me," says Saldowr. "Rest now. Talk to each other."

His cloak swirls around him as he re-enters his cave.

We sit together in silence, side by side. It's comforting just to be near Conor. We understand each other's feelings without having to speak. I have a confused hope that somehow Conor will know what we should do now. But he broods in silence, fists clenched on his knees, head down. At last he says, "I suppose you saw the same as I did."

"Yes."

"What a couple of idiots we were. Plunging into Ingo, believing Dad needed us. Thinking we were on some kind of rescue mission. I bet Dad had a good laugh."

His voice is so bitter that I exclaim in protest. "No, Conor! Dad's not like that. He *did* need us. He came to find me because he was unhappy. He does still want us; I know he does."

"He didn't want us enough, did he. He wants *her* more. And the – the..."

"The baby."

"The *Mer* baby, you mean."

"He's our *brother*, Con."

"He's no brother of mine. He's one of *them*, Sapphire. He's got a tail, for God's sake."

"He's our half-brother, then."

Conor shrugs angrily. I don't want to make things worse, but there's something I've got to say. "He's Elvira's cousin, too. And Faro's cousin."

Conor's eyes flash with anger. "And they never said a word to us. Not one word," he says.

"Maybe... maybe they wanted to, but they couldn't. Maybe Saldowr had forbidden it."

"Elvira never even tried."

"But couldn't it be why they came to find us in the first place, last summer? Because we're linked, through our blood. Faro has saved us twice now, Conor. He saved you last summer when the guardian seals attacked Roger. And just now he brought you safely here. He even tried to dive into the Deep to rescue me. Why would he do all that if he wasn't... wasn't part of us, somehow?"

Conor puts his head in his hands. "I don't want to think about Faro and Elvira any more, Saph. It's too much."

But I can't stop thinking about the baby. His soft, feathery hair. His plump little fists curled up by the side of his head as he slept. His tail. Yes, his tail. It wasn't horrific. It wasn't shocking. It was part of him. It would have looked strange if he *hadn't* had a tail. If he'd been *cleft*. My baby brother, and I don't even know his name.

"It's Mum I'm thinking about," continues Conor, looking up again. "What's it going to be like for her when she knows?"

I am shocked at myself. I haven't thought of Mum at all. I can't believe I could be so selfish. But when I'm in Ingo, Mum is never quite real. She is like a frozen image of herself that can't speak or move until I come home again.

"Oh, yes, Mum," I say feebly, trying to pretend that I've been thinking about her too.

"It will be terrible for her," goes on Conor with absolute conviction. It's clear that Mum isn't a frozen image to him, but just as real as if she were standing next to us.

"But does Mum have to know?"

"*Saph.* You can't be serious. Of course Mum's got to know what's happened. Dad's not only left her, he's completely betrayed her. She deserves the truth."

"Mum's got Roger."

"Mum would never even have looked at Roger if Dad hadn't disappeared."

I say nothing. I know that Conor's right in a way. Dad's entirely to blame, and we ought to hate him and support Mum. But I can't do it. I can't make it as simple as that. Good and bad. Black and white. Air and Mer. I belong to both sides and it's like standing on an ice floe which has cracked apart. One foot on one bank of ice, one on the other. I've got to choose, and either leap for safety, or else fall into freezing water. But I can't choose. I don't know how to. Maybe *I'm* a betrayer, too. Like Dad.

"Cheer up, Saph," says Conor suddenly, surprisingly. "It's not the end of the world."

"What?"

"This is *not* going to wreck our lives. I'm not going to let it. Listen, I'll tell you what I'm going to do. I'm going back home. I'm going to take care of Mum whatever happens, and make sure Roger treats her right. I think he will, anyway; he's a good bloke. And I'll tell you something, Saph: I'm never coming here again. *Ingo.*" He spits the word out with disgust. "All they do is lie to you. I thought Elvira was my friend, and all the time she knew…"

I nod as if I'm agreeing with Conor, but inside myself I am not so sure. The little Mer baby is my brother. All right, my half-brother, but still my brother. My brother in Ingo. And there's Faro and Saldowr and the whale and the dolphins, and everyone else I've met in Ingo. Even

Elvira. But this isn't the right time to explain how I feel to Conor.

"Elvira does like you," I say instead.

"She has a strange way of showing it."

"All the same, she does."

We don't talk any more after that. We know Saldowr's going to come back soon, and in a way we're glad to escape from what the mirror has shown us and concentrate on what Saldowr said. *A matter of the gravest urgency.* Saldowr is not the kind of person you doubt. There is a force in him which is invisible but real, like electricity. As he comes towards us, we both look at him eagerly.

"A true answer cuts to the heart," says Saldowr again as he reaches us, "but I see that your hearts are strong and capable of healing."

"If we want them to," retorts Conor.

"Just as you say. No one would wish to heal you against your will. But we must leave all that aside for now, and return to the matter I spoke of earlier. Have you not yet noticed the change in the tides?"

"Tides?" The change of subject is so complete that we just stare at him.

"Yes. There have been changes. You are creatures of Air and Earth; you must chart the progress of the tides on your shores. We know that you measure them. You make 'tide tables'?"

"Yes, I suppose so…" I say, bewildered. "I mean, I don't make them myself—"

"Are you talking about the way the tide came in when the dolphin was stranded?" asks Conor. "No one had ever seen it rise so fast."

Saldowr nods. "That is part of it. You did service to Ingo that night, and it won't be forgotten. But the change in the tides lies deeper than that. Too deep. We fear that the tides wish to reach beyond themselves. They struggle to release themselves from the knot that binds them. We mark it; we study it; we know it; we fear it.

"We fear the meaning of it. That is, those of us who are wise. There are enough hotheads in Ingo who welcome such changes. They rejoice when they hear rumours that the Tide Knot is loosening. Ingo will gain, they say. Ingo's strength will flow with the tides, and its power will surge to a height that has not been known since the days of our ancestors. They would like to see your world drowned where its borders fight with ours. But wisdom observes that if the balance is disturbed in one quarter, it will also be disturbed in another. If a balance tips too far one way, it must right itself. And it may right itself with violence. I have great fears. You might say," Saldowr goes on, smiling wryly, "that my fear has grown to match my wisdom. For I study the Tide Knot, and each day my fears increase."

"What is the Tide Knot?"

"Come with me."

Saldowr leads us through the thickness of the Groves towards the mouth of the cave Conor told me we could not enter. We halt outside again. Saldowr dives to the sea bed, and sand swirls around him, clouding the water. He appears to be struggling with something heavy which resists him. His cloak is thrown back, the muscles on his arms and shoulders bulge with the strain. The sand clears, and we see that he's lifting a heavy stone from the sea bed. A smooth black stone that looks as if it's been polished by thousands of years of water washing over it.

"It's a keystone," whispers Conor.

He is right. As Saldowr raises the keystone, the smooth and solid rock begins to move. A tiny crack appears, a zigzag of bluish light. Saldowr places the keystone in a basin of rock, and swims back towards us. He puts a hand on each of our shoulders. "Watch," he says.

The rock continues to separate. Through the gently swirling sand we see a circle opening in the rock. At first, the circle is small, about the size of a plum. It continues to widen. It's the size of an apple, then a watermelon, then suddenly the circle is so big that I could not put my arms around it.

"Not too close," warns Saldowr, his grip on my shoulder tightening. I've taken a step forward without realising it. "It is still opening."

We can see into the opening now. It's lit from within by a deep blue, restless, roiling light. A pang of terror shoots through me. All the stories I've ever heard about monsters of the Deep flood into my mind. This hole in the rock might hide an octopus with tentacles long enough to reach out and snatch us into its depth.

The rock stops moving.

"The Tide Mouth is open," says Saldowr. "Come a little way forward. Look within."

There are no monsters, no sea snake or octopus or giant crab. What we see is more like a jewel. The Tide Mouth holds a knot of water made up of hundreds and hundreds of strands tightly coiled together. The knot itself is twisted so intricately it looks as if the coils could never escape. Instead, they twist over and over one another. They pour themselves into patterns that only settle for a second before they spring apart. And then another pattern forms, and another. I wonder how many patterns there are?

"As many as the grains of sand on the sea bed," says Saldowr. "But you must not watch them too long. Even I have been caught by the beauty of their coils, and have only just managed to tear myself away in time."

I blink, and look away. The coils of the knot twist in my mind, sinuous and powerful as snakes.

"This is the Tide Knot," says Saldowr. "It holds the tides, and shows them the pattern they must follow."

"I thought that the tides followed the moon," says Conor.

"Yes," I say, remembering. "The tides are the moon talking to Ingo. Faro said that."

Saldowr nods. "You are right that the tides follow the same music as the moon," he says. "But they are not the moon's equals, and they cannot follow her any farther than the Tide Knot allows. This is the knot that binds the tides. It looses them, and it draws them back. They must follow its pattern – as long as the knot holds. We have always believed that the knot will hold until the end of time."

His voice is troubled. Saldowr stares at the Tide Knot like a doctor trying to treat a patient who has a disease he's never seen before. "But now we have reason to suspect that the Tide Knot is slipping," he goes on in a low voice. Another pang of terror goes through me. The Tide Knot continues to coil over and over. To me, the knot looks tight. The tides flex and turn, flashing like jewels. They are so powerful and so beautiful. I could watch them for ever and they would never repeat their pattern...

"Don't look too long!" repeats Saldowr sharply.

"Are they really loosening?" asks Conor quietly. "They look as if they are held tight."

"The changes I observe are very small. Your eyes may not see it yet, but I have observed the Tide Knot from childhood, and can detect that there is change."

I shudder. "The tides could do anything."

Saldowr looks at me. "You feel it too. You feel their power."

"Yes."

"You are right. The tides wish to free themselves. As I said before, there are some in Ingo – some among the Mer, even – who want the power of the tides to be unleashed. They would gladly drown your world."

"So why don't *you* want our world to be drowned?" asks Conor boldly. "We're always being told about the harm humans do to Ingo. Why do you want to protect us?"

"I have no great love for humans," says Saldowr. "I have had little reason to love them. But once the tides are unleashed, who will bring them back to the knot? I tell you, there is enough force held here to destroy the Mer, too. There is enough force to tear our world apart.

"The balance must be kept. I am Guardian of the Tide Knot, and that is my wisdom. There are other wisdoms, of course," he adds more lightly, "and you will have to choose yours."

I am listening, but not listening. The Tide Knot holds me like a hypnotist. If I look long enough, surely I'll see where the patterns begin and where they end. Saldowr says the knot is loosening. *Show me,* I say inside my head, *show me.*

The tides coil over and over like snakes. They are writhing now. The blue-green light is strong. A flash of blue illuminates the slippery sides of the hole. How far down does it goes? How deep is the Tide Knot? It's as blue as a sapphire – so blue…

I take a step forward. The Tide Knot weaves in its coils, glistening with power and life. It's much larger than I thought at first. Only a tiny part of the Tide Knot shows through the gap. It must run deep under the rock, way beneath the ocean. I'm only seeing a grain of its enormous pattern, but if I go just a little closer I'll see more—

Saldowr yanks me back. "Get back, child! The Tide Mouth is closing."

He is right. Very slowly, hypnotically slowly, the walls of rock are squeezing together. As the rock closes over it, the light from the Tide Knot shines even more brightly. We see it roll and coil for the last time as Saldowr lifts the heavy keystone, and slams it into place.

My arms hurt. I look down and see the marks of Saldowr's hands where he dragged me back from the Tide Mouth before it could swallow me.

CHAPTER THIRTEEN

"It's time for you to leave," says Saldowr. Saldowr and I have moved back from the sealed Tide Mouth, but Conor can't tear himself away. He has swum right down to the surface of the rock. The sand swirled violently when Saldowr dropped the keystone back into place, but now it has settled again. The water's clear, and Conor is scanning the rock, close-up. Now the keystone is back in place, you can't even see the join. I can hardly believe that the coiling mass of the Tide Knot is still there, hidden.

I want to see the Tide Knot again, even though it frightens me. All that power and energy, enough to light a thousand cities, all hidden away under this rock. Maybe if we wait, Saldowr might remove the keystone again—

"You must leave Ingo now," Saldowr repeats, more urgently this time. "A storm is on its way."

"But we can't go yet. We'll have to wait for Faro. Conor can't travel through Ingo without Faro. I know he's all right here with you in the Groves, but once he's outside he won't be able to get enough oxygen."

Saldowr's expression doesn't change. Obviously he doesn't realise just how dangerous it is for Conor to be in Ingo without support.

"His lips go blue, and then he can't swim. It's weird, because Conor's much stronger than I am when we're in the Air. I can support him for a while here in Ingo, but it's never long enough. Unless – well, unless *I've* grown stronger…" My voice trails off doubtfully, and Saldowr shakes his head.

"You are not strong enough yet, child. Your brother's will is set towards Air and Earth. That weakens him in Ingo. But *you* are divided equally between the human world and Ingo. Your will fights itself. If you were undivided, you would be stronger still. You would enter Ingo with all your heart— But enough of that. You must go back to the Air now. There's no time to lose."

"Will you take us then?"

"No. I cannot leave the Tide Knot."

"Then what are we going to do? What about Conor—"

"The dolphins will take you. You know them, and they know you. You have already travelled with them. Wherever the dolphins are, they bring Ingo with them, but they can also leap through the Air at will. Your brother will be able to breathe freely in the dolphins' company. They will swim with their backs above the water as much as possible to ease his passage. And yet all the time you will be safe in Ingo. The dolphins will be glad to make the journey with you. They have a greeting for you and it will give them pleasure to deliver it."

Riding with the dolphins again! Excitement thrills through me. I remember the glory of last summer's ride with the dolphins, leaping and crashing through the waves, as fast as an arrow and as wild as the wind. Maybe we'll even meet the dolphin who was stranded. And there'll be no danger for Conor. Perfect. I smile gratefully at Saldowr, and then I remember the sharks.

They're up above us, patrolling, guarding the Groves of Aleph as ruthlessly as the seals guarded Limina. Once we're outside Saldowr's protection, we'll have no defence against the sharks. They even attack the Mer sometimes. Faro said so last summer. *Sometimes sharks can't hear that we're Mer. They want to hear that we are seals.*

My thoughts tumble over and over as if terror is blowing a gale through them. The rush of a shark through the water towards me – its jaws opening as it swerves for the attack—

Are you unconscious by the time a shark eats you, or do you still know what's happening? "Those – those sharks," I begin. Saldowr puts up his hand to silence me.

"Fine fellows," he says. "Not the cleverest creatures in Ingo, but they know their duty and nothing will turn them from it. Come, you must meet them."

"Meet – meet a shark? Me?"

"Yes. Both of you. Don't look so terrified, child, it's for your own protection. Conor!"

But Conor's still absorbed in studying the rock face.

"*Conor!*" Saldowr repeats sternly.

Conor glances round. He sees Saldowr waiting with his arms folded, looking taller and more formidable than ever. With obvious reluctance, Conor pushes away from the rock face and swims to us. "Those patterns, Saldowr," he says eagerly, "they look like writing, but it's not like any writing I've seen before. What language is it?"

"Which patterns do you mean?"

"The ones cut into the rock. As soon as you put the keystone back into place, the patterns emerged. Like... like that magic writing we used to do with water and paintbrushes when we were little, remember, Saph? You saw the patterns come out on the rock, didn't you, Saph? I'm sure it's writing."

I say nothing. I didn't see any patterns or writing, but I don't want to contradict Conor in front of Saldowr. Conor tugs my hand. "Come and look, Saph. Maybe you'll be able to read them."

"Wait!" says Saldowr. "Could you read any of the words, my son?"

"No..." Conor hesitates. "Not quite. You know when something is only just out of focus? The writing's like that. If I study it a bit longer, I think I'll be able to read it—"

"Maybe. But there's no time for study now."

"Can *you* read the writing, Saldowr?" I ask him boldly.

"I am the Guardian of the Tide Knot," he says, as if that's a full answer.

"But, Saldowr—"

"This is no time for questions."

It never is, in Ingo, I think rebelliously. I can tell that Conor's just as curious as I am, but Saldowr's expression is a blank wall.

"Leave the rock for now," he says. "Trust me, Conor, the time will come. But now you must meet the sharks, for your protection, and get home before the storm."

"Won't you let us see Faro first, just for a moment? We really want to thank him," I say. There's so much I want to talk to Faro about. Conor's furious with Faro and Elvira for keeping so much hidden from us, but I'm not so sure. Maybe they didn't have a choice. Mer life is so different from human life. There's still so much I don't understand.

"Please let us see Faro," I beg.

But Conor says, "Leave it, Saph. I don't want to see him now."

Saldowr refuses, anyway, and I don't dare to ask again. Unwillingly, I follow Conor and Saldowr upwards, swimming through the dense branches and foliage of the swaying sea trees until we are out of the Groves of Aleph.

Saldowr glides to a halt. "Keep close together, behind me," he tells us. Saldowr is so much more powerful than Faro or Elvira that Conor doesn't need to hold his wrist for support. Just being close to him is enough. "Stay behind me. We are coming to the sharks' patrol grounds."

I feel sick with dread. If Saldowr wasn't here, I'd do a backflip and dive straight back into the Groves. But we swim on steadily, close together.

Suddenly they loom into view. The sharks, their huge grey-white bodies seeming to turn the sea itself as grey as death. Their long, powerful bodies, as wide as helicopters and as long as submarines, their underslung jaws, their small eyes. Pitiless eyes. All the things I know about sharks rush back into my mind. If even the Mer can't always convince sharks not to attack them, what chance have we got?

"I think they're Great Whites," murmurs Conor.

Then the rumours we've heard these past few years are true. Great Whites are coming farther north on the warm currents. The sharks turn towards us, and Saldowr spreads out his arms towards them in welcome. His cloak billows, shielding us.

"Come slowly, my friends," he calls. Two of the sharks break off from their patrol and head down towards us. Even under Saldowr's protection, to keep still and face the sharks' approach without flinching is the hardest thing I've ever done. My mouth tastes of fear, like metal. The sharks mustn't smell my fear. Probably they're like dangerous dogs, which can always tell if you're afraid of them. Conor puts his arm around my shoulders and holds me tight.

"It's OK, Saph," he whispers. "Saldowr won't let them hurt us."

The sharks' jaws gape as they slide to a halt before Saldowr. Their mouths are lined with rows and rows of teeth, each as long as my hand. I'm so close I can see the jags on their teeth. Do sharks ever see dentists? I have to swallow a hysterical giggle.

Those teeth would rip you apart like a power saw. The whale was awesome, but these sharks are terrifying. No echo of fellow-feeling comes from them. They are cold-blooded strangers.

"You have done your work well," Saldowr praises them. "Listen closely now. I bring you two friends of the Tide Knot. Learn them. Know them. Be sure you let them pass."

He pushes us forward a little, letting the folds of his cloak fall around us so that they protect us without hiding us. The sharks swing their great heads from side to side. I clench my fists tight and dig my nails into my palms.

Conor's grip on my shoulders tightens. "Keep cool, Saph. It's going to be OK," he murmurs.

"They are picking up your scent," says Saldowr quietly. A shark eye catches mine as the head swings. It is cold and dull, rapt with duty. I am not a person to this shark. It will not try to communicate.

"Learn them well," insists Saldowr. "Know them well. They are friends of the Tide Knot. Let the memory of their scent pass into the shoal."

"Come closer to them," Saldowr urges us. "We must be sure that they know you."

If I reached out my hand now, I would be able to touch the shark's flank. It is like a wall. The skin's so rough that it would scour mine to shreds if it rubbed against it. The shark's power throbs like an engine. I can sense it. I try to reach out to the shark with my thoughts, to show him that I'm not an enemy, but his mind is walled like his skin. I can't get into it.

But I'm not so scared now. I think I understand what the shark's doing. He is separating the thousand fibres of our scent and storing them in his mind. He'll pass on the imprint of our scent so that every shark who meets us will find us already in his memory, and will know to let us pass without harm. He'll do it, because Saldowr has ordered it.

Conor and I float, upright, dead still. The sharks hang in the water. *We're under Saldowr's protection. We're under Saldowr's protection,* I say over and over in my mind. I mustn't panic. The sharks will pick up the scent of panic. *We're under Saldowr's protection...*

"They have heard you. They have got your scent," says Saldowr at last, and there's relief in his voice, as if even Saldowr had not been absolutely sure of the sharks.

He stretches out his hands towards them. "You have done well and fittingly, my friends," he praises them. "You are great in the shoal and you will be remembered in the Groves of Aleph. Your children will be remembered, and your children's children. You have done well. Now return to your duty."

The shark closest to me swings sideways, almost touching me. As his jaw slides past, I catch an expression I recognise. Surely the shark is smirking as he laps up Saldowr's words of praise.

"Duty is everything to them," says Saldowr after the sharks have gone back to their patrol, and we've swum down again to the safety of the Groves of Aleph. "A shark would rather die a hundred times than fail in his duty." He pauses, then adds in a different voice, "But they can be touchy. They like to feel they are appreciated. They hate laughter, or mockery. Always remember that. An insult to one is an insult to all where sharks are concerned. And they don't like being asked to do anything outside their routine."

I was right. Saldowr was not absolutely sure of the sharks' reaction when he brought us to them. He was most certainly asking them to do something outside their routine.

Saldowr adds quickly, as if to make up for his criticism, "They do a magnificent job of protection. Absolutely tireless."

"I bet they are," murmurs Conor.

As soon as the first dolphin reaches us, I realise just how frightened of the sharks I was. It's like meeting a friend with a lantern in a dark, dangerous forest. My heart goes out to these beautiful warm-blooded creatures. Their eyes are alive with intelligence, and their voices reach out for us through the water.

"Greeting, little sister."

"Greeting, brother."

It's no effort to understand the dolphins now, as I had to struggle to understand them when we were on Mal's father's boat. I glance at Conor. He is smiling as he stretches out a hand in greeting.

"Can you understand them, Con?"

"Anyone could understand them," says Conor. "You don't need language."

But I did understand their language easily this time. Does that mean I'm speaking full Mer? I don't know. But Conor's right: the dolphin's language isn't just a matter of words. They wheel around us in the water, playfully nudging us and then arching in circles. It's a welcoming pattern, full of warmth and affection. With a surge of joy, I realise that we have won the trust of the dolphins because of that long night when we struggled to save their stranded sister. The dolphins are not here just because Saldowr has ordered them to come, but because they want to be here. They're happy to see us.

"They're thanking us, Conor!"

"I know."

"She must have survived, that dolphin who was stranded."

Saldowr smiles as he watches the dolphins. I remember what the whale told me. It is because the dolphins are so intelligent that their lives are made of play. The whale was envious, in her huge, gentle way. She would have liked to play, too. And she'd definitely have liked to be better at telling jokes.

"Greetings, brothers, and welcome," says Saldowr, and there's an affection in his voice that I haven't heard before. He turns to us. "They are ready to take you home now. They'll bear you out of Ingo before the storm comes."

These are young male dolphins. They swim alongside for us to climb on to their backs. I remember what Faro taught me last summer: I must ride with the dolphin, not on him.

I sit on the dolphin's back and lean forward, curving my body into his shape. My arms are round him, my face against his skin. I can sense the energy and eagerness in him. He can hardly wait to be flying through the water again. Conor and his dolphin are already moving forward. Conor turns to me, his face glowing with excitement. "Can you believe this, Saph?"

"I know. It's amazing."

Conor's dolphin swims a little faster, with a lazy flick of the tail that hints at the speed he could reach if he chose. Suddenly he plunges forward into a perfect somersault and brings Conor back to me in a swirl of bubbles. Both the dolphin and Conor are laughing.

"I can't believe you didn't fall off."

But Conor's already gone again. The dolphin's playing a new game with him. Conor and the dolphin rush forward and then stop dead, rush forward and stop dead again, making the water churn around them. They weave a figure of eight, curving in and out, round and round, upside down and then right side up in a way that would make the most brilliant figure skaters in the world look clumsy. I'm dizzy with watching them. I can hardly pick out which is the dolphin and which is Conor.

"Are you ready, little sister?" my dolphin reminds me gently.

"Yes."

I close my eyes. I know we've got to go through the sharks' territory, but I don't ever want to see those sharks again.

"Don't be afraid, child," says Saldowr. "Open your eyes. Look at me." I open my eyes reluctantly. Saldowr's face is quizzical. "You are a strange child," he says. "You survived the Deep, which should have destroyed you. When you should be afraid you are not afraid, but when you have no reason to fear you are full of terrors. I have told you that the sharks will not hurt you."

"I know, but—"

"Be brave. Each time you are brave, it grows easier. This is only the beginning."

"The beginning of what?"

"Of the times when you will need all your courage."

Saldowr is older than I thought. His face is smooth

and unlined, but his eyes look as if he's been alive for a thousand years and seen more than I can ever imagine. Conor's right – Saldowr is like Granny Carne, even though he's also her complete opposite. Her wisdom belongs to Earth and Air; his wisdom belongs to Ingo. But they share something deeper than their differences. I don't know exactly what it is, but I can feel it. Power isn't quite the right word. Granny Carne and Saldowr are like magnets, drawing everything to themselves. People and creatures and knowledge.

Maybe Saldowr really has been alive for a thousand years. Maybe he can look forward and backward through time, like Granny Carne. I shiver. It must be terrible to have so much knowledge.

As he floats there with his cloak swirling around him and his hand lifted in farewell, Saldowr is formidable, but maybe he's lonely too. He knows so much more than everyone. All that wisdom must be a lonely thing, like a cloak of ice around your shoulders.

Everybody goes to see Granny Carne, but all the time she stays separate, because her life is not like anyone else's. How could it be, if she really has lived for hundreds and hundreds of years – maybe even a thousand.

"Remember that you are protected, child," says Saldowr. "The sharks will not hurt you. If you keep this in your mind, then the sharks will remember it too. You must not show weakness."

He is very serious. I realise that Saldowr's protection

isn't a magic trick that he can wrap around us. We have to do our part to make the protection work.

"I know." But I can't help shivering again at the memory of the sharks' cold eyes as they roamed over me and Conor.

"Please tell Faro—" But I don't know what message to give. "Tell him – tell him I didn't want to go without seeing him. Tell him I'll come back."

"Of course. But hurry now. I feel the storm gathering."

Even though I keep my eyes tight shut, I know the moment that we reach the sharks. A searching chill passes over us, like a radar beam. My skin shrinks. Coldness, emptiness, enmity. The sharks are scanning us, and searching their memories for what they should do with us.

I have got to open my eyes. It's no good shutting them, like a baby playing hide-and-seek. *If I can't see you then you can't see me.* That's what babies think. But the sharks can see me all right. I open my eyes. The water is grey with the sharks' presence. Here they are, strung out in a line, on patrol. The chill creeps over me again as they reach out, probing and hungry.

Who goes there?

The voice is harsh, but empty of emotion. The shark will do his duty without emotion. The dolphins that carry us are side by side, almost touching.

"Don't be afraid, Saph," says Conor quietly. He raises his head. "Look at the sharks. Tell them who we are."

"We are – we are..." My voice is thin. Immediately, I sense the sharks picking up my weakness. From the corner of my eye I see the shark farthest from us start to circle towards us.

"We are under Saldowr's protection," says Conor. His voice is calm. Yes, that's what I must say. I gather my strength and try to swallow the crazy beating of my heart in my throat. My mouth is full of strong salt water. The taste of it gives me courage. Saldowr's voice is in my ear. *You must not show weakness. You've survived the Deep*, I tell myself. *You can face the sharks.*

"We are – we are under Saldowr's protection," I say more firmly, and then the right words come to me. "Remember us, friends, as we remember you. We pass under Saldowr's protection."

The icy grip of the sharks breaks. The dolphins gather their strength and surge upwards, rushing through the water. The sharks' patrol territory falls away behind us. It's like coming out of a clammy cave into a summer day. We're swept along with the dolphins into the freedom and wildness of their flight as we leap out of grey into blue, and then above the water's surface into the world of Air and gulls and flying foam, before we plunge back down into the waves. Conor's dolphin keeps close to the surface, never letting him stay underwater for longer than a few seconds. Our dolphins leap at the same moment, and water streams off us as their bodies arch high above the sea and then dive through the foaming crests of the waves.

Conor turns to me, his face glowing. This is what Conor wants – to be in Ingo and yet not in Ingo, riding the sea with a dolphin's freedom, and breathing easily, without pain.

The next time my dolphin surfaces I see a ship far off on the horizon, and a black rock and a lighthouse. The light of day dazzles me.

"The Bishop Rock!" Conor yells, "We're almost home."

Earth will always be home to Conor. I wish I could be so sure. I press my face into the dolphin's back and smell the saltiness of Ingo. I don't want to leave. As long as I'm riding on the dolphin's back, I am still in Ingo. Somewhere in a cradle of stone far beneath the water there's my baby brother. Somewhere beneath the water my father is living another life.

I can't leave – not now—

But I've got to. Without the dolphins, Conor can't survive, and the dolphins aren't tame creatures. They'll take us on our journey, but then they'll go back into their own lives. I wish... I wish...

We're travelling up the coast now, still in Ingo, rising into the Air but not yet needing to breathe it. We can see land now. There are the cliffs, their granite bulk plunging down to the water. On top of the cliffs there's a handful of cottages that look like toys. I can smell the land now. I never realised that land had such a strong smell. We're coming closer now. What if someone was out on those cliffs and saw me and Conor riding on the back of the dolphins? They wouldn't believe their eyes. Even if they did, no one else would believe them. Imagine telling your friends that you'd seen a boy and a girl riding on dolphins, far out to sea.

Soon the dolphins will turn and make their rush inland at full speed, just beneath the surface of the water. They'll bring us inshore, and we'll stagger out of the sea, our clothes dripping, the cold wind cutting us like a knife.

But how rough the sea's getting. The sun's disappeared and the water has changed from blue to pewter. Foam whips off the tops of the waves. Saldowr was right – there's a storm coming. The sky is growing dark. The clouds on the horizon look like a mass of bruises.

We're almost there. Only a few minutes more and the dolphins will leave us. Ingo will close behind us, just as the rock closed over the Tide Knot.

CHAPTER FOURTEEN

"My God, Conor! Sapphy! Look at the state of you!"

I expect Mum to leap up and grab hold of me, but instead she gets up slowly – very slowly – from the chair where she's sitting by the fire. "You're soaked through. Come here, let me feel your hands. You're freezing! Sapphy, your clothes— Is that blood on your arm? And, Conor, you're covered in bruises!"

"No, it's not really blood – it's just a little cut, Mum—"

"What's been going on?" Mum asks frantically. "Has there been an accident? You've been in the sea, haven't you?"

I haven't seen Mum's terror of the sea burst out like this since we moved to St Pirans.

"Calm down, Mum," says Conor. "Nothing terrible's happened. We were up beyond Pedn Enys, watching a pair of dolphins that had come close inshore. Saph slipped, and then I went in too. That's all."

"You could have drowned! The sea could have swept you away! Those rocks are so dangerous when there's a big sea—"

"Mum, we *weren't* swept off," says Conor patiently. Unlike me, he never gets angry with Mum. "It was just a big rock pool that we fell into. There's no way we could have drowned."

I crouch down by the fire and spread out my hands to its warmth. We ran all the way back from where the dolphins left us, wet clothes and all. Everything Conor has told Mum is true. There's no word of a lie in it. We've only been away for a day, just as we promised when we told Mum we were going for a day out.

I shall never understand about time in Ingo and time here. The relationship between the two times keeps shifting. It's not like a maths formula in which x hours of Ingo time equals y hours of human time. Ingo time seems to be as slippery as water. As soon as you think you've grasped it, it pours away through your fingers.

The dolphins were amazing. They brought us right in at Pen Tyr, where we would be protected by a rocky outcrop that breaks the force of the waves coming in from the southwest. The dolphins swam so close to shore that I was afraid they'd be stranded, but they knew exactly what they were doing.

The water is deep at Pen Tyr, and the rocks rise up sheer, but there are plenty of handholds and footholds.

Dolphins are so intelligent. They must have searched their minds for a place that would be the perfect combination of shelter, deep water and climbable rock.

Dolphins make everything seem so easy. There was only a short stretch of water for us to swim across, and then we could scramble up on to the rocks. Even in that sheltered place the water was quite rough, but Conor and I are used to climbing out of the sea on to rocks. You have to tread water until a wave lets you seize a handhold, and then you can scramble up.

We're bruised by the rocks, and I cut my arm on some mussel shells. It looks a lot of blood, but it's not too bad really. Conor helped me. We couldn't change into our dry clothes because huge waves were already smashing right over the rocks where Conor had hidden them. I love the way the sea shocks up behind the rocks in a cloud of spray and then spills all over them, making white rivers down the black rock. It's beautiful, but it's very dangerous. Dad always told us that the sea lets you make one mistake, and it can be your last.

I hope our clothes and trainers will be all right. They're wrapped in a plastic bag, and Conor wedged them right down between the rocks. Mum would go crazy if she had to buy new trainers for both of us.

We had to run home in wet clothes and bare feet. Luckily it was raining hard by then, so we didn't look too strange. Mum asked where our trainers were, and I said we'd left them outside because they were wet, which was true in a way. Conor's going to go back for our stuff first thing tomorrow morning. It's already getting dark now.

We did fall into a rock pool. That part is true as well. It was my fault because I was standing right on the edge of the rocks so that I could watch the dolphins swim back out to sea. I was waving at them, which was stupid because obviously they were looking ahead, not back at us.

The truth is, I could hardly bear to see them go. There I was, up on land, and I felt stranded. The rock was so hard and rough, and everything was too cold and too noisy and too – too *solid*, somehow. So I watched the dolphins until I couldn't see them any more. And then I slipped, like an idiot, and fell backwards into the pool and cut myself again. Conor jumped in after me because he thought I'd hit my head on the rock. The pool was quite deep, and I was under the water for a few seconds. But I wasn't in Ingo. I swallowed some water accidentally and it tasted of salt, and then some of it went into the back of my throat and made me cough and splutter. I knew for sure then that I was back in the Air. Ingo was closed to me.

"But where's Sadie?" I ask suddenly. I haven't thought of Sadie for hours and hours, but I don't feel as disloyal as I did the time I left her tied up by the beach. Sadie's been safe at home all day. She's used to the fact that we have to spend whole days away from her, at school. She didn't know that I was in Ingo, so she wouldn't have been pining for me.

"Roger's taken her for a walk," says Mum absently, rubbing my wet hair with the kitchen towel. "Up those stairs now, Sapphy, and straight into a hot shower. Conor, I'm going to throw a duvet down. Get that wet stuff off yourself and wrap up in the duvet in front of the fire. You go in the shower after Sapphy."

"Thanks," says Conor. "Why do girls always get the shower first?"

But it's a rhetorical question. He knows the answer: they just do.

"Mum," I ask as I go upstairs behind her, "why are you at home anyway?"

"My cold's got worse. I can't be sneezing all over the customers' plates."

No, she doesn't look well. I touch her hand. "Mum, you're burning hot. Why don't you go to bed?"

"That's what Roger said. But I can't settle. I don't know why. I've got a funny feeling..." Mum makes a face, as if she's trying to laugh at her own fears. "Stupid, isn't it?"

"What sort of feeling?"

"As if something's going to happen," says Mum very quietly as if she doesn't want anyone to overhear.

"But what could be going to happen? You mean here, in the house?"

"I don't know. I wish I did. I've just got this uneasy feeling all over my skin. I can't settle. Sadie was the same.

She kept whining and padding up and down and twitching until Roger got fed up with it and said he'd take her out."

"She was probably only wondering where I was."

"No. It wasn't that, Sapphy. The hair on the back of her neck was standing up. Bristling."

"But Sadie's got a smooth coat, Mum."

"You could see it, all the same. It made me think of the way dogs are supposed to know when an earthquake's coming."

"An *earthquake*! There can't be an earthquake here in St Pirans."

I'm quite relieved. If all that Mum's worried about is an earthquake, then I can relax.

"You know how they say cats and dogs run out of the house when an earthquake is on its way, but nobody understands how they sense it? I think something's in the air, and Sadie senses it. Something... something *ominous*. And that's what I feel too."

"What do you mean, Mum, *ominous*?"

"Oh, Sapphy, you're better with words than I am. You know what an omen is. It's a sign, a warning."

I open the bathroom door. I don't want to talk about imaginary earthquakes or signs or warnings. What is really going on is strange enough. "Mum, you should go to bed. Maybe you're having, you know, whatever it's called when people imagine things because they've got a high temperature."

"I'm not delirious," says Mum, folding her arms. "I thought *you'd* understand, Sapphy." She stares at me, her eyes very bright and swimmy, and her face full of trouble. Mum's not well at all. For a moment I feel as if I'm the mother and she is the daughter. Conor would put his arms round Mum and hug her if she looked like that, but I'm so cold and wet that it wouldn't be a good idea.

"If you don't want to go to bed, Mum, why not rest by the fire with Conor? You shouldn't be trying to do things when you're ill. I'll make you some tea as soon as I've had my shower."

"I don't like the sound of the wind," says Mum abruptly. "Listen to the way it's blowing over the top of the house. That horrible empty booming sound. And the waves were crashing right inside the harbour."

"Well, they do, don't they, when there's a storm?"

"The wind's still rising. I don't like it. I wish Roger hadn't gone out."

"He'll be back soon. We'll look after you, Mum," I say as gently as I can. When I was in Ingo, I couldn't properly remember that I loved her. How could I have forgotten? She's not a frozen image. She's Mum.

"It's only a storm coming," I tell her as reassuringly as I can. "It'll pass."

"I know," says Mum. "I know all that." She pauses, as if there's something more she wants to say but she isn't sure that she should.

"Mum, what is it? What's wrong?"

"It's nothing, Sapphy. Don't worry. I'm just being silly. It's only – it's just that I don't like the sound of that wind."

It's completely dark by the time Roger gets back with Sadie. He's walked the legs off her, he says jokingly, and now he hopes she'll settle down. But far from settling down, Sadie leaps on me as if she hasn't seen me for years, licks my hands, trembling with excitement, and then puts back her head and begins a volley of barks that are loud enough to be heard across three fields rather than one small living room. Mum puts her hands over her ears.

"Try and calm her down, Sapphy," says Roger.

"I'm trying to. Sadie, girl, what's the matter? Stop it now." I put my arms around her firmly, and she nuzzles into my shoulder, still barking so loudly that my ears hurt.

"That's *enough*, Sadie, or we'll have to put you out in the yard, and you don't like that. Mum's not well."

Sadie stops barking, but instead she stares at me reproachfully. I can almost see the thoughts in her soft brown eyes. *Don't you understand that I'm trying to tell you something? You go off without me, and I don't know what you're doing or when you're coming back, and then you make me stop talking. All right, I'll do as I'm told, but only because I've got no choice.*

"Sorry, Sadie," I whisper into her ear. "I can't explain to you properly now, but I *had* to go today. It was really important. I couldn't take you with me because dogs can't go to – well, to the place where I was. It's no use looking like that. You can't understand because you haven't got a single drop of Mer blood in you. Maybe that's lucky for you. "

Sadie whines deep in her throat. She's still uneasy, like Mum. There's something going on that unsettles her. Probably it's just the storm. Dogs are much more sensitive to weather than humans are.

"Oh, Roger, I've got such a headache," says Mum, as if she can't help herself. Mum hardly ever complains, just as she's hardly ever ill.

"Let's get you up to bed, Jennie," Roger says. "Sapphire will make your tea, and you'd better take some paracetamol. You're very hot. You need to lie down."

I jump up. "Tea'll be ready in a minute, Mum. You go on up with Roger."

Roger smiles at me. It's a warm, approving smile, and I can't help smiling back. I've got to admit that sometimes it's good to have Roger here. He *does* think about other people... and he's kind, too. It's not soft kindness, but it's real.

Anyway, it's all right to recognise Roger's good qualities. I'm certainly not going to start thinking he's my stepdad or something, just because I've stopped hating him.

Roger decides he's going to sit with Mum until she goes to sleep. "Your Mum's got a high fever. I'll call the doctor in the morning if she's no better. Keep the music down, kids."

But it's not music that'll keep Mum awake, I'm sure of that. It's the wind, and the angry roar of the sea. The storm is disturbing and exciting at the same time. The weather hasn't been as wild as this since we came to St Pirans.

"Barometer's dropped again," announces Conor from the doorway where the barometer hangs on the wall.

"What does it say?"

"Storm. Going down to severe storm, I think."

"What comes after that?"

"Hurricane. But there won't be a hurricane, Saph."

"Listen to it."

We both listen. I see what Mum meant about the booming sound. The house sounds like a drum and the wind is the drummer. Beyond the wind we can hear the shapeless roaring of the sea.

Just then the phone rings. It's Mal. His dad needs help, urgently, and he's asked Mal to call his friends.

"He's got a share in his brother's boat – you know, that big clinker-built one that does trips out to the seals," Conor explains, as he starts to cram his feet into his boots. "They want to bring it right up the wharf. Mal says conditions in the harbour are freaky."

"I'll come with you."

"*No*, Saph. Stay here. Mum'll get upset if you go out again on a night like this. She doesn't need the hassle."

"But I can help with the boat. I'm strong."

"Saph. Please. Just for once, could *you* be the one who stays in the house and keeps everybody happy?"

Reluctantly, I agree. I don't want to make Conor angry. But as soon as the door closes on him, I wish I'd gone too. The house doesn't feel like a drum any more, but like a cage, with the wind rattling its bars. A fierce draught whistles under the door, and then the weirdest thing happens. The draught lifts up the bright red rug Mum put there as a doormat. It doesn't lift the rug right off the floor, but it gets underneath and makes the thick red material ripple up and down like incoming waves. It's uncanny. After a few seconds the rug flops back against the boards and lies still. But just when I think I imagined it all, there's another twitch and the funnelled force of the wind under the door gets hold of the rug again and flip-flops it against the wooden boards. It's only a little sound, compared to the racket of the storm, but it makes my skin crawl. It's as if the wind is the cat and the rug is the mouse.

Sadie hates it. She cowers on the other side of the room, staring at the rug.

"I know, it's horrible, Sadie," I murmur, putting my arms around her. "I don't like it any more than you do."

Sadie whines plaintively, then gets up, shakes herself all over and pads towards the stairs, looking back at me for my reaction.

"You know you're not allowed upstairs, Sadie."

But Sadie's expression is so imploring that I give way.

"Oh, all right, just this once. As long as nobody hears, you can go up in my bedroom. But I'm not coming to bed yet, so you'll just have to wait for me."

I settle Sadie in my room alongside the bed. There's so little space in my room that I have to step over her in order to get to the doorway. My porthole window is firmly shut, and I draw the curtains too, to shut out the wild night.

"There now, is that better? Are you happier now?" Sadie thumps her tail softly on the floor. She understands that she mustn't make a noise up here. She's certainly a lot more relaxed now that she's upstairs. I wonder why?

"I'll be back soon, Sadie. I'm going to close the door so Mum and Roger don't see you. Hush now." I put my finger on my lips, and Sadie stares back conspiratorially. She knows perfectly well that we're breaking the rules.

I go back downstairs, put another log on the fire and clear the washing-up off the draining board. Perhaps I ought to go up to bed now. It's early, but at least I'd be with Sadie.

I feel too restless. I hate being shut in the house when the wind is like this. I never minded when we were at our cottage. We were so high up on the cliffs that it didn't matter how ferocious the sea became, because it could never reach us. Our cottage was made of granite and its walls were so thick that no wind could ever blow them down.

But this house doesn't feel so strong, and the sea's very close – less than fifty metres away, and almost on the same level as the house. It seems farther away because the road winds around the houses, but it's not. *Don't be stupid, Saph. This house has been standing since Victorian times. That is more than a hundred years. They wouldn't have built it here if there'd been any risk.*

I turn the TV on and then quickly switch it off again as a storm of static hits the screen. Something's happened to the reception.

The rug twitches again. A buffet of wind and rain hits the windows. Suddenly I feel completely alone. The living room ought to be safe and comforting with the log fire burning, but it isn't. Smoke blows back down the chimney and the fire's struggling to keep alive.

Maybe Mum's really bad. Maybe we should have called the doctor...

I'll go upstairs, creep in on tiptoe and see how she is. I can't believe she's really asleep, with the wind battering the house like this.

But she is. She's lying flat on her back in the middle of the big bed, fast asleep. The bedside lamp is still on. Mum's very pale, but there's a red blotch on her cheeks and she's breathing fast. Her lips look dry and cracked. Roger is asleep too, in the basket chair. Half the newspaper is on his lap and the other half has slid on to the floor. His mouth is open. He certainly doesn't look as handsome as usual, but when people are asleep you can't help feeling as if you should look after them... just a bit. I tiptoe to the bedside lamp and switch it off.

The click of the switch seems to disturb Mum. In the light from the landing I can see that her eyes are still shut, but she starts to toss from side to side, muttering. I stand dead still, not daring to move in case she wakes up.

"Mathew... Mathew... no... don't go out... not in the *Peggy Gordon*, Mathew, no..."

She sounds terrified. Oh Mum, don't. Please don't. What you were afraid of has already happened.

I wish I could make it not have happened. I wish with all my heart that we could go back in time, and change it so that Dad never left our cottage that night the summer before last. Dad, why did you do it?

Suddenly the Mer baby comes into my mind. His soft, plump little hands. His hair like dark feathers, drifting in the water. And his mother's face, full of love as she looks at my father.

Mum doesn't know about any of it. Again I have that feeling that I am the mother and she is the daughter. I don't want her ever to know. I don't want Mum ever to feel as sad as I know she will feel if she sees the Mer baby.

"No, Mathew. No... no..." Mum mutters again. I stand there frozen, hardly breathing. Go back to sleep, Mum, *please*.

At last, Mum is quiet. She stops tossing her head from side to side, and settles back on to the pillow. Very slowly, I tiptoe to the doorway, slip through and shut the door as gently as I can so that the catch doesn't even click. Maybe Mum will sleep peacefully until morning now.

I go to my bedroom door and listen. Not a sound. Sadie must have gone to sleep too. I won't go in, in case she starts barking again. Everyone's restless today. Everyone's on edge, as if something's about to happen.

Conor's not back yet. I'd like to go down to the harbour to find him, but he'd be angry. I really don't want to stay in this house a minute longer. It's like a cage full of sadness, as if Mum's anguish about Dad has drifted out of her dreams and into the air, and now it's flitting from room to room, touching everything.

I thought Mum had put Dad out of her mind. I thought she only cared about Roger now. But in her sleep, she talks to Dad.

I've got to get out of the house. I won't go far, just to the beach. I'll stay on the slipway and watch the waves. It's not even high tide yet, so it can't be dangerous.

Mum's asleep, so she's not going to know. Even Roger's asleep. Imagine sleeping through a storm like this.

I was right. It's not high tide yet. There are still about twenty metres of sand, glistening in the faint reflected lights of the town, and then the pounding waves. It's hard to measure the waves from here, but they're huge. The wind is so strong that it blows the top off them. The air is full of flying foam and when I lick my lips they taste of salt.

The wind has veered round, so I'm sheltered from the worst of it. It must be hitting St Pirans full on from the west now. The waves roar up the beach, dragging sand and stones and hurtling them on to shore. Not even the best surfer in the world could ride these waves. They are wild and jumbled, as if the sea itself doesn't know what it's doing. I don't think it's raining any more, because the moon is coming out from the clouds, but there's so much spray that I'm glad I put on my waterproof. I wonder if Conor and the others have got that boat to a safe place yet?

I can't go back in the house. I'm restless, prickling all over. The wind hits me like slaps from huge invisible hands. But it's not the wind that worries me. It's something else, beyond the storm. That's what is making me have that horrible prickling, frustrated feeling. Maybe that's how Mum felt earlier on, but I'm sure I haven't got a fever.

The moon slips right out of the clouds, and shines on the raging water. Just for a second it doesn't look like the sea at all. Instead, the sea is like a mass of coiling snakes, whipping the water and lashing at the air.

Ingo is angry.

Who said that? I spin round. I'm sure that I heard a voice, but there's no one there. Only the night, and the storm.

Ingo is angry.

It must be inside my own head. Maybe *I* have got a fever. Maybe *I'm* del-i-whateveritis.

Ingo is angry.

The third time is when I realise that it is not a voice at all. Not a real voice speaking from outside me, that is. It is a voice inside me. It is my Mer blood speaking to me.

Sometimes you know more than you think you know. All the pieces of the puzzle are coming together. The raging and raving of the waves no longer sounds like any normal storm which will blow itself out by the morning. Saldowr's words about the Tide Knot leap into my mind. Saldowr was afraid because the Tide Knot was beginning to loosen, and soon it wouldn't be able to hold the tides in place. And then he said that there were some in Ingo who would welcome that. They'd like to see our world drowned, if that made Ingo stronger.

To see our world drowned. My blood shudders in my veins as if the fierce wind that blew under our door is blowing straight through me. Can our world be drowned like that village on the Lost Islands? Could it really happen?

Another heavy bank of clouds is about to swallow the moon. What the moon showed me is burnt on to my mind. A mass of coiling, writhing snakes. When I looked down into the Tide Knot, it was like a nest of snakes, twisting and twining. But then, they were prisoners of the rock...

I glance back at the row of cottages. Cracks of light show between the curtains. Patrick and Rainbow live in one of those cottages: that one, down by the end. They'll be sitting by their fire in the living room, listening to the wind but feeling quite safe because they believe the storm will blow itself out, like every other storm there has ever been. And they know that the tide only ever comes so far, and no farther.

Saldowr didn't want our world to drown. He didn't want the balance between this world and Ingo to be destroyed. But the tides are so powerful. The strength of them was awesome, coiling endlessly, shining blue against the sheer dark sides of the rock that enclosed them. When you look at the Tide Knot for more than a few moments, it starts to hypnotise you. Maybe the tides can do whatever they want now.

"*Sapphy...*"

This time the voice is no more than a breath. It's very faint and faraway, but it's struggling with all its power to reach me. I know straight away whose voice it is. I don't answer; I just stand there, every fibre of my body tense. Listening, listening for the voice to come again. It fades then breaks through again, like a voice on a radio from a country thousands of miles away.

"Myrgh... myrgh..."

The voice is struggling through a nightmare, trying to cry out a warning as loud as it can, but only managing a whisper. It's my father. He's desperate to tell me something but he can't get close enough.

Suddenly I'm sure I know where he is. He's out there in the bay, coming as close to shore as he dares before the waves grab him and smash him on to the rocks. He's broken the laws of Ingo: he's left the Mer baby and the Mer woman to find me again and tell me the secrets that only Ingo should know. But I can't even hear what he's trying to tell me.

I shout back into the mouth of the wind, "Dad! Dad! Where are you? I can't hear you!" But the wind snatches my voice away.

"Dad!"

I wait, willing the noise of the storm to part and let me hear Dad's voice. The wind rips my hood back and my hair flies free, tangling over my face. And then the voice comes again. Or is it a voice? Maybe it's just my imagination. The voice is so far away now, as thin as a spider's web. But if it's as thin as a spider's web, it's also as strong. The urgency in it burns me like fire.

"Sapphy..."

The voice is real; I know it is. Dad wants me to come to him. I know it as surely as if the words were written on the sand. And I can do it. If I run along the top of the beach, past the café and the beach shop, past the lifeguard station and round on to the headland, I can clamber on to those rocks below. It's not dangerous, I tell myself. I'll stay well above the tide line. Down below the rocks, the water's deep. Maybe, just maybe, it'll be possible for Dad to swim closer in and speak to me.

I don't stop to think twice. As if the moon has heard my thoughts, it chooses this moment to break out of the cloud bank again. There's enough light for me to make my way round to the rocks.

I daren't stand up once I'm out on the headland for fear of being blown off into the sea. I get down on hands and knees and crawl forward, clinging on to clumps of thrift and grass. The moonlight is strong now, but I don't want to look at the sea for fear of seeing those coiling snakes again. I look just a little way ahead, the way I've got to go.

I crawl down a little way on to the rocks. A huge wave hits the other side of the headland, and the rock shivers. I hear an explosion of water far below me, then a dragging, sucking sound as the water is forced into all the cracks of the rock. I don't dare even crawl now. I'm flat on my stomach, wriggling along, clinging to every handhold I can find, flattening my body against the rock so the wind won't be able to prise me loose.

The churning of the sea sounds more violent than ever. It's no good. Dad will never be able to come close. He'd be smashed against the rocks.

Very cautiously, I turn my head and peer down to the right, where the rocks protect the water. The sea isn't boiling quite so furiously just here. The rocks create a bulwark which breaks the force of the storm. If I can crawl just a little closer to the edge, I'll be able to look down. If Dad comes in anywhere, it will be just here. But I mustn't go too far. I mustn't risk falling.

"Sapphy..."

The voice is faint, half-snatched away by the wind. But it comes from down there in the water. I cup my hands to my mouth and shout as loud as I can: *"Daa-aaaad!* I'm here."

And as I raise my head, I see him for a second, in the path of the moonlight on the wild water. He's swimming with all his strength against the power of the tide, which is trying to drag him towards the rocks. He's coming too close in.

"Dad!"

He hears me. He turns towards me. I see the glisten of moonlight on his face and his hair, then a wave swamps him. When he rises again he is even closer to the rock. He stops swimming to raise his hands to his face. He cups his hands, just as I did.

"*The Tide Knot is unloosed. Run and tell them that the Tide Knot is unloosed. Make for high ground. Can you hear me?*"

The current is dragging him into danger. He's got to swim clear. "*Dad, swim! Swim away from the rocks! Can you hear me?*"

I kneel up on the rock. The wind fills my mouth so I can hardly breathe. As loud as I can, I scream into it: "*Yes, I heard you!*"

He raises a hand in acknowledgment. But he's got to escape. He's got to swim with all his strength now, away from the rocks. Doesn't he understand that?

"*Dad! SWIM OUT! It's dangerous! Go now! Go now! DAD!*"

Cloud sweeps over the moon again, and the water goes dark as ink. I think I saw Dad dive, a split second before it went dark. I think he plunged deep beneath the waves, to swim with all his power away from the rocks. But I can't be sure.

CHAPTER FIFTEEN

"Conor! Oh, Con, I'm so glad you're back."

I push the house door shut behind me, and pull off my boots and waterproof. Conor is kneeling by the fire, warming himself.

"I should have guessed you wouldn't do what you said, Saph," he says coldly, without turning round.

"What?"

"You were going to stay here, *remember*? So Mum wouldn't be worried?"

"Oh! Oh... I'd forgotten all about that—"

"Very convenient."

"Don't be like that, Con. Listen, it's important. Something's happened. I've seen Dad."

He does turn round then. His eyes are wide with shock. "Dad? What do you mean, you saw Dad? He's not here. We know where *he* is."

"No, Conor, listen—"

"Keep your voice down, Saph. They'll wake up if we're

not careful. Mum's restless. She was muttering stuff when I went upstairs just now."

"What sort of stuff?"

"I couldn't really hear what she was saying," says Conor, after a pause which tells me that he could. He looks stressed and unhappy, and I feel a pang of guilt that again it's me who has seen Dad, not him. But I've got to tell him what Dad said.

Conor listens very carefully, without interrupting. He doesn't show fear, or surprise, or any other emotion. His face is pale under its usual brown. When I've finished, he says nothing.

"Conor, don't you believe me?"

"Give me a minute, Saph. I've got to think."

I wait tensely. I'm so afraid that Conor's not going to believe me. That he'll think I only imagined that I saw Dad, because I wanted him to be there.

"Conor—"

"The problem is, Saph, that if we go out now and start knocking on doors telling people to get out of their houses and run up the hill because we've had a message from our father who hasn't really drowned but has turned into a Mer man, and he tells us that St Pirans is going to be drowned because it's on the border of Ingo... They're really not going to believe us."

"But you believe me."

"Yes, but that could be because I'm just as crazy as you are," says Conor.

"We can't *not* do anything!"

"No. We can't not do anything. Listen, Saph. I'm going to wake up Roger."

"*Roger!*"

"Yes. Wait, don't start exploding. He might believe us, and if he does, everybody else will believe him. People respect Roger."

"But it's all taking too long! How long's it going to take to convince Roger? Quick, Conor, we've got to do something straight away. Dad said the Tide Knot was loose already."

"Dad's not here. Roger's what we've got."

I follow Conor up the stairs, still frantically trying to convince him not to wake Roger. But I can only whisper, because of Mum. It makes everything seem even more unreal, like trying to scream in a nightmare. You never can, can you...

Roger wakes up immediately, and to my amazement he not only understands that Conor's got something urgent to tell him, but also that we're trying not to wake Mum. "Is she worse?" he whispers.

"No, it's not Mum."

Roger stumbles a bit as he heaves himself out of the basket chair, and the rest of the newspaper falls to the floor. But he's impressively *there* – present, in control and ready to take charge. I suppose he must be trained to deal with emergencies, being a dive leader...

As soon as we're downstairs, Conor says quickly, "We've

got something very important to tell you. It's going to sound completely weird and you're probably not going to believe it, but please, please, listen till I've finished."

He doesn't say a word about Dad. He only says that we know for certain that there is going to be a tidal surge, right here in St Pirans, and it's coming soon. The storm is only part of it. He can't tell Roger *how* we know, but he is sure. We are both sure. We have got to wake people now and warn them, so they can get up on to high ground.

The words sound so feeble. So pathetic. *We know there's going to be a tidal surge.* Who would believe two kids who said a thing like that, and told everybody to get out of their houses and head for high ground? They'd just laugh. *Oh yeah, I'll stay in bed if you don't mind.*

But the way that Conor says it doesn't make me want to laugh. He's impressive, my brother. Serious, determined, his eyes blazing with conviction. Roger stares from one of us another. His face tightens in a frown that makes him look angry, but I don't think he is angry. Suddenly he points at me as if he's remembering something. "You're the girl who always knows when the tide is turning, am I right?"

Yes, Roger would remember that. I blurted it out one day, back at our old home. I let it slip that I could feel when the tide was turning, and Roger questioned me. He was interested because the tides are vital to him, too, as a diver.

"Yes," I say.

"And what do you say to this idea of Conor's? Can *you* feel that a tidal surge is on its way?"

"Yes," I say. I don't dare to go much beyond what Conor has told him, or mention Dad's name. But almost before I know that they are in my mouth, the words are out. "It's the Tide Knot. It won't hold any longer."

"The *Tide Knot*? Sapphire, what is this? Are you telling me some kind of a children's story? These are people's lives you're playing with."

In desperation, I take an even bigger risk. "Roger," I say, keeping my eyes fixed on his face and praying that he'll see the seriousness and the truth in me. "You know how things happen maybe once or twice in your life that you can't ever find an explanation for? Nothing fits together because there's a part that's... well, it's hidden from you. Like the time when you had your diving accident and we were there when you woke up, and you could never really work out how we swam out all that way. Because we shouldn't have been able to do it, should we? *This is the same, Roger.* And remember that time you were out in your boat and you looked down into the water and you saw a girl who looked just like me, looking back at you. And you could never work it out."

Roger starts violently. "How did you know—"

"I can't explain how I know. You wouldn't believe me if I did. But it's real. It's real in exactly the same way as what we're telling you now is real."

I can see in Roger's face that he's remembering everything. That time he saw me looking up at him from the sunwater, when I was in Ingo and he was in his boat, looking down into the sea. I remember his astonished, upside-down face. Roger would never forget that moment, or the day last summer when he nearly died. He must have thought of it many times since. The way he woke up bruised and battered and never knowing what had attacked him. Somewhere, deep inside him, maybe Roger did know that he had strayed into Ingo, and almost been killed by the guardian seals. Even nightmares stay with you somewhere.

Roger stares at me, remembering, thinking, not knowing what to trust. "Can I believe you?" he asks slowly.

"You *have* to. *Please.* Even if you can't find a reason for it. You *have* to believe me."

The moment holds and holds, like a long close-up in a film. It feels as if time has stopped. There is no human time or Ingo time any more, only this moment when Roger has to choose whether he's going to trust something that seems impossible, or turn his back on it. His frown deepens. His eyes are sharp, hard, searching. He's weighing it all in the balance; I can see him doing it. On one side there's normality and reality and practicality and reason and all the other things Roger lives by. On the other there are all the things that are irrational, don't add up and don't make sense.

At that moment the heaviest blow of wind yet thuds against the front door. The roar of the sea is suddenly magnified, as if the volume has been turned up by someone who loves its wild music. Upstairs, Sadie breaks into another volley of furious, terrified barking. And as if in answer, we hear other dogs too, a whole chorus of them, some in the next house, some in the next street, but all of them barking and barking against the noise of the wind, as if every dog in St Pirans has been roused by danger.

"Dogs always know," says Roger slowly, like a man in a trance. "I remember Rufie—"

He breaks off. The tension builds and builds as the barking of dogs grows to a crescendo. I can't move or speak. Inside myself the pounding of my heart is even louder than the words pounding inside my head: *Make him believe us. Make him believe us. Make him believe us.* And then Roger swings into action so fast that it takes my breath away.

"OK, let's go. Sapphire, upstairs! Wake your Mum, help her get dressed, wrap her in a duvet. I'll be back with the car as soon as I can. Conor, we're going to hit the streets. *There's an official warning of an immediate tidal surge in the area,* that's all you say. Don't stop, don't answer questions, straight on to the next house. Bang on the doors; yell it out. As soon as they're up, get them to warn the neighbours too. Tell everybody to get on to high ground, up the hill. Anyone sick, anyone housebound, get them to get up to the top floor and wait for help. Don't stop to argue the toss. If one gets moving, they'll all get moving. I'll contact the coastguard and the lifeboat service. And God help us all if you've got this wrong."

In a few minutes Conor and Roger are out of the house. I stand on the doorstep, holding the door against the wind, and peer down the street. Shadows jump and dance. Rain is streaming down again. There's Roger, thundering on the Trevails' front door. After a few seconds, lights come on upstairs. The Trevails are old; they are always in bed by nine o'clock. They'll be shocked, frightened. The upstairs window opens, and then there's Roger's voice shouting, *"It's an emergency! Tidal surge! Everyone's got to be evacuated."*

And then old Mr Trevail's creaking voice, "What's that you're saying, boy?"

I slam the door shut. I should be helping Mum. But as I rush up the stairs, Sadie lets out such a pitiful, terrorised howl that I have to go to her. I open my bedroom door and there she is behind it, shivering all over, her coat bristling just the way Mum said it was earlier on.

We are right to rouse the town. If I had any doubts left, they melt when I see Sadie. She whines urgently, fixing her eyes on me. She is so desperate to warn me that she seizes a corner of my sleeve in her teeth, and begins to pull me towards the door.

"Sadie, I know. I understand. It's coming, isn't it? But first of all we've got to help Mum."

Sadie presses against me like a shadow as we go into Mum's room. Mum is still deeply asleep, hearing nothing and sensing nothing. I switch on the bedside light, but this time the click of the switch doesn't disturb her. A burst of rain slashes across the window. The tumult of the storm isn't quite so bad here, because Mum's room faces away from the sea. Mum always chooses a room that faces away from the sea. But just then I hear a siren, coming closer. A police car, or an ambulance. Maybe the emergency services are already responding to Roger's call.

Very cautiously, I reach out and touch Mum's hand. I don't want to shock her. "Mum?"

But she only mutters, and turns her head away.

"Mum!" I say more loudly.

At last she opens her eyes. They are very bright, but she looks confused. She doesn't seem to realise who I am.

"Mum, we've got to get up. Roger's coming to get us soon. There's an emergency." I daren't tell Mum what it is until she's woken up properly. She has such a terrible fear of the sea.

"Sapphy!" Mum struggles to raise her head from the pillow. Her voice is dry and croaky. I reach over to her bedside table, where there's a glass of water, and hold it to her lips. She takes a tiny sip, then falls back on the pillow as if she's exhausted. "Such a pain in my chest, Sapphy," she whispers.

Mum is really ill. I can see that even though I have no idea about illness at all. She is very hot, and she's breathing so fast, almost panting.

"Mum, listen! You're going to have to get up and get dressed. Roger thinks there's going to be a tidal surge."

Mum's face goes still. I know she's heard and understood. Her hand seizes mine in a surprisingly strong grip.

"He's waking people up, getting them to leave their houses and go to high ground. So is Conor. Roger said for you to get dressed and wait and he'll be back as soon as he can."

With a huge effort, Mum pushes back the covers, swings her legs over the side of the bed and tries to stand. I grab hold of her as she wobbles on her feet and then collapses back on the bed. "Sorry, Sapphy. Feel so dizzy."

I give her some more water. Sadie begins to tug at Mum's nightdress, as if she thinks she can rescue her single-handed, like a dog in a story.

"Stop it, Sadie! That's not very helpful."

Everything is going wrong. I should be out there with Conor and Dad, warning people. What about Rainbow and Patrick? Rainbow's like Mum: she'll be terrified of a flood. What if Roger and Conor haven't remembered to go to their cottage? They are right by the water, and when the tide surges they will be the first in its path.

Mum opens her eyes again. "You go, Sapphy. Go now. I'll be fine here."

She's just like Dad, I think in exasperation. Both of them telling me to *go*, as if it doesn't matter what happens to them. "I've lost one parent," I say grimly. "I'm not going to lose two. Either you come as well, or we're all staying here."

"No, Sapphy, you've got to go—"

"I mean it, Mum. I'm staying here. You just need to get your strength up," I go on as reassuringly as I can. "In a little while you'll be able to walk."

I rummage in Mum's drawers to find the warmest clothes I can.

"Sadie, please! Stop pulling me. I want to go as much as you do, but we can't, not now."

With what is clearly a superhuman effort, Mum begins to struggle up again. It's not going to work, though. I can already see that horrible faint, dizzy look coming over her again. But this time Mum has an idea. "Brandy, Sapphy. Get the brandy from downstairs."

Sadie and I rush downstairs. Sadie won't leave my side for a second. I pull open the kitchen cupboards and begin to search for the brandy. I didn't even know we had any, but Mum keeps all the drink together, so it must be behind this weird-looking bottle of tequila somebody gave her after a holiday in Mexico... ah, yes.

My hands are shaking so much as I slop the brandy into a glass that half of it floods over the worktop. No time to bother about that. Suddenly Sadie barks violently again, making me jump and spill even more brandy. Maybe she should have some as well, to calm her down. Can dogs drink brandy?

Get a grip, Sapphire, I tell myself firmly. And just then, there's a tremendous banging on the front door. For a muddled few seconds I think it's Roger, come to shout, *"Emergency! There's going to be a tidal surge!"*

It's Rainbow. She's wearing waterproofs but no hood, and her hair is soaked. Her face is frantic. "Quick, you've got to get out, Sapphire! It's coming!"

"What... now?"

"The sea's all wrong. The wind dropped and suddenly the sea went all flat as if something was pressing down on it. And then it started going backwards. It's being sucked out, Sapphire. It's horrible. Everybody's running. I ran—"

"Where's Patrick?"

"Gone with Conor."

"Oh my God, Rainbow! Look..."

Down at the end of the street, in the light of the streetlamps, something is standing. Black and glistening, a wall of water. We don't speak; we don't even think. We hurtle up the stairs with Sadie. A few seconds later there's a shuddering crack as the water hits the house.

CHAPTER SIXTEEN

Just as we reach the top of the stairs, the lights go out. I grab Rainbow's hand. "This way!"

Sadie's barking wildly. I can hear Mum's voice too: "Sapphire! *Sapphy!* Are you all right?"

"It's all right, Mum. We're here. Steady! Steady, Sadie."

"I'll hold her," says Rainbow, suddenly sounding calm and sure what to do. "All right, girl, everything's going to be OK. Let Sapphire go now." Rainbow must have caught hold of Sadie's collar, because Sadie's weight is off me. We all shuffle along the landing towards Mum's room.

The dark is as thick as a blanket. From downstairs come eerie, disturbing sounds that I have never heard inside a house before. There's a suck, and then a splosh. A thud, as if something has come loose and is floating about, bumping into the walls. The sound of water is everywhere. The sea has got into the house and is making itself at home downstairs, in our living room.

Rainbow and I cling to each other's hands, silent,

listening. Sadie's panting sounds very loud. Rainbow is shivering. "The water's going to come up the stairs," she says in a terrified whisper.

We push open Mum's door and stumble towards the bed.

"Sapphy! Sapphy! Thank God you're all right," comes Mum's voice out of the darkness. "What's going on?"

"It's the tidal surge, Mum. We saw all this water coming down the street."

"I felt it hit the house," says Mum. Her voice is sounding stronger. "Go to the window, Sapphy! Look out and see how deep it is."

"I can't see anything. I can't even see the window."

"It's those blinds Roger put up."

Of course it is. Roger put up some blackout blinds so Mum could sleep on in the mornings after her late shifts. Maybe it's not quite as dark as this outside.

Suddenly I realise that I am still holding the glass of brandy. "Rainbow, hold on to this a moment."

"What is it?"

"Brandy."

"I didn't know you drank, Sapphire."

It's so good to hear Rainbow trying to make a joke instead of sounding terrified. "It's for Mum."

Rainbow takes the glass, and I edge round the bed to the window. There's a horrible moment when I get caught up in the curtains, then I find the edge of the blackout blind behind a fold of curtain and tug hard.

With a tearing, rattling sound, the blind comes down.

"Mum, I think I've broken the blind."

"It doesn't matter," says Mum. "I mean, when everything's being flooded anyway..." and she laughs a bit hysterically.

Mum was right. Once the blind is down, it's not completely dark. There's a faint bluish light. I look up and there's the moon again, riding safe and serene, as if nothing's changed. I look down into the street.

There isn't any street. Only a black, glistening spread of water. It is halfway up the front door of the house opposite. As I watch, there's a pulse in the water, and it rises a little higher, as if it's licking the paint. Rainbow has come to the window to look out too. I hear her sharp intake of breath.

"It's OK. We've got plenty of time. I'm going to open the window," I say.

"Don't, Sapphire!"

"If I lean out, I'll be able to see right down the street."

The window swings open. At once a smell of sea rushes into the room. With it come sounds that make me shiver. The thunder of the sea must have been there all the time, but without the muffle of the blind and curtains and window it sounds terrifyingly near. The volume's been turned up as high as it will go. There's shouting, sirens, gulls screaming somewhere in the black sky, more shouting, a confusion of voices in the dark. From all over town comes the furious, terrified barking of dogs.

"Hold me round the waist, Rainbow. I'm going to lean out. I can't see properly from here. Maybe there's a boat coming."

I'm thinking of TV news pictures, where boats sail up streets to rescue people from the upper floors of flooded houses. Surely the lifeboat must have been launched by now. "Did you hear the maroons, Rainbow?"

"No. Would the men even have been able to get down to the lifeboat station? The sea came in so fast." Rainbow's voice is steadier. She's being so brave, controlling her fear. It's not too bad for me, because I don't share Mum and Rainbow's dread of the sea.

"Hold on tight, Rainbow. Don't let go whatever you do."

I lean out as far as I can, staring down the street, scouring it for a sign of life. A light bobs for a second right down at the end, but then it vanishes. The strange thing is that the wind has died down completely, as if the bursting of the sea's boundaries has killed the storm. But the water is definitely rising. It's not so wild now, but there's a deadly seriousness about the whirlpool swirling below me, and the slow, rising pulse of the tide against the houses. The sea looks as if nothing can stop it.

There's a light on next door. I stretch out just a little farther. Their window is open too. It's old Mr Trevail, peering out. His features are clear in the moonlight. He doesn't look terrified. He looks like a sailor out at sea, staring into an oncoming storm.

"Mr Trevail!"

He turns to me. "You all right in there, my girl?" he calls.

"Yes, we're all right. Is Mrs Trevail OK?"

"Gone up in the attic. Looks like he's rising fast. You'd better get on up yourselves, high as you can. Lifeboat'll be here, don't you fret, my girl. Keep your powder dry."

Keep my powder dry? What does he mean? But with a wave, Mr Trevail disappears. *He* doesn't seem too scared, anyway.

But we haven't got an attic. I think about it for a second, then cup my hands and yell as loud as I can, "Help! We need help! *Please, somebody help us!*"
Another swirl of water surges past the house, carrying something dark and bulky that I can't identify. The house shudders under the weight of rising water. Is it going to be able to stand?

"Please help!" I shout again, but the night swallows my words and nobody answers.

"There's no one out there," says Rainbow. She doesn't say, *We'll have to help ourselves,* but I know that's what she means. "Come back in, Sapphire," and she hauls me back into the room.

"Candles!" says Mum. She's struggling out of bed.

"Careful, Mum—"

But she stumbles to her chest of drawers, and I remember that Mum always keeps scented candles in her bedroom. "Here we are," she mutters. A few seconds later the light of a struck match flares up, filling the dark spaces of the room. "Thank God, it's a new candle," says Mum. "It'll last us for hours."

I've never realised until now how comforting the light of just one candle can be. It wavers, then settles into a strong, steady flame. Mum sits down on the side of the bed, and rests her head in her hands. A faint smell of vanilla starts to drift from the candle.

It is the strangest moment, like an island of peace in the middle of a war. Sadie is perfectly quiet, pressing up close to me. Rainbow goes over and puts her arm around Mum's shoulders. "You not feeling so good, Mrs Trewhella?"

"A bit shaky," says Mum's muffled voice. "Be all right in a minute."

Sadie thrusts her nose into my hand. She is still scared, but she isn't panicking any more. She nuzzles me, watching the candle flame. I can see it reflected in her eyes.

"Conor!" says Mum suddenly, as if she's only just realised he's not here. "Where is he? Is he all right?"

"He's with Roger, Mum. He'll be fine. Roger won't let anything happen to him."

"I always knew something like this would come," Mum goes on, as if she's talking to herself. Suddenly I guess what she is thinking of: the fortune-teller. The fortune-teller who told her years and years ago that the one she loved would lose her by water, and gave Mum the terror of the sea that has blighted her life. And now she thinks the prophecy is coming true. *Beware the sea. The sea is your gravest danger.*

I remember the brandy. Where did Rainbow put it? Ah yes, on the floor. Lucky I didn't kick it over. I hold it out to Mum. She doesn't seem too sure at first but suddenly she lifts the glass, takes a swig, coughs and chokes.

"Are you OK, Mum?"

"Mm… I think so," gasps Mum when she can stop coughing.

"Maybe we should all have some," says Rainbow.

"Definitely not!" says Mum, sounding quite a bit stronger.

I go over to the window again. The water seems a little higher against the front door opposite. I watch carefully. Yes, it is still rising. Slowly, inexorably—

"We've got to get up higher."

"How?" asks Rainbow.

"I don't know. I've got to think… Is there a loft?"

"Yes," says Mum, "the trapdoor's in the bathroom."

"Where's the ladder?"

"Cupboard under the stairs," says Mum. She is certainly sounding a bit better. "Listen, Sapphy, while you're down there, get my mobile. It's on that little table by the fire."

"Oh."

Rainbow and I look at each other. Obviously Mum doesn't realise how high the water has come already. "I'm going to see how deep it is down there," I whisper.

"I'm coming with you."

"It might not be that deep yet. Sadie, stay! Stay, girl. Stay with Mum."

Sadie doesn't really want to come, I can see that. She knows there's water down there, and she's afraid. But she thinks she ought to be with me. Sadie's so loyal, but this isn't the time for it. "No, Sadie! Stay and look after Mum! Stay!"

At last she obeys. We close the bedroom door behind us. I lift the candle high as we cross the landing and peer down the stairs. The water swirls below us, dark and oily. But the front door is still closed. The water must be coming in underneath it. It's hard to tell how deep it is.

"Count how many stairs are left," says Rainbow.

There are eight stairs rising from the water.

"How many are there normally?"

"I don't know. Twelve or thirteen, I think."

Stuff is floating about: a book, an orange. All the wooden spoons have floated out of the jar Mum keeps on the worktop and are bobbing at the bottom of the stairs. As we watch, the water gives a little push, and swallows another stair.

"They'll rescue us," says Rainbow, but her voice trembles. "We've just got to keep calm and wait."

"I don't know." I want to reassure Rainbow, but there's no point pretending. "If all the houses are flooded – all the houses on the level, I mean – there are all the old people, like the Trevails. They'll have to rescue them first. They might not be able to get boats to us for ages…"

Rainbow shivers. I realise again how incredibly brave she is being. She's controlling her terror, trying to think what to do.

"How deep do you think it is?" I ask.

"I don't know. Sapphire, you're not to go down. Look how it's swirling round. You'll get trapped."

"We can't get up into the loft without the ladder."

"Maybe if we get a chair and stand on it, and then one of us pushes the other up from behind, and then the one who's up reaches down and pulls—"

"Mum won't be able to do that. She's ill. Rainbow, I'm going down to get the ladder. Hold the candle up high."

"Please, Sapphire, don't—"

"I've got to."

I strip off my jeans and top and throw them back on to the landing. The water eddies coldly around me. Black, scary water. Not Ingo, but something very different. I take a deep breath, and lower myself into it. It's very cold. I want to shut my eyes so as not to see what might be lurking in the water. Something brushes against my leg and I stifle a scream. *Look down, Sapphire. Be brave.*

It was only the wooden fruit bowl. *You've got to stop this, Sapphire. You can do it. Let go of the banister.*

I swim away from the stairs. All I have to do now is dive. The cupboard is immediately under the stairs, only a couple of metres away.

I dive. But at that moment the front door gives way under the pressure of the flood outside, and bursts open. The rush of incoming water scoops me up, drags me across the room and pins me to the wall. I kick desperately, fighting my way to the surface. How deep is the water? I can just touch the floor but I can't stay on my feet.

"Sapphire!"

"M'OK."

I spit out water, and brace my feet against the wall. My right foot slips into space. A flash of fear goes over me. Maybe the walls are caving in! But then my foot strikes metal and I realise what's happened. I have put my foot into the back of the fireplace, that's all. The fireplace where the log fire was burning just a short time ago.

"Sapphire! Sapphire! Hold on, I'm coming."

"No, don't—"

But she's already plunged off the stairs and she's swimming towards me. The candle flame flares behind her. Water is still pouring in through the front door, but more slowly now, without the terrifying pressure behind it. We've got to get the ladder fast, before this room fills up to the ceiling and we're trapped.

"Can we still get the ladder out?" gasps Rainbow as she reaches me.

"We can try – but I'm afraid we'll get trapped. Water's rising fast."

The swilling water is full of rubbish swept up from the streets. I don't want to dive down into it, but I've got to. We doggy-paddle across the room.

"Under the stairs, that's where the door is. I'll swim down – see if I can open it—"

"I'm coming too."

We both take in a deep breath, and dive. It's so murky I can't see the cupboard door. I've got to feel my way along the panel - but my fingers keep getting pushed away. I kick harder. The water's trying to carry me away from the cupboard. And then my fingers catch on the cupboard door handle. I pull as hard as I can, but it won't open. Rainbow is beside me. I grab her hand and guide it to the handle. We both pull with all our strength, but it's impossible. The door won't budge.

We shoot up to the surface. The water is slopping up the walls, higher than my head now. Whatever happens we mustn't get cut off from our escape route up the stairs.

We swim back to the stairs to rest for a moment. "I think it's the pressure that's stopping the cupboard from opening," Rainbow says. "We need to smash the door. Once the pressure on the inside is the same as the pressure on the outside, the door should open."

"How do you know?"

"I'm not sure, but it's worth trying."

I scour my mind, trying to think of something that we

could use to smash the door. But everything's already under the water. Maybe we're going to have to abandon the ladder. What's Mum going to do then? She'll never be able to climb up to the trapdoor from a chair, even if Rainbow and I hold her. And there's Sadie. She'd panic. She wouldn't understand what we were trying to do for her. I'm not even sure that Rainbow and I could climb up without a ladder. The bathroom ceiling is pitched, and it's high. But if Mum and Sadie can't get into the loft, then I'm staying in the bedroom with them.

"Let's try again."

Down into the dark water. The same struggle to find the door, the same agonising, hopeless battle to open it. It won't open. We pull and pull, and by the time we surface Rainbow is choking. Back to the stairs.

"This isn't going to work."

"I know."

And at that moment I realise something. I knew it already, but now the knowledge starts to mean something. "Rainbow – the front door's open."

Water isn't rushing through it any more, but it's still pushing steadily in, as if there's an endless flood behind it, waiting.

There *is* an endless flood behind it. There isn't a shore where the sea stops any more. There isn't a tide line. The barrier between Ingo and the human world has broken. In St Pirans the sea is everywhere. It doesn't look like Ingo, and it doesn't feel like Ingo. The water is too dirty and mixed up with household rubbish for that. But there's an open path between Ingo and where we are—

And between me and the Mer. I could call my father. He'd come. I know he would. Fathers always come to their children when they are in danger.

But it's not safe to call Dad. What if Mum sees him? I can't begin to imagine what might happen then. What if she finds out everything that's happened since Dad left us?

There's another fear, too, so deep in my mind that I can barely put it into words. It sounds so... so disloyal. But it's my deepest fear of all. If I do call Dad, and then he doesn't come—

No. Don't think of that.

But I could call Faro. Faro is bold and he loves an adventure. He would come. His strength is much greater than mine. Faro could break open the cupboard door.

Maybe Faro doesn't even know about the flood, if he's still deep in Ingo, in the Groves of Aleph with Saldowr. Has Saldowr finished healing him yet?

My thoughts whirl, as fast and confused as the flood water. Rainbow mustn't see Faro. No one else must see the Mer: it's dangerous for them. But I *must* call Faro. He's our only hope now.

"Sapphire, quick, we've got to get upstairs," Rainbow urges me. "It's no good. We'll never get that cupboard open."

The right answer comes to me. "You go up. Mum shouldn't be on her own. I'm going to have one more try."

"Don't be crazy. I'm not leaving you."

"*Please*, Rainbow. Listen, Mum's calling! She's ill; she needs us. And I'm really good at holding my breath. I'll just do one more dive."

As if in answer to a prayer, I hear Mum's voice. "Sapphy! Quick! *Quick!*"

Rainbow and I stare at each other in the light of the candle.

"Go up to her," I say rapidly. "Leave the candle on the top stair. It's worth one more try. I'll yell if I get the door open, then you come down and help me with the ladder."

The water is lapping around my feet, even though I'm halfway up the stairs. I watch the struggle in Rainbow's face. Fear, responsibility, the anguish of not knowing what to do—

"*Sapphy!*"

Reluctantly, Rainbow backs away up the stairs, towards Mum. "I'll see how she is and I'll come back."

Faro, where are you?

What's the best way to call him? Suddenly I know. Faro won't be able to find me easily, in the jumble of drowned streets and houses. He's never even been in a town before. I'll have to show him the way.

I open my mind and create a picture inside my head. This room, full of water. The stairs and the open front door. And then I let my mind travel outside, like a camera, showing him the route he must take. The narrow street that turns a sharp corner and leads down to the slipway, the steps and the beach. But there won't be any beach now. *Look down, Faro. Follow the pattern of the road. Follow the houses. Can you see the way?*

But come quickly, quickly. There isn't much time left. Come now.

Time slips. I feel it move inside me. Human time or Ingo time, I don't know which it is. Time won't hold steady any more. It wants to swirl like the water. The seconds stretch, becoming minutes, hours...

And there he is in the doorway, diving gracefully through the shadowy water. I know it's Faro before I see his face. Who else could have read my thoughts and known where I was, and come to rescue me?

"Greetings, little sister," says Faro, pushing back his hair and smiling calmly, just as if we're sitting on a rock in summer sunshine.

"Faro!"

"I've been *everywhere* looking for you. I kept seeing humans, but nobody who looked like you. I've been going in and out of all these caves where you humans live, searching—"

"They're called houses, Faro. You know that perfectly well."

But Faro ignores this. "And you didn't even send me a message until now."

"So you were here in St Pirans already!"

"Of course. How could I miss what is happening tonight, little sister? Ingo has broken her bounds." He looks at me with sparkling, triumphant eyes. "Do you understand what that means? All the territory that was closed to us is now open. I can go anywhere!"

"Yes, Faro. I've been trying to dive into a cupboard in my own living room. I certainly do understand what it means. There's water everywhere. Nice for you, but not so great for humans."

"Don't be cross, Sapphire."

"Cross! These are people's lives we're talking about," I hiss furiously, then realise that I'm echoing Roger.

"Why are you angry? I came to make sure that you were safe."

"Only me?"

"And Conor, of course."

"There are other people in this town besides me and Conor."

Faro shrugs. He steadies himself against the incoming water with a flick of his tail. It seems incredible that Faro is really here, inside our house, sculling the water with his hands. Faro belongs to Ingo, not to St Pirans. But now Ingo is everywhere. A dreamlike feeling washes over me. Can any of this really be happening?

"I came to help you," announces Faro. "As long as you remember your Mer blood, you are perfectly safe, Sapphire. You can swim with me, wherever the sea goes. You can even swim alone. Come. Ingo is here. You don't have to go and find it any more. Ingo has come to you."

But at that moment reality rushes back. *Mum.* Conor's safe with Roger, I'm sure he is, but Mum's in terrible danger. And Rainbow too. Danger's everywhere. I can't just save myself.

"Faro, you've got to help me. If we can open the cupboard under the stairs and get out the ladder then I can take it upstairs and help Mum climb into the loft through the trapdoor in the bathroom."

Faro looks blank.

"Down there, under the water. Look, Faro, there's a door. I've got to open that door and get out a ladder. You know what I mean? To help us climb up high to the top of the house. But the water's too strong for me to open the door."

At that moment Mum calls again, her voice full of fear, "*Sapphire!* Come up! It's not safe down there. *Sapphire!*"

"I'm OK, Mum," I yell back up the stairs. "I'll be up in a minute." My voice echoes as if I'm in a swimming pool.

Faro stares at me. "Whose was that voice?"

"My mother's."

"Your *mother?*"

It's strange. It's almost as if Faro hasn't really believed until now that I have a real mother at all. She was just an Air thought that he needn't bother about.

"I'm going to dive down again, Faro. I've got to open that cupboard. If you can't help, I'll do it on my own."

But Faro is beside me as I plunge into the murky water again. I know for sure that this has to be the last attempt. Down we go, into the darkness.

"Your caves are very strange," says Faro's voice in my

ear, still light and teasing in spite of everything. "They have so many sharp corners."

I realise with a shock that I can hear his voice just as clearly as I can hear it when we're swimming together in Ingo. I turn and peer through the gloom and there he is, still with the faint mocking smile on his lips that I know so well. And my lungs are not bursting with pain. My body is flooded with strength and oxygen. I am in my own living room, but also, unbelievably, it seems that I'm in Ingo.

"Faro, help me open the cupboard. *Please.*"

"Where is this cupboard?"

"Here."

Faro touches the handle curiously.

"You have to pull it, Faro. But the water's too strong; it won't let the door open."

"I think it will open," says Faro casually. He grasps the handle and tests it. "Yes, you are right. There is a problem with the weight of the water. We must balance it. Put your hand on my arm to help me."

The muscles in Faro's arms bulge. The cupboard door resists for a few seconds, and then yields.

Thank God Roger is so tidy. There is no jumble of rubbish under the stairs because he cleared it all out and took it to the dump a few weeks ago. There is only the ladder, shining with a dull fish-like gleam in the darkness.

"There it is!"

"That's the thing you want?"

"Yes, the ladder."

Faro eases the ladder backwards and I help to pull it around the angle of the cupboard. It is long and awkward. "Are you sure you need it?"

The water surges against me, nearly pinning me to the wall again. I fight my way back to the ladder. "Pull more that way," I gasp.

And the ladder is out. We haul it to the surface. Faro takes most of the weight, as we swim around to the stairs. I tread water as Faro skilfully angles the ladder so that it points up the stairs. I'll be able to drag it into the bathroom. The water's lapping close to the ceiling now.

"*Sapphy!*"

"*Coming.* Rainbow, I've got the ladder."

Faro slips beneath the water, into the shadow of the wall, as Rainbow rushes to the head of the stairs.

"Oh, Sapphire, I'm so sorry, your mum was faint and I had to hold her, I couldn't leave her... Wow, you got the ladder! I can't believe it! However did you drag it out of that cupboard?"

"Can you – can you lift it up the stairs? Got to rest a minute – out of breath."

"I'll set it up beneath the trapdoor."

Rainbow seizes the ladder, hauls it to the top of the stairs, and bumps it away towards the bathroom. Faro surfaces. "Faro, you shouldn't keep doing that. It hurts you to breathe Air, you know it does. You should stay under the water."

"Ingo is strong everywhere tonight," says Faro. "Even the pain of breathing your Air is not so bad."

"But you've been ill, Faro. You've got to be careful."

"Saldowr healed me," says Faro proudly. "I told you, he is a great teacher."

But not such a great keeper of the Tide Knot, I think, making sure to keep this disloyal thought hidden from Faro. Whatever's been going on in Ingo tonight, Saldowr hasn't been able to control it.

"And you are safe," says Faro. For a moment his smile sparkles, but then a look of exhaustion crosses his face. The ladder must have been too heavy for him. Maybe he's not really recovered yet.

"Oh, Faro, you're always rescuing me. And I never even thanked you last time." Faro swims close. He stretches forward and takes my hand in his. The water level is only about six inches from the ceiling now.

"There's no need for you to thank me," he says. His voice isn't mocking now, and his eyes look into mine with deep seriousness. "We are joined by our blood, little sister. We two can never be strangers to each other. Whenever you call me, I will come. Even in this cupboard place we can find each other."

"Faro, believe me, I'm grateful."

A quick, glancing smile crosses Faro's face, and then he slips beneath the surface in an eddy of water, and is gone. I think I see his shadow pass across the threshold, but I can't be sure.

CHAPTER SEVENTEEN

I wake suddenly, jolted out of a deep sleep. Did my alarm clock go off? No, everything's silent. Where am I? I stare around, struggling to remember. There's a light. A candle burning. A jumble of shapes in its flickering light. Boxes, bags, old furniture. And three other shapes, curled up on the floor.

Mum, Sadie and Rainbow, on the other side of Sadie. I don't even remember falling asleep. We were so exhausted. Rainbow and I got Sadie up the ladder into the loft first, which was quite hard because Sadie kept trying to help us by scrabbling her paws on the ladder's rungs and licking our faces to encourage us. She knew we were trying to rescue her, and she wanted to do her bit. I was wrong to think she would panic. Sadie was like a lion for courage.

Helping Mum up the ladder was a nightmare, even though Mum was so brave and kept saying she could manage. But she couldn't. We were afraid of hurting her and making her even more ill than she was already. In the end Rainbow supported Mum on the ladder, and lifted her while I pulled her through the loft trapdoor. Mum couldn't really stand up on her own. As soon as we got her into the loft she gave a funny little gasp and collapsed on to the floor. After a bit she started saying, "I'm all right, I'm all right," but even in the light of one candle she looked so far from all right that we gave her more of the brandy in case she fainted.

Rainbow climbed down again, collected our duvets and pillows and pushed them up through the trapdoor, one by one. We spread them out on the floor and then we lay down to rest just for a while. We must have fallen asleep.

The candle is on top of a packing case, where Rainbow put it so that it couldn't set fire to anything. Mum said this candle should last for forty hours. Forty hours! What if we have to wait for forty hours before anybody rescues us? This loft isn't meant for human beings. It's cramped and low, full of spider webs and dust. Maybe there are mice too. I don't really mind mice, as long as there aren't any rats.

I wish I were still asleep like Mum and Sadie and Rainbow. They look so peaceful. I wonder if I can crawl over to the window without waking them, then I'll be able to look out and see what's happening. Surely they'll be sending boats out soon? We heard a helicopter go over while we were helping Mum up the ladder. Rainbow and I thought it was a rescue helicopter. It came down low, beating the air, and we saw the flash of a searchlight. But then it went away again. I thought all the rescue services would be here by now. That's what happens on TV when there's a flood. Helicopters everywhere, and boats, and even TV and radio crews to cover the drama. I can only think of one reason why they aren't here, and it's alarming. Maybe this flood is so big that there just aren't enough rescue vehicles and helicopters to cover all the flooded towns and villages up and down the coast.

I shiver. *Ingo has broken her bounds.* Did the Mer understand what would happen when the sea flooded in? Did Faro? Is this devastation what they wanted?

The little square window in the eaves is like Conor's window in our cottage. It's full of moonlight. Can I get to it without disturbing Sadie?

And then I hear the sound. Straight away I know it's the same sound that woke me. A whistle. Somebody's whistling.

Cautiously, I wriggle to the trapdoor. Sadie doesn't even twitch, although usually I can't move without her wanting to come with me. I'm so close to her that I can feel the warmth of her body and hear her breathing. It's the deep, regular breathing of a dog who is lost in dreams of sunlit fields full of rabbits. I reach the open trapdoor, and peer down. Nobody's there. How could there be anybody whistling inside a flooded house?

The ladder stands in water now. The flood has come up on to the landing, and it's swilling ominously against the lower rungs of the ladder. A stab of terror runs through me. *No, Sapphire, you are not going to panic. The water can't keep on and on rising. It's got to stop soon. We're safe up here in the loft. No flood is ever going to come right over the top of a house. Sadie wouldn't be sleeping so peacefully if we were really in danger.*

I tell myself all these things, and then I turn away from the trapdoor and the dark, threatening water and try to shut them out of my mind. I've got to think, got to make a plan. If no one's coming to rescue us, then we'll have to find a way of rescuing ourselves.

That whistle again! But louder this time. Closer. Two notes – one long, one short. My heart lurches with excitement. Surely no one else whistles in exactly that way. It's a signal. It's Conor. It must be. It's got to be Conor.

But where? Surely he can't be outside, in the flood. He's bound to be safe somewhere. Roger wouldn't let Conor take any risks.

Maybe Roger's here with him! Maybe they've come in Roger's boat. That must be it. Roger has come to take us to safety on high ground. I open my mouth to wake Mum and Rainbow with the good news, then shut it again. What if there's no boat and the whistle was what Dad used to call "a figment of Sapphire's lively imagination"?

I turn and crawl over the rough, splintery floor, pushing aside boxes that send clouds of dust into my face. Mustn't cough or sneeze. The window is filthy, but strong moonlight still pours through it. I brace my elbows on the window frame and stare down.

Water. Black, oily water, gulping up the walls. The houses opposite are almost swallowed now. That side of the street stands lower than this. The sea is right up to the top of their bedroom windows. Their roofs and chimneys are sharp and black.

And then the moonlight glints on two faces, upturned, in the water beneath me. It's them. Not Roger with a boat, but Conor and Faro, swimming.

For a moment I can't believe it. It must be a dream that I'm having because I so much want it to be true. I blink to see if the faces vanish. But when I look again they are clearer than ever. Faro and Conor, looking up at the window. I wave, and they see the movement. Faro waves back, then dips down beneath the surface to breathe. I fumble the rusty window catch. My fingers shake so much that I can't undo it at first. Even when I do, the window is stuck tight. It probably hasn't been opened for about a hundred years. I glance behind me. There they are, Mum and Rainbow and Sadie, fast asleep. I decide to take the risk, and bang the window as hard as I can. It flies open. Another backward glance. No one has moved.

"Is Mum there?" Conor calls up. "Is she all right?"

I look to see if Mum and Rainbow are stirring at the sound of his voice. But no, they lie still, as if a spell has been laid on them. Ingo is strong tonight, and Earth is weak. Sadie whines and shivers all over, then sinks back into sleep.

"Mum's here, Conor," I call back as softly as I can. "She's OK. Rainbow's here too. They're all asleep."

"Don't wake them. Roger's on his way with an inflatable. He'll be here soon. His boat's smashed. But, Saph, it's you we've come for. It's you we need."

"What for, Conor?"

"Is that window big enough for you to climb out?"

"Yes, I—"

"Climb out quick. We'll catch you."

"But—"

"Don't be afraid, little sister," comes Faro's teasing voice.

"I'm not *afraid*," I whisper angrily, "I just want to know what's going on." I glance behind me again. Mum, Rainbow and Sadie are sunk so deep in sleep that even if I went over and shook them, I don't believe they'd wake.

"Quick, Saph!" Conor urges me. "Saldowr has called us. He wants us to come. He needs our help."

"Saldowr!"

"Yes," says Faro quietly, and now there's no teasing in his voice. I look down at them. With their wet hair slicked back, their faces are strangely similar. "It's the first time I've known Saldowr to ask for help," Faro goes on. "He has called you both to the Tide Knot, and asked me to be your companion on the journey. You must hurry."

How far below me is the water? About three metres, maybe less. If I climb out of the window feet first and then twist round when I'm sitting on the sill, I'll be able to lower myself from the ledge and drop into the water. It won't make too big a splash, and Conor and Faro are there waiting. They won't let the flood sweep me away.

But is it really Ingo down there? It looks so dark, so unfriendly. Not like the sea I know so well. It's as if Ingo changed its nature when it broke its bounds. But I've got no choice. I can't wait for Roger and the inflatable to rescue me if Saldowr has called us.

Mum, will you be all right? You'll be terrified again when you wake up and find I'm not there. And poor Sadie will run up and down the loft, barking frantically. She'll know where I've gone. But I can't do anything about that. I'm not abandoning you, my darling Sadie, I'm trying to help us all. Please stay asleep, and then you won't be frightened. Mum, don't be afraid. Nothing bad is going to happen to me and Conor. We have to go; we've got no choice. Sadie and Rainbow will look after you.

Once I'm down in the water with Conor and Faro, there's no time for talk. It's too dangerous. Just by our house the water is relatively calm, but as soon as we swim away there are swirls and currents and eddies and whirlpools that want to buffet us against buildings, and drag us into doorways, and trap us inside houses. It takes all my strength to swim against the flow of the water. Faro dives, but Conor and I swim on the surface, our mouths just above the water. I'm not sure if I dare dive. Is this Ingo, or not Ingo? Is it an enemy, or a friend? At the moment it looks more like an enemy. It has swept into town, and conquered.

A cat floats by on an upturned table, its back arched, its wet fur flattened against its body.

"Oh, Conor, look at the cat! Can't we rescue it?"

"No," says Conor shortly.

I've never known moonlight as strong as this. It makes everything look as unearthly as a dream, but the pitiful yowling of the cat is all too real. It stares back at us while the flood carries it away, as if asking why we don't help it.

Conor and I swim close together. I'm afraid to lose him in this mess of debris. I've never tried to swim through water like this. It carries a swirling mass of rubbish: furniture, traffic bollards, apples, nappies, plastic bags, sodden plants and flowers. In the distance we see a car, half-full of water, spinning slowly round on the current. At that moment, Faro surfaces by my side. "Dive!" he says urgently. "That car's going to hit us—"

There's no choice. The three of us plunge into the murk, and swim down as deep as we can. We flip on to our backs, and watch the car pass overhead like a shark, outlined in moonlight.

"Swim away!" orders Faro sharply.

Things are happening too fast. Houses loom to the right and the left, windows gaping like eyes. Where are all the people? What has happened to them? This is like the drowned island Faro took me to. I never guessed that the same thing could happen here in St Pirans. The water pushes against us like a giant hand as we try to swim around the corner of the street.

"Dive deeper," says Faro. His voice is tense. "We've got to go deeper, then we'll be under the current."

We swim down. The current weakens, but just as I think we're out of its power it grabs me, tears me away from the others, and slams me savagely against a granite wall. The pain is so fierce that I scream, and Conor seizes my hand as we are swept into a backwater beside the sea wall. There's no current here.

"You all right, Saph?"

I can't speak. They are on either side of me, holding me up.

"Are you OK, Saph? Saph, say something!"

I make a huge effort, and pull myself together. "M'all right. Hurt my leg."

"I can't see – is it bleeding?"

"Think so."

"Is it broken?"

Cautiously, I move my leg. It hurts, but not in the way I think a broken leg would hurt.

"Do you want to go back?" asks Conor.

"Saldowr told me to fetch *both* of you. This is no time for weakness," interrupts Faro. Tears rush to my eyes, partly because of the pain but mostly because of what Faro's just said.

"I'm not weak."

"He knows you're not," says Conor, and gives my hand a squeeze. "Everyone knows you're tough, Saph. But can you still swim? It's a long journey."

"M'OK."

"Sure?"

I think of Mum and Sadie and Rainbow, sleeping as the water rises. Will Roger be there by now? And all the other people whose houses are being swallowed one by one... Can Saldowr really help them? Can the tides ever return to their knot, so that the water will stop rising and drowning more and more homes? Compared to that, nothing else matters. I can swim.

"Hold her wrist, Faro," says Conor. "I'll swim on her other side."

"But you won't – you won't be able to breathe, Con, unless Faro's helping you."

"Don't worry about me. This isn't too bad. Not like being deep in Ingo. More like – half and half – half Air, half Ingo."

It's wonderful to have them there, so close, one at each side of me like bodyguards against the flood. Suddenly I know where I am. We're close to where the cottages look out over the slipway and the beach. Rainbow's home is near here. All these cottages are completely underwater now. Even their chimneys are covered. They loom dimly through the water.

We swim low, grazing the road. I put my hand down and feel Tarmac. It's almost impossible to see through this water now. It's so filthy and full of rubbish. Trying to draw oxygen through it is like trying to breathe in a garage with the car engine belching out exhaust. I can't believe that Conor thinks this is easier than breathing deep in Ingo.

This is what it must be like to be a sea bird when there's an oil leak. This is what it must be like to be a fish gasping in water that's full of chemicals. This is what it must be like to be a dolphin thrashing in a tuna net.

"Hold on," says Faro in my ear.

Suddenly the colour of what is beneath us changes. It's not Tarmac any more. It's white sand, glinting in reflected moonlight. The water grows wilder, but cleaner. We're in the sea, the real sea at last. This is true Ingo, not the robber Ingo that has stolen our town. Hope floods into me. Maybe Ingo is still itself, after all. And that means that our world can return to itself, too.

"Look out!" yells Conor, dragging me sideways. An ice-cream van rears up a few metres away, lunging towards us. It misses us by less than an arm's length, as we dive for the sand.

"Usually I'm happy to see an ice-cream van," says Conor, once we've recovered a little, "but I'm not in the mood today."

"Conor, you've got to hold on to Faro. This is true Ingo now."

"I know," says Conor. "Can you manage without me, Saph?"

"I think so."

I want to look at my leg and my side, but it's too dark down here. The moon gives only a faint glimmer of light. I think my leg is bleeding, maybe bleeding quite heavily. I feel strange, as if my body doesn't belong to me. I wish I didn't feel so dizzy. *Don't be stupid, Sapphire, you are safe in Ingo. Ingo, remember?*

I feel sick, too. But how can anyone be sick underwater? I'm not going to tell Faro or Conor. Faro will think I'm weak, and anyway it's much too late to go back. And if Conor thinks I'm struggling, he'll try to swim on my other side to support me, and that will mean he can't hold on to Faro... and then he won't get enough oxygen... and then... it's too much to think about. It's making me even dizzier.

"Can you get us to Saldowr, Faro?" Conor asks. "Do you know the current we should take?"

"I hope so." I've never heard Faro sound so unsure, even fearful. "But tonight – Ingo doesn't feel as she should. The currents have become strangers. The loosening of the Tide Knot has changed everything."

"I thought it was going to be so wonderful, when Ingo grew strong and we humans grew weak," observes Conor coldly. But this time Faro doesn't reply. I haven't got enough energy to think of talking. I'm not even really swimming any more. I'm still moving my arms and kicking the leg that isn't injured, but there's no power in my strokes.

"We need my sister," says Faro abruptly. He stops swimming. Conor treads water, Faro balances on his tail and I hang there, limp, wondering vaguely if I'll ever be able to move again. The sea booms in my ears like underwater thunder.

"Elvira?" Even through a fog of pain and weariness, I hear the change in Conor's voice. He can't hide his eagerness.

"Yes. My sister will help yours. Elvira is a healer: that is, one day she will be a healer. She has a gift."

"Can you call her?"

"I've been trying to find her with my mind ever since Sapphire was hurt. But the message from Saldowr is so powerful that all I can hear is his voice, telling me to come quickly, and to bring you both with me. It leaves no space for me to call Elvira. But Sapphire needs her help."

"Could I…" I mumble, meaning could I call Elvira.

"No. Save your strength. But, Conor, maybe you could? Can you speak to my sister? Can you ask her to come to us?"

"How?"

"Show her what is in your mind. Show her that Sapphire is injured. Show her that you want her to come here."

That shouldn't be too difficult for Conor, I think to myself, with a feeble inner giggle.

"But I don't know how," says Conor. "I'm not like you and Sapphire. I've never been able to – to share my thoughts."

"Just try," says Faro impatiently. "Think of Elvira. Come close to her in your mind. Call her to you. Once you feel that she is listening, show her our predicament. Show her that Sapphire is hurt, and that we need her to be healed so that we can get to Saldowr. She'll come if you can get the message to her. Even if Elvira was at the bottom of the world where the ice mountains live, she would come to my help."

"I'll try," says Conor.

A long time passes, or at least it feels like a long time. Conor is concentrating desperately, struggling to reach Elvira. I wish I could help him, but a foggy curtain of exhaustion hangs between me and the others. Maybe we'll never get to Saldowr. Maybe the water will just keep on rising and rising until it gets to the top of the highest hills in Cornwall. The water is so powerful, and I feel so weak...

"Sapphire. *Sapphire.*"

"What is it, Faro? 'M just having a rest—"

"You're falling asleep. Wake up, Sapphire! Elvira's on her way. She'll be here soon."

And then Conor's voice, too, full of relief. "I reached her, Saph! I did it! I kept trying and trying and it wouldn't work, and then I just sort of let my mind empty and then I thought about her, and she was there."

"Fantastic, Conor."

"Hold on, Saph. She'll be here as soon as she can."

It seems a long time before Elvira comes. I keep drifting in and out of a dream. I want to stay in my dream, but Conor and Faro won't let me. They keep waking me up.

"Whassamaaer Con... m'only sleeping—"

"Wake up, Saph. *Wake up!*"

And then the dream breaks. Elvira's here, breathless.

"I came on the fastest current I could find. Is she still with us?"

"Yes."

"I wish we had more light. I can't see what's wrong."

"We'll bring her closer to the surface. Is the moon still strong?"

"The strongest I've ever seen," says Elvira.

When Faro said Elvira was going to be healer, I thought he meant she wanted to be a doctor one day. I expected her to have some kind of Mer first-aid kit with her. But she hasn't got anything. Only her hands. As soon as she touches me, I understand what Faro meant. Elvira's hands have got healing in them. I couldn't have let anyone else touch my leg, but Elvira's hands don't hurt. She frowns.

"She's got a bad gash, look, there. It's still bleeding, that's why she's weak. And she's terribly bruised. Oh, Faro, I have no experience of human flesh and blood. I'm afraid of doing the wrong thing."

"You won't," says Conor, gazing at Elvira.

I catch Faro's eye, and he winks. "It's true that you're only beginning your training," he says in a patronising voice that has an instant effect on Elvira.

"I'll do what I can," she says. Her long dark hair swirls around us like a cloud, making a private world where she and I are alone. She puts the heel of one hand on the cut and presses down with the other. "Look into my mind, Sapphire," she says very quietly so that no one else can hear. I obey. It's easy to look into Elvira's mind. It's as if her mind is a mirror, showing me myself. Look, there's the wound on my leg. But it's not bleeding any more. It's healing. The edges of the wound are drawing together. The bruises are fading.

"Look," says Elvira again, "look deep."

I concentrate as hard as I can. I'm not afraid any more. It's a cut, that's all. It's not so terrible, and I'm certainly not going to die from it. Elvira's healing flows into me, like warmth from a fire. I'm not dizzy now. I don't feel as if I'm slipping away into a dream place. My leg still hurts, but not in the same way.

"There," says Elvira at last, "that's as much as I can do for now. You'll need to see another healer, Sapphire, to stitch your leg, but I think you have enough strength to reach Saldowr."

"Will you come with us?"

"Yes."

CHAPTER EIGHTEEN

The Groves of Aleph look as if a hurricane has torn through them. Great underwater trees lie uprooted. Boulders are scattered, the white sand piled into heaps. We force our way through a dense mat of weed that has been ripped off the ocean floor. All the colours are dim and muddied. This place was so beautiful, and now it looks as if it's dying. It's as much a scene of devastation as St Pirans.

At least the sharks have gone. I was so afraid as the current swept us close to the Groves. Saldowr promised that the sharks would know us again, and we would be protected, but I've heard too many stories about sharks scenting blood from miles away, and homing in on their victim. I was afraid they'd attack me because of the wound on my leg. I could tell that the others were afraid, too, because they closed tight around me.

We needn't have worried. There is no sign of a living creature as we drop off the current and swim down to where Saldowr keeps the Tide Knot. Everything is eerily still. Even the water itself looks lifeless. Dawn is coming up, but it's a grey, cold dawn that filters drearily down through the water.

We're not even sure that we're close to Saldowr's cave. The whole seascape has changed. Even Faro, who spent so long inside the cave for his healing, isn't sure where it is. Boulders are almost buried in sand, as if there's been an underwater whirlwind. The same whirlwind has exposed a long line of fanged black rocks. They look as if they want to reach out and rip us to pieces.

"Where is Saldowr, Faro? Can you still hear him in your mind?"

Faro frowns. "He's close. He knows we're here. Wait."

And then we see him. He must have been there all the time, watching us. He's in the shadow of the one remaining tree, wrapped in his cloak, as if a freezing wind has blown over him.

"Saldowr!"

"Yes," he answers, swimming forward slowly, as if movement is an effort. "It was I who called you. But you know that. Perhaps I was wrong to do so, but I had no choice."

I look at him and think at first that his power is broken, but then I look into his eyes and realise that isn't true. His power is still there but it has sunk deep inside him. His beautiful cloak is ragged, as if some animal has torn the cloth with its teeth. Saldowr has dark bruises of exhaustion under his eyes. "The tides destroyed everything in freeing themselves," he says. "I was fortunate. I survived."

"Are all the sharks dead?" I ask quickly.

"The tides took them. Whether they are alive or no, who can say? They would not turn from their duty. They refused to flee, even when I told them I could no longer hold the Tide Knot."

Conor and I glance at each other. We can't feel as sorry as Saldowr about the sharks' absence.

"What – what happened to the Tide Knot?"

"See for yourselves."

He swims a little way, and we follow him. He halts, and points into the distance. "Faro, do you see my cave?"

There's no cave left. Its mouth is stuffed with sand. Even the smallest fish wouldn't be able to wriggle inside. If that's Saldowr's cave, then somewhere close, on the sea bed, is the Tide Mouth...

"You are right," says Saldowr, as if he's reading my thoughts. "The Tide Mouth is still here, even though the tides have gone. Come."

Conor and Elvira are on one side of Saldowr, and Faro and I on the other. Saldowr dives to the sea bed, as he did before. Sand swirls around us, clouding the water. But this time there's no heavy stone for him to lift. Only an open, gaping mouth. The Tide Mouth. There's no blue light, no sinuous, coiling tides, flexing and turning, flashing like jewels. The Tide Mouth is empty. The tides have gone.

"But where is the keystone?" asks Conor. Saldowr looks at him sharply. "You remember the keystone?"

"Of course."

"You remember the patterns engraved on it?"

"Yes, the writing. But where is it?"

Saldowr sighs. "This is why I called you here. Could you read those patterns?"

"No. No, but—"

"I understand you. You saw some meaning in them."

"Yes."

"Your sister survived the Deep, which has never been known before. You saw those patterns, which no one saw before. I called you here because after everything that has happened here, Ingo needs a new and different power. No one can drag the tides back. They are too strong. They burst the keystone and it shattered into fifty pieces, like my mirror. Those patterns are words, my children. They are words that have never been spoken since the tides were first sealed into their knot, in the time of our farthest ancestors. Perhaps – perhaps those same words, once spoken, may seal them again."

"Do you really think they can?" I ask.

Saldowr's sombre face lightens a little. "It's not very likely, *myrgh kerenza*. But all the same we must try it, since there's nothing else. Nothing else but destruction."

"I thought Ingo wanted to grow strong," Conor challenges him. "I thought the Mer wanted to defeat the power of humans."

"Some in Ingo wanted it, and now they know their error. Look around you." We all stare at the pallid, wrecked, lifeless seascape. "This scene will be repeated a thousand times in Ingo, and a thousand times on Earth, unless the tides return. The balance between Earth and Ingo has failed. I have failed. *Keeper of the Tide Knot*," he says, with bitter self-contempt. "What have I kept safe? But perhaps my failure can still be redeemed."

I don't think I want to be here. It's all too sad and fearful. What chance is there that we can do anything, when someone as powerful as Saldowr is helpless?

"We'll try," says Conor.

Saldowr holds out his hands to us.

Our first task is to find all the scattered fragments of the keystone, and gather them together. It looks impossible. So much is buried under sand or masses of weed.

"We've got to have method," says Conor. "If we all spread out and move inwards, we won't miss any of it. As soon as you find a piece, either mark where it's lying, or bring it to the cave if you can carry it. Saph, don't try to do too much."

Saldowr seems content to let Conor take charge for

now. Faro, Elvira, Conor and I swim backwards, separating until we are out of sight of each other. "Ready?" calls Conor. "Come forward slowly. Mark everything you find. Search everywhere. Plunge your hands deep into the sand. Feel through the weed. Lift every stone."

Saldowr is close to me. I expect him to help with the search, but he does nothing. When I find my first shard of the keystone I hold it up triumphantly. "Here, Saldowr, this is part of the stone, isn't it?"

He nods. "Well done, my daughter. But your brother was right, you must not exhaust yourself. That injury needs care."

"But – but Saldowr, aren't you going to help us?"

"I am helping you. Your brother is free to search, isn't he? He can draw in oxygen without Faro's help?"

"Yes, I suppose so – I hadn't thought—"

"I may be a poor keeper of the Tide Knot, but I am still Guardian of the Groves." His voice is stern, and I daren't ask any more questions. But Saldowr continues, "Understand me, Sapphire. I am not one of those teachers who ask questions to which they already know the answers. I would not have called you here if I thought I could carry out this task without you."

I don't fully understand, but it's not the time to ask for explanations. Finding every single fragment of the keystone is what matters, and it's a long, exhausting task. I keep having to rest, but Elvira, Conor and Faro work on tirelessly. Piece by piece, we bring what we've found to the silted-up cave. Some of the pieces aren't much more than splinters, sharp enough to slice our fingers to the bone if we handle them carelessly. Others are heavy chunks of rock that have to be dragged through the sand by two or three of us. Each piece of the keystone is dense and heavy, far heavier than any rock I've ever lifted onshore. The scatter of broken rock is like a jigsaw puzzle in three dimensions. It's hard to believe that the keystone can ever be put together again.

But Conor has always liked jigsaw puzzles. When we've got about thirty pieces of rock together, he starts to pore over them, swimming around them, viewing them from one angle and then another.

"Can you see any sense in it?" asks Faro, peering over Conor's shoulder.

"Look, those two pieces will fit together – if that splinter is slotted in just there, along the seam of the rock..."

Faro shrugs. "You see more than I do, brother. You had better work on it, while we keep on with the search."

Elvira lays down three jagged pieces of rock. "We must work faster," she says, her voice tense. Conor looks up at her.

"What are you afraid of, Elvira? The flood has already happened."

"Can't you feel it? The force of the tides has gone wild. It's tearing Ingo apart. It will destroy us all."

"And Ingo is all that matters, is it? Why should I try to

put the keystone together? You let my world drown. You were glad of it, weren't you?"

"No, Conor, no, believe me, I wasn't glad of it. I'm a healer. Don't you understand what that means?"

"A trainee healer," adds Faro. Elvira ignores him.

"How can I be a healer and be happy when there's injury – death – fear everywhere?"

Conor looks into her face. "I believe you, Elvira," says Conor gently, "but don't ask me to believe that everyone in Ingo is like you."

Wearily, I push myself up off the sea bed and swim back to the interminable search. I can't put that jigsaw puzzle together. I didn't even see that there was any writing on the keystone when it was whole. But perhaps I can find just one more sliver of rock, buried under the sand...

Finally, we have to give up the search. Maybe there are fragments of the keystone where we'll never find them, but we have scoured through sand, rummaged in weed, levered up boulders and lifted stones. Our hands are scratched and bruised. We've brought every fragment of rock we could find. Conor is still at work, and now we can begin to see a shape emerging. But of course the pieces won't hold together, even when Conor works out where they fit. A puzzle in three dimensions can't be solved flat on the sand.

"I'll never be able to put them together properly," says Conor at last. He looks so frustrated, as if he'd like to sweep the pieces of rock into a jumble again. But that isn't the kind of thing Conor does. "We're just wasting time."

"We could ask Saldowr."

"Where is he?"

"He was here just now."

"He's resting behind those rocks," says Elvira, pointing. Sure enough, there's the ragged hem of his cloak trailing in the water.

"Shall we wake him?"

"Saldowr!"

As he swims towards us, very slowly, I realise with a shock how old he looks now.

"Have you found all the pieces?" asks Saldowr.

"We don't know. We've looked everywhere. But what's the point? We'll never be able to put this rock together."

"When you find the last piece, the keystone will come together of itself," says Saldowr.

"Are you saying we haven't found the last piece? But we've searched and searched. There's nowhere else it can be."

"The missing piece may be closer than you think," says Saldowr, and he pulls his cloak back from his shoulder. There, lodged in his flesh, is a small, dagger-shaped splinter of rock. "I was too close when the keystone broke," says Saldowr, "or maybe not close enough. One of you four must pull it out for me, so that the keystone can make itself whole again."

Without meaning to, we all shrink back a little.

"Which – which one of us?" I know my voice is shaky. *Not me, not me, not me.* The words drum in my head so loudly that I'm sure Saldowr can hear them. He looks at me piercingly.

"I don't know," he says. "I only know that one of you will be able to draw out the rock, and heal the keystone."

"But you are my teacher!" exclaims Faro. "How can I do such a thing?"

"I don't know, Faro. That question is for you to answer, not me."

"Elvira, can't you do it? You're a healer. You made my leg better."

"I'll try," Elvira says bravely. "Sometimes a healer must hurt her patient in order for the patient to recover."

She puts out her hand tentatively, touches the dagger splinter, and then takes hold of the part which has not entered Saldowr's shoulder.

"You have good hands," says Saldowr. "Pull."

Elvira tosses her hair back, braces herself, and pulls as hard as she can. Saldowr sways, but the blade of rock does not move. "I couldn't do it. I'm so sorry. My hands won't—"

"It's not your fault, child."

Faro is next. He's very pale and I know he is hating this. Saldowr is the teacher he loves like a father. He braces himself, and then lays his hand on the dagger of rock. But unlike Elvira, he doesn't even try to pull it out. He shakes his head and lets his hand fall to his side. "This is not for me."

"What do you mean?" asks Conor.

"This isn't my task. It's pushing me away."

No one could doubt that Faro's telling the truth.

"I'll try, then," says Conor. He braces himself, and reaches for the dark, shiny splinter of rock that has buried itself in Saldowr's shoulder. Delicately, so as not to hurt Saldowr, he takes hold of it.

"I can't do it," he says at last. "My fingers keep slipping."

"Your turn, Sapphire," says Faro.

I wanted to be the last to try, because I was afraid. Now I wish I'd gone first, and then it would be over. Too much depends on it now. If I can't shift that dagger of keystone, then there's nothing left to try. Cautiously, I raise my right hand and touch what looks like the handle of a dagger. Immediately, my fingers close around it, as if the keystone had wrapped them there.

Everything is silent, tense. Everybody's waiting. I know, deep inside me, that if I pull, the dagger of rock will come out. But what will happen then? Will Saldowr die from the wound the rock has made in his shoulder? I'm afraid.

"I think you are the one, *myrgh kerenza*," says Saldowr gently.

"But – but I don't want to hurt you."

"It's not you who has hurt me. The keystone has done so already."

I look into his eyes and find the courage to say what I really mean. "What if you die, Saldowr?"

His lips quirk into a smile. "I'm not so easy to kill, my child. Pull out the dagger."

I press my lips tight together, look straight into Saldowr's eyes again, and pull as hard as I can. The dagger of rock glides smoothly out of Saldowr's flesh, and into my hand. Behind me I hear Faro gasp. The hole in Saldowr's flesh gapes, raw and ugly. His blood wells from the hole the stone dagger made, and for a terrifying moment it's like staring into the Tide Knot again, at the tides coiling like snakes. The feel of the stone dagger in my hand makes me shudder. I pass it to Conor and he grips it firmly, like a weapon. Saldowr raises his fist and presses it hard against the wound. Even so, a smoke of blood unrolls through the water. Saldowr's eyes are shut, his lips pressed tightly together. He's very pale and his face is clenched. Slowly, very slowly, he sinks down on to the sea bed.

"Can't Elvira heal him?" I whisper to Faro. But he doesn't answer. I don't think he even hears me.

"Elvira," says Conor, "surely you can do something?"

Elvira bites her lip. "I don't know enough. I'm not the right healer."

A wave of fury sweeps through me. Are the Mer going to wait and do nothing while Saldowr bleeds to death? I dive down to the sand where Saldowr's lying. "Let me help you. Tell me what to do."

His eyes open and meet mine. They are dull with pain, but they are still Saldowr's eyes. "*Myrgh kerenza*," he says gently, "there's nothing to be done now. But don't be afraid, I'm not going to die."

"But you're bleeding so badly, Saldowr. We can't just do nothing."

A gleam of a smile crosses Saldowr's face. "My dear child, sometimes you are very human. We're not doing nothing. We're healing…" He coughs, and presses his fist hard against the wound. "…healing the Tide Knot. There's no time for anything else. Don't be afraid. Conor…" He stops, gasping for breath. Conor leans forward to catch the words. "…the keystone is complete. Conor, lay the last piece."

"Where, Saldowr?"

"With the rest. You know where it should go."

Conor's eyes meet mine. He doesn't know. How can Saldowr think that he does?

"Quick, Conor, lay the last piece. *Now*. See if the keystone – if the keystone – remember—"

Saldowr says he's not going to die, but I'm terrified that he will.

"The last piece – now, Conor – now—"

We swim to the pile of stone we've gathered, Conor holding the last piece, the stone dagger. "It's not going to work," he says. "How can it work? The writing's smashed."

"Do it!" says Faro. "Saldowr commands it."

We gather around the jumble of fragments and boulders that was once the keystone. Conor weighs the stone dagger in his hand, his eyes narrowed, searching for the place where it will fit. But there's no clue. It's impossible. A puzzle in three dimensions that I can't believe we'll ever be able to solve.

"The keystone is wounded too," says Elvira suddenly, like a doctor making a diagnosis. "Wounded exactly as Saldowr is wounded."

"But I don't suppose you're the right healer for the keystone either, are you, Elvira?" I snap.

"Saph!" says Conor, but Elvira just goes on eagerly, "That's true, Sapphire, but the keystone doesn't need me. It wants to heal itself. I'm sure it knows how to heal itself. Conor, you can lay down the piece of stone that hurt Saldowr."

Conor hesitates. "What, just put it anywhere?"

"Yes."

Gently, Conor clears a small patch of sand. He glances round the circle of our faces, and then stretches out his hand, holding the stone dagger down. Instinctively, we all move back.

There's complete silence as Conor places the last piece of stone in the place he's made for it. We wait, tense, staring, willing something to happen.

Silence. I don't dare look at Conor or anyone. We've failed. Saldowr might die, and we've failed.

Suddenly, the silence starts to thrum with life. It's like the sound of the heating coming on in the dark of a winter morning. The thrumming sound grows louder. It's coming from the shattered fragments of the keystone. Another sound joins it, a rushing sound from far away. I don't know where it's coming from but I'm sure it's from something immensely powerful. It's like the distant roar of a waterfall when your boat is gliding along a peaceful river. There's something a million times stronger than you are just around the bend in the river, waiting for you.

"Get back!" shouts Conor. We somersault backwards through the water as the noise swells, beating on our eardrums. I put my hands over my ears, but the sound keeps on growing.

Something wonderful and terrible is happening on the sand where the pieces of the keystone are laid. As if the thrumming noise has charged them with life, the pieces of the keystone begin to move. Heavy chunks of stone slide towards each other. Tiny splinters whirl around the heavy, smashed heart of the jigsaw. It looks as if all the fragments of the keystone are trying to dance their way back into place. For a few seconds its core is veiled in a cloud of flying shards, and then, as we watch, the stone starts to solidify. In the centre of the cloud, piercing it through, there's the stone dagger.

Faro's hands are outstretched, holding off the magic. Elvira's hair swirls around her, hiding her. But Conor's arm is strong around my shoulder as the rushing sound reaches its climax. Streaks of light zizz around the segments of rock as they join. The stone dagger shows one last time, and then disappears into the heart of the rock. The keystone has healed itself.

The keystone rests on the sand, smooth and solid. Nobody moves for a few long moments, and then Saldowr's voice, very faint now, calls us from where he's lying. We swim to him. His face is colourless, but illuminated with relief. "The keystone – read it, Conor – now – no time—"

We move forward to the keystone. It's surface is black and as highly polished as glass. I can't see any sign of carving, or patterns, or words. I glance sideways at Faro and Elvira. They look as blank as I feel. "You're not looking the right way," says Conor, touching my arm. "Look. Look there, where the light catches it."

I strain my eyes. I think I see something, and then I know that I don't. The stone is smooth and unreadable.

"Can you read it, my son?" whispers Saldowr urgently.

"It's coming." Conor's fingers are digging into my arms. "It's coming into focus. Can't you see it, Saph?"

"I'm not sure—"

"There! There, Saph. Look!"

And then I see something, or I think I do. Marks in the smooth stone. Marks that seem to write themselves as we watch. But I can't make out any words. I can't read them. "Conor, I—"

Conor lets go of my arms. He draws himself up to his full height, and the water lifts his hair like a crown. Like Faro, he raises his hands, but Conor's hands are palm up as if he's calling the words out of the stone.

I remember the song that Conor sang to the guardian seals, long ago on the borders of Limina. But this song is even more powerful. It thunders like water being pulled over the lip of a waterfall and pouring down on to the rocks below. As he sings, just for a second, I see the pattern cut deep into the keystone.

And then the song is gone. The keystone is smooth. Conor's my brother again, shaking his head in bewilderment. "What was that?" he asks, as if he doesn't know what he's done.

I wait for Saldowr to rouse himself up again. But Saldowr doesn't thank Conor, or explain what's going on. *Maybe he hasn't got the strength*, I think, then I realise that Saldowr's listening to something. "Hush," he mutters, although none of us has spoken. Slowly, a look of infinite relief dawns on his face. "They're coming."

"Who's coming?" I whisper to Conor. He shakes his head.

"Saldowr," I ask boldly, "who is it?"

He looks at us as if he'd forgotten we were here. "Go," he says. "Now."

"What?"

"Now." With a huge effort, Saldowr turns back to face us. "Faro, Elvira, help your friends. Join hands. Take them home."

"But Saldowr, what's happening?" I ask him.

Saldowr pauses, clearly gathering strength to speak again. His fist is still pressed against the wound, but maybe – maybe it's bleeding less now. "The tides – back to the Tide Knot. The keystone called them – home." He coughs, and bites his lips. "Go. The force of it – will crush you..."

The sound of the tides bulges in our ears like a million waterfalls packed together, surging from every corner of the globe. Far away still, but coming closer, closer...

What will the noise be like when the tides arrive? "Saldowr, won't the tides hurt you when they come?"

"I am – their keeper."

"Don't let them hurt you, Saldowr!" I plead.

The ghost of a smile crosses his face again. "The tides are not – to blame. Join hands. Faro, Elvira, take them home."

CHAPTER NINETEEN

lvira and Faro bring us in at Rake's Point. Faro thinks it's not safe to risk the currents and narrow passages of St Pirans if the flood is still in the town. From Rake's Point there's a footpath that will take us across the fields to the hill above the houses.

I know Rake's Point, but not when it looks like this. The coast path should run above a shallow cliff. As we swim in, there's the path beneath us, with the sea bubbling around a signpost that points through the water and reads ST PIRANS, 1 MILE. I clutch Faro's arm. "Faro, nothing's changed. The tides are still here. The flood hasn't gone down. Do you think Saldowr was wrong?"

Water surges as Faro spins in a tight circle to face me. "Look at those two," he says, nodding towards Elvira and Conor.

"I know." Conor and Elvira notice nothing. They see each other and no one else.

"Saldowr told us that the tides would go back to the

Tide Knot," continues Faro, as if that's the end of any possible argument.

"But, Faro, look at that signpost! It should be pointing in the air."

"We have to trust him."

"You don't really care, do you?" I burst out. "You wouldn't care if St Pirans lay underwater for ever, like that village you took me to."

But Faro isn't having this. "Didn't I help you?" he demands. "Would you have got safely back here without me? And think, Sapphire, of what Saldowr has done for us."

I feel ashamed. We left Saldowr to face the force of the tides as they swept back to their knot. No wonder Faro's face is heavy with anxiety. "I'm sorry, Faro."

"Saldowr won't die," says Faro quickly. "You heard him. He'll find a healer. If Saldowr says he will live, he will live."

Faro's voice rouses up a strange echo in my head. He reminds me of someone... My thoughts grope for the answer, and then it comes like a sheet of lightning. Faro reminds me of myself. Believing against all the odds that Dad was still alive.

"Yes," I say gently, "Saldowr is strong. But all the same, Faro, the flood is still everywhere. Look around you."

"Don't worry," says Faro with maddening calm, "You want everything to happen immediately. You think the Tide Knot is like a magic trick. It's your Air thinking, Sapphire."

"*My Air thinking!* Faro, this is real water—"

"Anyway," Faro goes on, as if making a huge concession, "my thinking was also mistaken."

"How?"

"I thought that if Ingo grew strong in your world, it would bring peace and happiness."

"So it would be all right if thousands of people lost their homes, and maybe their lives," I snap, "as long as everybody in Ingo is happy."

Faro goes on as if he hasn't heard me, "But thousands of the Mer were harmed, too. Swept away by the tides, trapped in caves, searching for lost children."

Maybe that's what happened to Dad! Of course he didn't abandon us. He came to warn us, didn't he? He would have come to find us in the flood, but he couldn't. Maybe he was trapped in a cave by a boulder that the tides had rolled over its entrance. Maybe he was hurt—

"Faro, do you know what happened to my father when the tides broke loose?"

Faro executes a perfect back somersault, as if we're playing together on a summer day. "Yes."

"You didn't tell me!"

"He had to save the baby. They were almost swept away. My aunt was injured."

"Oh." He saved the baby. Of course I understand that he had to do it. I would never want any harm to come to a baby. He was so small and helpless. But *we* were Dad's children first...

Faro takes my hands and clasps them in his own. "We will put our lives together again, little sister," he says seriously. "We belong to each other, you know that. Whatever the tides do, it can't change what we are."

The firm clasp of his hands and his intent gaze are strangely comforting. I'm not leaving Ingo, not altogether. Part of me will always be here.

St Pirans, 1 mile, says the signpost. The words waver through the flood water. I'm still in Ingo, but the human world is growing clear and sharp. Suddenly I want to see Mum, more than anything. I trust Roger, I know he'll have made sure Mum's safe, but I need to see her with my own eyes. I need to put my arms around her and hug her and know that she's still here, and I'm still here. And Sadie will leap into my arms and lick my face with her rough, warm tongue. So much has been swept away, but not everything.

"Conor, come on."

Conor doesn't reply. He and Elvira are still talking intently, their voices too low for us to hear. Faro and I raise our eyebrows at each other.

"*Conor!*"

I'm shivering with cold and tiredness by the time Conor and I stumble up the last slope of the hill. Below us, the town is silent. A rescue worker in a bright yellow jacket met us on the footpath and pointed us up to the relief centre in St Mark's church hall, which is the highest point above the town. He wanted to ask us questions, but we said we had to find our family. I suppose we must have looked strange, appearing out of nowhere after a night of devastation. There are lots of rescue workers down in the town, steering inflatables along the flooded streets. From the distance we can see the yellow of their fluorescent jackets and the orange of the boats.

"I bet one of those rescue workers is Roger," says Conor, shading his eyes. A helicopter clatters overhead, then flies away. "Are you OK, Saph? Can you make it?"

"My leg hurts a bit, that's all."

"I wish Elvira was here."

I bet you do, I think. It's only a few minutes since we said goodbye to Faro and Elvira, but already they seem to belong to another life. But I hold on to Faro's words. *We will put our lives together again, little sister.* From the look on Conor's face, he's remembering Elvira's words, too.

Conor's arm is around me, supporting me, as we reach the path to the church hall. There are people standing around, wrapped in blankets, drinking out of plastic cups.

"Look, TV," whispers Conor. A reporter is standing with a mike, and a camera on him.

"This is Alex McGovern reporting from the stricken town of St Pirans, as the grey light of morning reveals the extent of the devastation..." He is wearing warm waterproof clothing and he looks excited. The rest of us look like refugees beside him. Suddenly, the camera swings on to me and Conor. "...This morning more homeless people are making their way to the emergency centre. Among them are the injured, and those who have become separated from their families..." And now the mike is right in Conor's face, and the reporter is blocking our way into the hall. "Are you brother and sister? Can you tell us what happened to you?"

Conor is silent for a moment, and then he says with great dignity, "No, I can't tell you what happened. Please let us past; my sister is injured."

As we go into the church hall, we hear the reporter's voice behind us, saying, "So far, miraculously, there are no reports of any fatalities. But once rescue workers are able to enter the flooded houses, this situation may change... All along this part of the Cornish coast, similar scenes of flood havoc are being reported."

The church hall is lined with rows and rows of people. Some lie down wrapped in blankets, some lean against the walls. Babies are crying, but everyone else is silent, as if they've been stunned. One by one, I recognise some faces. There's Mr Trevail and his wife. They are wrapped in foil blankets, sipping drinks. Mr Trevail sees me and waves. He doesn't look too bad. But where's Mum?

"There she is!" exclaims Conor.

Mum hasn't seen us. She's got a plastic cup in her hand and she's talking to a policeman, who is writing stuff down in a notebook.

"Mum!" I shout, much louder than I meant to. People turn to look but I don't care. I rush forward, tripping over blankets and feet, desperate to get to her. "Mum, Mum, are you all right?"

Mum drops the cup she's holding. She moves so fast that she looks as if she's flying across the hall. Her arms grab us both like a vice, and she hugs and hugs as if she'll never let go. "Sapphy! Con! I thought I'd lost you."

"Mum, you're hurting me!"

"Sorry, Sapphy." Mum wipes her face with the back of her hand and then clutches hold of us again. She's got mud on her cheek and her hair is wet and straggly. She looks beautiful.

"I can't let go of you," she says at last. "I can't believe I've really got you back. I've been watching that door for hours, praying you'd walk in. I asked everyone if they'd seen you—"

"It's all right, Mum," says Conor. "We're here now. We got trapped by the flood for a while, that was all. We were never in danger."

"It's all jumbled up in my head," says Mum, pulling us down to sit on the floor beside her. "I thought you were in the loft with me, Sapphy, but when I woke up you were gone. I can't tell you how scared I was. Rainbow said you must have been picked up by boat and gone to get help for us, and then Roger came."

"You had a fever, Mum. That's why it's all jumbled up. Conor came and fetched me, and he said Roger was on his way to rescue you and Rainbow and Sadie. We're all safe."

"Yes," says Mum, "you're safe. Nothing else matters." And she pulls us close again and hugs us as if she's never going to let go of us. I shut my eyes and lean against her. I'm so tired. I just want to go to sleep now—

Suddenly a terrible realisation flashes into my mind and I sit bolt upright. "Sadie! Mum, where is she?"

"It's all right, Sapphy, calm down. Rainbow's taken her for a walk. Sadie was so restless, she was driving everybody crazy."

"Which way did they go?"

"Sapphy, you're not going out again. You've got to rest. We need a doctor to look at that leg."

A shadow falls over us. I look up, and there is a figure as tall and strong as a sheltering tree. She's dressed in earth-coloured clothes, with a red scarf tied around her neck. She carries a brown earthenware jug. "Granny Carne! What are *you* doing here?"

"*Sapphy!*" says Mum.

"Let me see your leg, Sapphire," says Granny Carne. She bends and examines the cuts and the bruising carefully. At last she says, "This has been well tended."

"Did you find a first-aid post, then, Sapphy? You didn't tell me," says Mum. Granny Carne looks me in the eye.

"Is our cottage all right?" I ask her. The sight of her reminds me of home. Our cottage door, wide open all day long, the path down to our cove and the garden Dad planted...

"Yes, the sea couldn't rise that far. The Fortunes are quite safe too." The Fortunes? Who are they? And then I remember Gloria and her husband. I'd forgotten all about them. Gloria wouldn't have found it easy to escape the flood on her crutches. What if the water had kept on rising...

Did she know it was Ingo on the move? I wonder if I was right about the look of Ingo on Gloria's face. I must find a way of asking her one day – a way of finding out if she's one of us.

Mum shivers, and clutches me close. "I always knew you could never trust the sea, or anything in it," she says. I open my mouth to argue, thinking of Saldowr and Faro and Elvira, and the whale who helped me in the Deep, and the dolphins, and even the sharks who risked their lives for their duty. But I meet Granny Carne's piercing gaze, and close my mouth again, and say nothing.

"Come outside," says Granny Carne. "I hear that the water's falling at last. Come and see."

"Granny Carne's been here all night, helping," whispers Mum. "People said she walked all the way over from Senara as soon as the flood broke."

"More likely they said she flew," whispers Conor.

"Conor! That's enough!" says Mum, sounding like herself again.